Hans Andersen's

FAIRY TALES

Hans Andersen's

FAIRY TALES

Translated by
L. W. Kingsland

Illustrated by
ERNEST H. SHEPARD

London
OXFORD UNIVERSITY
PRESS

Oxford University Press, Ely House, London W. 1

GLASGOW NEW YORK TORONTO MELBOURNE WELLINGTON
CAPE TOWN IBADAN NAIROBI DAR ES SALAAM LUSAKA ADDIS ABABA
DELHI BOMBAY CALCUTTA MADRAS KARACHI LAHORE DACCA
KUALA LUMPUR SINGAPORE HONG KONG TOKYO

ISBN 0 19 274505 0

*Printed in Great Britain
at the University Press, Oxford
by Vivian Ridler
Printer to the University*

CONTENTS

The Tinder-Box

A SOLDIER came marching down the road—
left, right! left, right! He had his pack upon his
back and a sword by his side, for he had been to
the wars and was now on his way home. On the road he
met an old witch; she was so ugly her nether-lip hung
right down upon her breast. 'Good evening, soldier!'
she said. 'That's a fine sword you've got there, and a
great pack, too—you look a proper soldier, if ever there
was one! And now, if you do as I say, you shall have as
much money as you like!'

'Thanks very much, old witch!' said the soldier.

'Do you see that big tree?' said the witch, as she pointed to the tree that was standing by their side. 'It's quite hollow inside. Climb up to the top of the trunk and you'll see a hole you can slip through. Then you can drop right down into the tree. I'll tie a cord round your waist so that I can hoist you up again when you shout for me!'

'What have I got to do when I'm down in the tree?' asked the soldier.

'Fetch the money!' said the witch. 'When you get down to the bottom of the tree, you'll find yourself in a large passage. It's quite light, for there are more than a hundred lamps burning there. Then you'll see three doors: you can open them because the keys are in the locks. Go into the first room and you'll see in the middle of the floor a big chest with a dog sitting on it. He's got a pair of eyes as big as tea-cups—but don't let that worry you! I'll give you my blue-checked apron; you can spread it out on the floor, go boldly up to the dog, take hold of him and set him down on my apron. Then open the chest and take out as much money as you like. It's all coppers; but if you'd rather have silver, you'll have to go into the next room. The dog that sits there has a pair of eyes each as big as a millstone, but don't let that worry you—put him on my apron and help yourself to the money! If you want gold, however, you can get that, too—and as much as you can carry—when you go into the third room. But the dog that sits on the money-chest there has two eyes each as big as the Round Tower in Copenhagen. He's a real dog, you can take it from me! But don't you worry about that! Just put him down on my apron and he'll do you no harm. And then you can take as much gold as you like from the chest!'

'That doesn't sound so bad!' said the soldier. 'But what

have I got to give you, old witch? I'm pretty certain you want something out of it!'

'No,' said the witch, 'not a single penny do I want! All you have to do is to fetch me an old tinder-box my grandmother left behind the last time she was down there!'

'Well, let me get the cord round my waist!' said the soldier.

'Here it is!' said the witch. 'And here's my blue-checked apron!'

So the soldier climbed up the tree and dropped down the hole. There he stood, just as the witch had told him, down below in a large passage where hundreds of lamps were burning.

Then he unlocked the first door. Ooh!—There sat the dog with eyes as big as tea-cups glaring at him.

'Nice dog! Good boy!' said the soldier. He put him on the witch's apron and took as many coppers as he could carry in his pockets: then he shut the chest, put the dog back again and went into the second room. Whew!—There sat the dog with eyes as big as mill-stones!

'You shouldn't look at me so hard!' said the soldier. 'You might get eyestrain!' And so he put the dog on the witch's apron, but when he saw the mass of silver coins in the chest, he threw away all the coppers he had taken, and filled his pockets and his pack with nothing but silver. Then he went into the third room! Oh, it was terrible! The dog there really did have two eyes each as big as the Round Tower—and they were turning round in his head just like wheels!

'Good evening!' said the soldier and touched his cap, for he had never seen a dog like that before. But when he had looked at him a bit, he thought he had better get a move on, so he lifted him on to the floor and opened the chest. Heavens above, what masses of gold there were! With that he could buy the whole of Copenhagen, and all the sugar-pigs, tin-soldiers, whips, and rocking-horses in the world as well! That was something like money! And now the soldier threw away all the silver coins he had filled his pockets and his pack with, and took the gold instead—yes, he filled all his pockets, his pack, his cap, and his boots so that he could hardly walk! He had money enough now! He put the dog back on the chest, slammed the door to, and shouted up the tree, 'Haul me up now, old witch!'

'Have you got the tinder-box?' asked the witch.

''Strewth!' said the soldier. 'I've clean forgotten it!' Then he went and fetched it. The witch hauled him up, and so he stood upon the road once more with pockets, boots, pack, and cap all crammed full of money.

'What do you want with that tinder-box?' asked the soldier.

'That's nothing to do with you!' said the witch. 'You've got your money—now give me my tinder-box!'

'Rubbish!' said the soldier. 'Either tell me right now what you want with it, or I'll draw my sword and hack your head off!'

'No, I won't!' said the witch.

So the soldier cut her head off. And there she lay. Then he tied all his money up in her apron, heaved the bundle on to his back, put the tinder-box in his pocket, and marched straight off to the town.

It was a fine town, and he took himself into the finest inn, where he booked the very best rooms, and ordered all the things he liked best to eat, for he was rich now with all that money.

The boot-boy who took his boots to clean thought it decidedly odd that such a rich gentleman should have such an old pair. He had not yet bought himself new ones, but the next day he got new boots and fine new clothes to wear! The soldier had now become a gentleman of note, and people told him about all the fine things to be found in their town, and about their king, and what a lovely princess his daughter was.

'How can you get to see her?' asked the soldier.

'It's quite impossible to get to see her!' everybody said. 'She lives in a great castle made of copper, with ever so many walls and towers round it! No one but the king dare go in and out to her, because it's been foretold that she'll marry an ordinary common soldier, and the king doesn't like the idea at all!'

'I'd very much like to see her!' thought the soldier, but that was something he would certainly never get leave to do!

He was living a life of pleasure now, going to plays, riding in the royal gardens, and giving a great deal of money to the poor—and that was noble of him! He knew well enough from the old days how wretched it can be not to own a penny! He was rich now, he had fine clothes, and he made very many friends who all said he was a rare fellow, a proper gentleman—and that pleased the soldier greatly! But since he was spending his money every day and not getting a penny to replace it, he was left at last with no more than two shillings, and he had to move from the beautiful rooms where he had been living, up to a narrow little attic right under the roof. He had to brush his own boots and mend them with a darning-needle, and none of his friends would come to visit him because there were far too many stairs to go up.

It was quite dark in the evening, and he could not even buy himself a candle, but then he remembered that there was a little stump in the tinder-box he had taken from the hollow tree the witch had helped him to go down. He got the tinder-box and took out the candle-end, but just as he was striking a light and the sparks were flying from the flint, the door sprang open, and the dog with eyes as big as tea-cups, which he had seen down under the tree, stood before him and said, 'What are my master's commands?'

'What on earth!' said the soldier. 'This tinder-box is certainly something, if I can get what I want like this! Fetch me some money!' he said to the dog. He was off in a flash. In another flash he was back again, holding a big bag full of coppers in his mouth!

The soldier now knew what a delightful tinder-box it was! If he struck once, the dog that sat on the chest of copper coins came; if he struck twice, the one that had the silver coins came; and if he struck three times, the one with the gold came. And now the soldier moved down into his beautiful rooms again and went about in good clothes, and so all his friends recognized him immediately, and they were very fond of him. . . .

Then one day he thought, 'It's a very rum thing, though, that you can't get to see the princess! They all say how lovely she must be! But what's the good of that when she's always shut up in that great copper castle

with all those towers! Can't I get to see her somehow?
. . . I've got it!—Where's my tinder-box!' And so he
struck a light, and in a flash there was the dog with eyes
as big as tea-cups!

'I know it's the middle of the night,' said the soldier,
'but I would so love to see the princess, just for a
second!'

The dog was outside the door at once, and before the
soldier had time to realize it, he saw he was back again
with the princess. She was sitting sound asleep on the
dog's back, and she was so lovely anyone could see she
was a real princess. The soldier could not stop himself—
he had to kiss her, for he was a real soldier.

Then the dog ran back again with the princess, but when the morning came and the king and queen were pouring out tea, the princess said she had had such a strange dream during the night about a dog and a soldier. She had ridden on the dog, and the soldier had kissed her.

'That's a fine story, I'm sure!' said the queen.

One of the old ladies-in-waiting now had to keep watch by the princess's bed the next night to see whether it had really been a dream or what else it could be.

The soldier longed terribly to see the lovely princess again, and so the dog came during the night, took her and ran off as fast as he could. But the old lady-in-waiting put her wellingtons on, and ran just as hard after him. When she saw them disappear into a large house, she thought, 'Now I know where it is!' And she drew a large cross on the gate with a piece of chalk. Then she went home and lay down, and the dog came back, too, with the princess. But when he saw that a cross had been drawn on the gate where the soldier lived, he took a piece of chalk, too, and marked crosses on all the gates throughout the whole town. And that was a clever thing to do, for now the lady-in-waiting would certainly not be able to find the right gate when there were crosses on all of them.

Early in the morning the king and the queen, the old lady-in-waiting, and all the officers of the court went to see where it was the princess had been to.

'There it is!' said the king when he saw the first gate with a cross on it.

'No, my dear husband, it's there!' said the queen, who was looking at the second gate with a cross on.

'But there's one there—and one there!' they all cried together, and wherever they looked, there were crosses on the gates. Then they could see it was not any use trying to find it.

Now the queen was a very clever woman, who could do other things besides riding in a coach. She took her big pair of gold scissors, cut out some pieces of silk, and made a pretty little bag from them. She filled it with fine small grains of buckwheat, tied it on the princess's back, and when that was done, she clipped a little hole in the bag so that the grains would be sprinkled all the way along where the princess went.

During the night the dog came again, took the princess on his back, and ran off with her to the soldier, who was so very fond of her and wished so much he had been a prince so that he could have her for his wife.

The dog did not notice the grain sprinkled all along the road from the castle right up to the soldier's window, where he leapt up the wall with the princess. But in the morning the king and queen saw quite clearly where their daughter had been, and so they seized the soldier and threw him into prison.

And there he sat. Oh, how dark and miserable it was—and added to that, they said to him, 'Tomorrow you must be hanged!' That was not at all funny—and he had left his tinder-box behind at the inn. In the morning he looked between the iron bars of his little window and could see people hurrying out of town to see him hanged. He heard the drums and saw the soldiers marching by. Everybody was off to watch, and among them was a cobbler's boy wearing his leather apron and a pair of slippers. He was trotting along at such a gallop that one of his slippers flew off and landed against the wall where the soldier sat peering out between the iron bars.

'Hi, you cobbler's boy! There's no need to be in such a hurry,' the soldier said to him. 'There won't be anything

B

doing before I get there! Just run along to where I live and fetch me my tinder-box, and I'll give you a shilling! But you must make good use of your legs!' The cobbler's boy was anxious to have his shilling and scurried off after the tinder-box. He gave it to the soldier—and now we shall hear what happened!

Outside the town a great gallows had been built, and all round it stood the soldiers and hundreds of thousands of people. The king and queen were sitting on a beautiful throne immediately opposite the judge and the whole council.

The soldier had already mounted the ladder, but just as they were going to fasten the rope about his neck, he said that a wrong-doer was always granted a harmless request before he underwent his punishment. He would dearly love to smoke a pipe of tobacco—it would be his last pipe in this world.

Now the king could not say no to that, and so the soldier took his tinder-box and struck a light—one, two, three! And there stood all the dogs, the one with eyes as big as tea-cups, the one with eyes like millstones, and the one that had eyes as big as the Round Tower!

'Now help me, so that I shan't be hanged!' said the soldier, and so the dogs pounced upon the judge and the whole council, took one by the legs and one by the nose, and hurled them many fathoms up in the air so that when they fell down they were smashed to pieces.

'I will not...!' said the king, but the biggest of the dogs seized both him and the queen, and hurled them up after the rest of them. The soldiers were terrified, and all the people cried out, 'Little soldier, you shall be our king and have our lovely princess!'

So they sat the soldier in the king's coach, and the three dogs all frisked about in front of him and shouted, 'Hurray!' And the boys whistled through their fingers, and the soldiers presented arms. The princess left the copper castle and became queen—she liked that! The wedding lasted a week, and the dogs sat with them at table, their eyes wide with astonishment.

Little Claus and Big Claus

THERE lived in a village two men with the same name. Both were called Claus, but one of them owned four horses, and the other only one. Now to distinguish them one from the other, the one who had four horses was called Big Claus, and the one who had only one was called Little Claus. And now we shall hear what happened to them, for this is a true story!

The whole week through, Little Claus had to plough for Big Claus and lend him his one horse; in return Big Claus helped him with all four of his, but only once a week, and that was on Sundays. Hurray!—How Little Claus cracked his whip over all five horses, for they were certainly as good as his for that one day! The sun was shining beautifully, and all the bells in the church-tower were ringing for church. As the people of the village, all in their Sunday best, went by with their hymn-books under their arms, on their way to hear the parson preach his sermon, they looked at Little Claus ploughing there with five horses, and he was so delighted he cracked his whip again and again, and shouted, 'Gee-up, there, all my horses!'

'You mustn't say that!' said Big Claus. 'You know quite well only one of them is yours!'

But as soon as someone else went by on his way to church, Little Claus forgot that he mustn't say it, and shouted again, 'Gee-up, there, all my horses!'

'Now,' said Big Claus, 'I must ask you to stop it! If you say that once again, I shall strike your horse over the head. Then he'll fall dead on the spot, and that'll be the end of him!'

'I really won't say it any more!' said Little Claus, but as soon as people went past again and nodded good day to him, he was so delighted and thought it looked so grand to have five horses to plough his field with, that he cracked his whip once more and shouted, 'Gee-up, there, all my horses!'

'I'll gee your horses up!' said Big Claus, and he took a mallet and struck Little Claus's horse over the forehead so that it fell down quite dead.

'Oh, now I've no horse at all!' said Little Claus, and started crying. Shortly afterwards he flayed his horse, took the hide and let it dry thoroughly in the wind: then he put it in a bag, slung it over his shoulders and trudged off to the town to sell his horsehide.

He had a very long way to go. He had to go through a great dark wood, and the weather had now turned frightful: he lost his way completely, and before he came upon the right road again it was evening, and it was much too far either to go on to the town or to turn back home before it was night.

Close by the roadside there lay a large farmhouse. The shutters outside the windows were closed, but a light was shining out over the top of them. 'Perhaps they might let me stay the night here,' thought Little Claus. So he went up to the door and knocked.

The farmer's wife opened the door, but when she heard what he wanted, she said he'd better be on his way, her husband was not at home, and she didn't let strangers in.

'Well then, I must find somewhere to lie down outside,' said Little Claus, and the farmer's wife shut the door in his face.

Close by stood a haystack, and between it and the house was built a little shed with a flat thatched roof.

'I can lie down up there!' said Little Claus, as he noticed

the roof. 'That'll make a very nice bed, so long as the stork doesn't fly down and nip me in the leg.' For there was a stork standing wide awake up on the roof, where it had its nest.

Then Little Claus climbed up on to the shed, and there he lay twisting and turning until he was comfortable. The wooden shutters in front of the windows did not meet properly at the top, and so he could see right into the living-room.

There was a great table set there, with wine and a roast joint and a lovely fish. The farmer's wife and the parish clerk were sitting at the table, and there was no one else there at all. She was pouring out for him, and he was tucking into the fish, for that was something he was very fond of.

'I'd like a bit of that, too!' said Little Claus, craning his neck towards the window. My, what lovely cakes he could see down there on the table! It was a regular feast!

Then he heard someone riding along the road towards the house—it was the farmer coming home.

He was a real good-hearted man, but he had one odd weakness—he just couldn't bear to see a parish clerk. If ever he caught sight of one, he became quite frantic. And so that was why the parish clerk had come to say good evening to the farmer's wife while he knew her husband was away from home, and the good woman had set before him all the nicest things she had to eat. Then when they heard her husband coming, they were so terrified that the wife told the parish clerk to crawl into a big empty chest that stood over in the corner. And that's what he did, for he was well aware that the poor farmer couldn't stand the sight of a parish clerk. The farmer's wife hastily hid all the lovely food and wine inside her baking-oven, for if her husband caught sight of them, he would undoubtedly ask what it was all about.

'Ah, well!' sighed Little Claus, up on the shed, as he saw all the food put away.

'Is there anyone up there?' asked the farmer, peering up at Little Claus. 'What are you lying up there for? You'd better come in with me!'

So Little Claus told him how he had lost his way, and asked if he could put him up for the night.

'Why, of course!' said the farmer. 'But we must have a bit to eat first!'

The farmer's wife seemed very pleased to see them both, spread a cloth on a long table, and gave them a large basin of porridge. The farmer was hungry and ate with a good appetite, but Little Claus couldn't stop thinking of the lovely roast joint, fish, and cakes he knew were standing inside the oven.

He had put the sack with the horsehide down by his feet under the table, for, you remember, it was to sell this in the town that he had left home that day. He didn't fancy the porridge a bit, and so he trod on the sack and the dry skin inside squeaked quite loudly.

'Sh!' said Little Claus to his sack, but at the same time he trod on it again, and it squeaked much louder than before.

'What's that you've got in your sack?' asked the farmer.

'Oh, that's a wizard!' said Little Claus. 'He says there's no need for us to eat porridge. He's conjured up a whole ovenful of roast beef, fish, and cake.'

'What!' cried the farmer, and had the oven open in a flash. There he saw all the good food his wife had hidden, but of course he believed the wizard in the sack had conjured it up for them. His wife dared not say a word. She set the food on the table at once, and they ate the fish and the roast beef and the cake. Little Claus thereupon trod on the sack again and made the hide squeak.

'What does he say now?' asked the farmer.

'He says,' said Little Claus, 'that he's also conjured up three bottles of wine for us, and they're standing in the oven, too!' And now the farmer's wife had to take out the wine she had hidden, and the farmer drank and grew quite merry: he would dearly love to own a wizard like the one Little Claus had in his sack.

'Can he conjure up the devil, too?' asked the farmer. 'I'd like to see him, for I'm feeling merry now!'

'Yes,' said Little Claus, 'my wizard can do anything I ask him. True, isn't it?' he asked, treading on the sack and making it squeak. 'Did you hear him say, "Of course!"? But the devil looks horrible. I shouldn't ask to see him if I were you!'

'Oh, I'm not frightened of him! What does he look like?'

'Why, he'll be the spitting image of a parish clerk!'

'Ugh!' said the farmer. 'That'd be horrible! I'd better warn you that I just can't stand the sight of a parish clerk! But now that I know that it's only the devil, I shan't mind so much! I've got my courage back now—but he mustn't come too near me!'

'I'll ask my wizard now,' said Little Claus, treading on his sack and bending his ear down to listen.

'What's he say?'

'He says if you go and open that chest over there in the corner, you'll see the devil skulking inside, but you must keep hold of the lid so that he can't slip out.'

'Will you help me to hold it?' asked the farmer, as he went over to the chest where his wife had hidden the real parish clerk, who was crouching inside, much afraid.

The farmer lifted up the lid a little way and peeped under it. 'Ugh!' he shrieked, springing backwards. 'You're right! As I caught sight of him, he looked just like our parish clerk! Oh, it was ghastly!'

They had to have a drink to recover, and then they went on drinking far into the night.

'You must sell me your wizard,' said the farmer. 'Ask whatever you like for him! Tell you what, I'll give you a bushel of money right away!'

'No, I couldn't do that!' said Little Claus. 'Just think how much my wizard can do for me!'

'Ah, I'd dearly love to have him,' said the farmer. And he went on pleading.

'Well,' said Little Claus at last, 'since you've been good

enough to give me house-room for the night, I don't mind if I do. You shall have the wizard for a bushel of money—but the bushel must be brim-full, mind!'

'That it shall!' said the farmer. 'But you must take the chest away with you. I'll not have it in the house an hour longer—you can never tell but what he's still inside it!'

Little Claus gave the farmer the sack with the dry hide inside it, and got a bushelful of money—top measure, too —in exchange. The farmer also made him a present of a large wheelbarrow to carry away the money and the chest.

'Good-bye!' said Little Claus, as he wheeled off the money and the great chest where the parish clerk was still crouched.

On the other side of the wood was a deep wide stream, its current running so strongly that one could hardly swim against it. A big new bridge had been built over it, and Little Claus stopped in the middle of it and said quite loudly so that the parish clerk inside the chest could hear him:

'What on earth do I want with this damn-fool chest? It's so heavy, it might be full of stones! I'm much too tired to push it any farther, so I'll just tip it over into the stream: if it floats down to the house, well and good; if it doesn't, it's all the same to me.'

Then he took hold of the chest with one hand and lifted it a little, as if he were about to push it over into the water.

'No! No! Stop it!' cried the parish clerk from inside the chest. 'Let me out first!'

'Ooh,' said Little Claus, pretending to be frightened, 'he's still there! I must topple it over into the stream right away and drown him!'

'Oh, no, no!' cried the parish clerk. 'I'll give you a whole bushelful of money if you'll only stop!'

'Well, that's another matter!' said Little Claus, and opened the chest. The parish clerk crawled out at once,

kicked the empty chest into the water, and went to his house, where he gave Little Claus a whole bushelful of money. With the one he had already got from the farmer, he now had a whole wheelbarrow full!

'Well, I've been pretty well paid for my horse!' he said to himself, when he was home again in his own room, and had tipped out all the money in a great heap in the middle of the floor. 'Won't Big Claus be annoyed when he gets to know how rich I've become from my one horse—but I won't tell him right out just like that!'

Then he sent a boy over to Big Claus to borrow a bushel-measure.

'I wonder what he wants with that!' thought Big Claus,

and smeared some tar on the bottom so that a little of whatever was measured in it should stick to it. And it did, too, for when he got his bushel-measure back, there were three new half-crowns sticking to it.

'What on earth!' said Big Claus, and ran straight over to Little Claus. 'Where have you got all that money from?'

'Oh, I got that for my horsehide I sold last night!'

'You got a pretty good price for it, I'll say!' said Big Claus. He ran home, took an axe and struck all four of his horses over the head with it. Then he flayed them and drove into the town with the hides.

'Hides! Hides! Who'll buy my hides!' he cried through the streets.

All the cobblers and tanners came running out and asked what he wanted for them.

'A bushel of money each!' said Big Claus.

'Are you mad?' they all said. 'Do you think we have money by the bushel?'

'Hides! Hides! Who'll buy my hides!' he cried again, but to everyone who asked what the hides cost he answered, 'A bushel of money!'

'He's trying to make fools of us,' they all said, and so the cobblers took their straps and the tanners their leather aprons, and they all set about Big Claus.

'Hides! Hides!' they mocked. 'We'll give you a hide all right—one that will spit red! Out of the town with him!' they cried, and Big Claus, thrashed as he had never been before, had to take to his heels for all he was worth.

'All right!' he said when he got home. 'Little Claus shall pay for this! I'll strike him dead!'

But Little Claus's grandmother lay dead in the house: true, she had always been very ill-tempered and unkind to him, but he was still quite sorry. He took the dead woman and laid her in his own warm bed to see if that would bring her back to life again. He would let her stay there all night, while he himself would sit on a chair over in the corner and go to sleep, as he had often done before.

During the night while he was sitting there, the door opened and in came Big Claus with his axe. He knew quite well where Little Claus's bed stood, and so he went straight over to it and struck the dead grandmother over the head, believing, of course, that it was Little Claus.

'There !' he said. 'Now you won't make a fool of me again!' And so he went back home.

'He's a bad wicked man!' said Little Claus. 'He wanted to strike me dead. It's a good thing the old woman was dead already, otherwise he'd have killed her!'

Then he dressed his old grandmother up in her Sunday best, borrowed a horse from one of the neighbours, harnessed it to the cart, and sat his old grandmother up in the back seat so that she couldn't fall out when he was driving, and then they drove off through the wood. When the sun rose, they were outside a large inn, where Little Claus drew up and went in to get something to eat.

The innkeeper was very, very rich: he was a very good man, too, but so quick-tempered you would have thought he was made of pepper and snuff.

'Good morning!' he said to Little Claus. 'You're up very early today in all your best clothes!'

'Yes,' said Little Claus, 'I have to go into town with my old grandmother. She's sitting outside in the cart. I can't get her inside, but would you mind taking her a glass of mead? You must speak fairly loud to her: her hearing's none too good.'

'Righto, I will!' said the innkeeper, and he poured a large glass of mead which he took out to the dead grandmother propped up in the cart.

'Here's a glass of mead from your grandson!' said the innkeeper, but the dead woman said never a word and sat quite still.

'Can't you hear!' bawled the innkeeper as loud as he could. 'Here's a glass of mead from your grandson!'

Once more he shouted the same thing, and then yet again. But as she did not make the slightest movement, he lost his temper and threw the glass right in her face so that the mead ran down her nose and she fell backwards into the cart, for she was only propped up and not fastened in any way.

'Good God!' cried Little Claus, rushing out of the door and seizing the innkeeper by his lapels. 'You've killed my grandmother! Just look at that great hole in her forehead!'

'Oh dear, oh dear, it was an accident!' wailed the innkeeper, beating his hands together. 'It's all because of my bad temper! My dear Little Claus, I'll give you a whole bushel of money and have your grandmother buried as if she were my own, if only you'll say nothing—otherwise they'll have my head off, and that'd be frightful!'

So Little Claus got a whole bushel of money, and the innkeeper buried his old grandmother as if she were his own.

Now when Little Claus got home again with all this money, he sent his lad over to Big Claus right away to ask if he might borrow a bushel-measure.

'What on earth?' said Big Claus. 'Haven't I killed him after all? I must look into this myself!' And so he took the measure over to Little Claus.

'My, where did you get all this money from?' he asked, opening his eyes wide at the sight of all the money he had come by.

'It was my grandmother you struck dead—not me!' said Little Claus. 'I've just sold her and got a bushel of money for her!'

'That was a good price, I must say!' said Big Claus, and he hurried home, took an axe and struck his own old grandmother dead straight away. He sat her up in a cart, drove into town to where the apothecary lived and asked if he would like to buy a dead body.

'Who is it, and where have you got it from?' asked the apothecary.

'It's my grandmother!' said Big Claus. 'I hit her over the head so that I can get a bushel of money for her!'

'Heaven preserve us!' said the apothecary. 'You can't know what you're saying! For God's sake, don't say things like that or you'll lose your head!' And then he told him plainly what a terribly wicked thing he had done, and what a bad man he was, and how he ought to be punished; whereupon Big Claus was so terrified, he rushed straight out of the apothecary's shop and into his cart, whipped up the horses and made for home. But the apothecary and everybody else thought he was mad, and so they let him go wherever he would.

'You shall pay for this!' said Big Claus, when he was out on the open road. 'Yes, you shall pay for this all right, Little Claus!' And then, as soon as he got home, he took the biggest sack he could find, went over to Little Claus and said, 'Now you've made a fool of me again! First I kill my horses, and then I kill my old grandmother! And it's all your fault! But you shall never make a fool of me again!' And then he took hold of Little Claus round the waist and thrust him into the sack. He heaved him up on his shoulders and cried, 'Now I'm going out to drown you!'

It was quite a long way to go before he came to the stream, and Little Claus was not so light to carry. The road went close by the church, where the organ was playing and the congregation singing. So Big Claus put down the sack with Little Claus inside close by the church door. He thought it would be rather nice to go in and listen to a hymn first before he went any farther: Little Claus couldn't possibly get out, and everyone was in church: so in he went.

'Oh, dear! Oh, dear!' sighed Little Claus inside the sack: he turned and he twisted, but it was quite impossible to loosen the string. At that moment an old cattle-drover came along: he had snow-white hair and he leant upon a stout staff. He was driving a whole drove of cows and bulls in front of him, and some of them bumped against the sack where Little Claus sat huddled up, and knocked it over.

'Oh, dear!' sighed Little Claus. 'I'm so young, and I'm on my way to heaven already!'

'And poor old me!' said the cattle-drover. 'I'm so old, and I can't get there yet!'

'Open the sack!' cried Little Claus. 'If you crawl inside and take my place, you'll get to heaven right away!'

'I'd dearly love to!' said the cattle-drover, and opened the sack for Little Claus who scrambled out at once.

'Will you look after the cattle?' said the old man, as he crawled into the sack. Little Claus tied it up, and then went on his way with all the cows and bulls.

A little later Big Claus came out of the church. He

c

heaved the sack upon his shoulders again, and thought it
had become much lighter. He was quite right, for the old
cattle-drover was scarcely half the weight of Little Claus.
'He feels a lot lighter now—it must be because I listened
to that hymn!' So he went on to the stream that ran deep
and wide, threw the sack with the old cattle-drover inside
over into the water, and shouted after him—he still believed he was Little Claus, of course—'There, now you
shan't make a fool of me any more!'

So he turned homewards, but when he came to the
cross-roads, he met Little Claus driving his cattle along.

'What on earth!' cried Big Claus. 'Haven't I just
drowned you?'

'Yes, of course you have!' said Little Claus. 'You threw
me into the river not half an hour ago!'

'But where did you get all those fine cattle from?'
asked Big Claus.

'They're sea-cattle!' said Little Claus. 'I must tell you

the whole story—but first I must thank you for drowning me, for I'm well off now: I'm really rich, believe me!— I was very frightened when I was in that sack, and the wind whistled in my ears as you threw me over the bridge into the cold water. I sank at once to the bottom, but I didn't hurt myself, for it was covered in fine soft grass. I landed on this, and the sack was opened at once, and the loveliest young lady in a snow-white dress with a green wreath on her wet hair took me by the hand and said, "So it's you, Little Claus? First of all, here are some cattle for you! And five or six miles along the road, there's another drove waiting—and I'm going to make you a present of them, too!" Then I saw that the river was like a main road for the sea-folk: down there on the river-bed they were walking and riding all the way from the sea right up into the land where the stream comes to an end. It was lovely down there, with flowers and fresh grass and fishes swimming in the water and playing round my ears, just like birds in the sky. They were such nice-looking people there, and you should have seen the cattle walking along by the ditches and fences!'

'But why have you come up here again so soon?' asked Big Claus. 'I shouldn't have, if it was so nice down there!'

'Well,' said Little Claus, 'that's just my artfulness! You remember I told you the sea-lady said that five or six miles up the road—and by road she meant the river, of course, because she can't go anywhere else—there was another whole drove of cattle awaiting me? But you know how the river twists and turns, now this way, now that, taking you a long way out of your way. If you can do it, it's much shorter to cut across the land and join the river again higher up. I shall save about half the journey that way, and get to my sea-cattle all the more quickly!'

'What a lucky fellow you are!' said Big Claus. 'Do you

think I should get some sea-cattle if I went down to the bed of the river?'

'Yes, I should think so!' said Little Claus. 'But I can't carry you in a sack all the way to the river. You're too heavy for me. But if you like to walk there by yourself and then crawl into the sack, I'll throw you into the water with the greatest pleasure!'

'Thank you very much!' said Big Claus. 'But, mind, if I don't get any sea-cattle when I get down there, I'll give you a good hiding, you trust me!'

'Oh, please, you wouldn't be so unkind!' And so they walked along to the river. As soon as the cattle, who were thirsty, saw the water, they ran as hard as they could so that they could go down and drink.

'Look at the hurry they're in!' said Little Claus. 'They're longing to get down on the river-bed again!'

'Yes, but you must help me first!' said Big Claus. 'Or else you'll get that hiding!' And so he crawled into a big sack which they had found lying across the back of one of the bulls. 'Put a stone in, else I'm afraid I shan't sink!' said Big Claus.

'You'll do that all right!' said Little Claus, but he put a big stone in the sack all the same, tied the string tight, and then gave it a good push. Splash! Over went Big Claus into the river and he sank down to the bottom at once.

'I'm afraid he won't find his sea-cattle!' said Little Claus, as he made his way home with what he had got.

The Princess and the Pea

THERE was once a prince who wanted to marry a princess. But she had to be a real princess. So he travelled all round the world to find one, but there was always something wrong—there were plenty of princesses, though whether they were real princesses he could never quite find out: there was always something that was not just right. So he came home again and was very unhappy because he wanted so much to have a real princess.

One evening there was a dreadful storm: it thundered and lightened and the rain poured down in torrents—it was really quite frightening! Then there came a knock at the town gate, and the old king went out and opened it.

It was a princess who stood outside. But my, what a sight she was with the rain and the storm! Her hair and her clothes were running with water: water was running in through the toes of her shoes and out at the heels. But she said she was a real princess.

'Well, we shall soon find out!' thought the old queen to herself. She went into the bedroom, took all the bedclothes off and put a pea on the bottom of the bed. Then she took twenty mattresses and laid them on top of the pea, and then twenty eiderdowns on top of the mattresses.

And there the princess had to spend the night.

In the morning they asked her how she had slept.

'Oh, terribly badly!' said the princess. 'I have hardly shut my eyes the whole night! Heaven knows what there was in the bed! I have been lying on something hard—I am black and blue all over! It's really dreadful!'

And so they could see she was a real princess, because she had felt the pea through twenty mattresses and twenty eiderdowns. No one but a real princess could possibly be so sensitive.

Then the prince married her, for he was now sure that he had found a real princess, and the pea was placed in the art museum, where it can still be seen if no one has taken it.

And that's a true story!

Little Ida's Flowers

'MY poor flowers are quite dead!' said little Ida.
'They were so pretty yesterday evening, and
now all their petals are drooping and withered!
Why have they gone like that?' she asked the student who
was sitting on the sofa. She was very fond of him: he
knew the loveliest stories and would cut out such amusing pictures—hearts with little ladies dancing in them,
flowers and great castles with doors that could open: he
was such good fun! 'Why do the flowers look so poorly
today?' she asked again, and she showed him a whole
bunch that were quite withered.

'Do you know what's the matter with them?' said the
student. 'The flowers have been to a ball during the
night, and that's why they're hanging their heads!'

'But surely flowers can't dance!' said little Ida.

'Oh, yes, they can!' said the student. 'When it's dark
and we're all asleep, they dance around quite gaily—
they have a ball nearly every night!'

'Can't children go with them to the ball?'

'Why, yes,' said the student: 'tiny daisies and lilies-of-
the-valley!'

'Where do the nicest flowers dance?' asked little
Ida.

'Haven't you often been out through the gate near the
great palace where the king lives in the summer-time and
where the beautiful garden is with all the flowers in it?
You must have seen the swans that swim right up to you
when you want to give them bread-crumbs. There's a
ball there right enough—you can be sure of that!'

'I was over there in the garden yesterday with my

mother!' said Ida. 'But all the leaves were off the trees, and there wasn't one flower left anywhere! Where are they? I saw so many in the summer!'

'They're inside the palace!' said the student. 'As soon as the king and all the people of the court move over here into the city, the flowers, you know, run straight up from the garden into the palace and enjoy themselves. You should see them! The two most beautiful roses seat themselves upon the throne, and then they're king and queen. The red coxcombs all line up beside them, and there they stand bowing and pretending to be gentlemen of the chamber. Then along come all the prettiest of the flowers and they hold a great ball; the blue violets, look-ing like little midshipmen, dance with the hyacinths and crocuses, whom they call young ladies! The tulips and the great yellow lilies are the elderly ladies who see to it that the dancing is nicely conducted and that everything is done properly!'

'But,' asked little Ida, 'doesn't anyone do anything to the flowers for dancing in the king's palace?'

'There isn't anyone who really knows about it!' said the student. 'Sometimes, it's true, the old palace steward, whose job it is to keep an eye on everything, will pass by during the night, but he carries a great bunch of keys with him, and as soon as the flowers hear the keys rattling, they stay quite still, and they hide behind the long curtains and poke their heads out. "I can smell something—there are flowers in here!" says the old palace steward—but he can't see them!'

'That is funny!' said little Ida, clapping her hands. 'But couldn't I see the flowers either?'

'Of course you could!' said the student. 'Just re-member, when you're there next time, to peep in through the window, and you'll see them right enough! I looked in today, and there was a tall yellow daffodil lying on the sofa, stretching and fancying herself a lady of the court!'

'Can the flowers in the Botanical Gardens go there as well? Can they go all that way?'

'Yes, you bet they can!' said the student. 'When they want to, they can fly. You must have seen those beautiful butterflies, red and yellow and white, that look almost like flowers. That's what they once were. They jump off their stalks high up into the air, beat their petals as if they were little wings, and off they fly—and if they behave themselves, they're free to fly about during the day-time as well: they don't have to go home again and sit still on their stalks: and so in the end their petals become real wings. You must have noticed that yourself! Of course, it could be that the flowers in the Botanical Gardens have never been to the king's palace or even been told what merry times they have there at night. And if that should be so, I'll tell you something that'll make him ever so surprised—the Professor of Botany, I mean, who lives next door to the gardens—you know him, don't you? The next time you go into his gardens, you must tell one of the flowers that there's going to be a great ball at the palace, and then it will tell all the others and off they'll fly. Then when the professor goes out into the gardens, there won't be a single flower left, and he won't have the faintest idea where they've got to!'

'But how can the flower tell the others? Surely flowers can't talk!'

'No, you're quite right, they can't!' answered the student. 'But they can mime! Haven't you noticed how flowers nod their heads in a light breeze and sway all their leaves!—Their meaning's just as plain as if they were speaking!'

'And can the professor understand their miming?' asked Ida.

'Rather! Of course he can! One morning he went down into the gardens and saw a tall stinging-nettle standing there miming with its leaves to a lovely red carnation: it was saying, "You're so pretty, and I do love you so much!" But the professor can't stand that sort of thing and slapped the stinging-nettle at once across the leaves, which are, of course, its fingers, and so he got stung and from that time he's never dared to meddle with a stinging-nettle.'

'That was funny!' said little Ida, laughing.

'Fancy putting such ideas into the child's head!' said the dull old councillor who had come visiting and was sitting on the sofa: he couldn't bear the student and always grew irritated when he saw him cutting out his queer amusing pictures: sometimes a man hanging from the gallows and holding a heart in his hand to show he had been a stealer of hearts; sometimes an old witch riding on a broomstick and carrying her husband on her nose—the councillor couldn't abide such things, and so he would say, as he did now, 'Putting such ideas into the child's head! Nothing but foolish fancies!'

But what the student had told her about her flowers seemed great fun to little Ida, and she thought a lot about it: the flowers were hanging their heads because they were tired from dancing the whole night, and they were really unwell. So she took them over to where all her toys stood on a neat little table with its drawer full of odds and ends. In the doll's bed her dolly, Sophie, lay asleep, but little Ida said to her, 'You really must get up, Sophie, and make do with the drawer to lie in tonight. The poor flowers aren't well and so they must lie in your bed, and then perhaps they'll feel better!' And so she took her dolly up, but Sophie looked very sullen and refused to say a single word, she was so cross at not being allowed to stay in her own bed.

So Ida laid the flowers down in the doll's bed, drew the little coverlet right up round them and said they must now lie nice and quiet and then she would make them a cup of tea so that they would feel well enough to get up in the morning. Then she drew the curtains close round the little bed to prevent the sun from shining into their eyes.

All through the evening she could not stop thinking of what the student had told her, and when it was time for her to go to bed herself, she had first to peep behind the curtains that hung down in front of the windows where her mother's beautiful flowers stood, both hyacinths and tulips, and she whispered quite softly, 'I know you're going to the ball tonight!' The flowers pretended they had not understood and did not stir a leaf, but little Ida knew what she knew.

When she was in bed, she lay awake a long time thinking how nice it would be to see the beautiful flowers dancing in the king's palace. 'I wonder whether my flowers have really been there?' But at that point she fell asleep. Far into the night she woke again: she had been dreaming about the flowers and the student whom the councillor had been telling off for putting ideas into her head. It was quite quiet in the bedroom where Ida lay: the night-light was burning over on the table, and her mother and father were asleep.

'I wonder whether my flowers are still lying in Sophie's bed?' she said to herself. 'I'd love to know!' She raised herself up a little and looked towards the door that stood half open: through there lay the flowers and all her toys. She listened, and it was just as if she heard someone playing the piano in the living-room, but very softly and much more prettily than she had ever heard it before.

'The flowers must all be dancing in there now!' she said. 'Oh, how I'd love to see them!' But she dared not get up for fear of waking her father and mother. 'If only they'd come in here!' she said; but the flowers did not come and the music went on playing so prettily that at last she could contain herself no longer, it was so lovely. She crept out of her little bed, tip-toed quietly to the door, and peeped into the living-room. Oh, what she saw there! What fun it was!

There was no night-light there, and yet it was quite light, for the moon was shining through the window right on to the middle of the floor! It was almost like day. All the hyacinths and tulips were standing in two long rows on the floor—there were none at all left in the window where the empty pots stood. Down upon the floor the flowers were all dancing so prettily round about one another, making proper chains and holding each other by their long green leaves as they swung round. And over at the piano sat a large yellow lily that little Ida was certain she had seen during the summer, for she clearly remembered the student's saying, 'My, doesn't it look like Miss Line!' They had all laughed at him, but now Ida, too, thought the tall yellow lily really did look like her, and it played with the same mannerisms as well, leaning its long yellow face now to one side, now to the other, and nodding in time to the lovely music. Not one of them noticed little Ida. And now she saw a big blue crocus jump right up on to the middle of the table where her toys were standing, go straight to the doll's bed and draw aside the curtains: there lay the sick flowers, but they got up at once and nodded to the others down below to show that they wanted to join in the dancing. The old

man with the pipe, whose
lower lip was broken off,
stood bowing before the beautiful flowers, not looking at
all unwell as they jumped
down among the others and
enjoyed themselves.

There was a sound just
like something falling off the
table. Ida looked up: it was
her Shrove-Monday birch-
rod[1] which had jumped
down, thinking, no doubt,
that it belonged where the
flowers were. It was a very prettily decorated rod, and
right on top of it sat a little wax doll which wore upon
its head a broad-brimmed hat exactly like the councillor's.
The birch-rod hopped upon its three red wooden legs in
among the flowers, and it stamped quite hard for it was
dancing the mazurka, and that was a dance the flowers
could not do as they were so light-footed and quite unable to stamp.

All at once the wax doll on top of the birch-rod grew
big and tall, spun round above the paper flowers on the
rod and shouted quite loudly, 'Putting such ideas into the
child's head! Nothing but foolish fancies!' And the wax
doll looked exactly like the councillor in his broad-
brimmed hat, and its face was just as sallow and bad-
tempered. But the paper flowers smacked its thin legs,

[1] On the day before our Shrove Tuesday, Danish children wake
their parents up by hitting them with small bundles of two or three
birch twigs tied together and decorated with little flags and paper
flowers. It is all done in fun, of course, and is one of several Danish
customs quite unknown in this country. L. W. K.

and so it shrank once more into a tiny little wax doll. It was very funny! Little Ida could not stop herself from laughing. The birch-rod went on dancing and the councillor-doll had to dance with it—no matter whether it made itself big and tall or remained a little yellow wax doll with a big black hat. Then the flowers, and especially

those that had lain in the doll's bed, pleaded for him, and so the birch-rod stopped. At that moment there was a loud knocking inside the drawer where Ida's doll, Sophie, was lying with all the other toys. The man with the pipe ran to the edge of the table, and, lying full-length upon his tummy, reached down and gave the drawer a little pull. Sophie raised herself up and looked round in wonder. 'Why, there's a ball!' she said. 'Why didn't anyone tell me?'

'Will you dance with me?' asked the man with the pipe.

'Well, you're a fine one to dance with!' she said, turning her back on him. And so she sat down on the edge of the drawer and thought that one of the flowers would be sure to come and ask for a dance. But none came, so she coughed, 'Hm, hm, hm!' but still no one came. And the man with the pipe danced all by himself—and not so badly either!

As none of the flowers seemed to have noticed Sophie, she let herself drop right down from the drawer to the floor; that made a great stir; all the flowers came running round her and asked whether she had hurt herself, and they were all very nice to her, especially the flowers that had been lying in her bed. But she had not hurt herself at all, and all Ida's flowers said thank you for her lovely bed and made a fuss of her. They led her to the middle of the floor where the moon was shining, and as they danced with her, all the other flowers made a ring about them. Sophie was now quite happy, and she said they could keep her bed with pleasure, she didn't at all mind lying in the drawer.

But the flowers said, 'Thank you very much indeed, but we shan't live long enough for that! Tomorrow we shall be quite dead. But tell little Ida that she must bury us out in the garden where the canary lies, and then we shall grow up again in the summer and be even more beautiful!'

'No, you mustn't die!' said Sophie, as she kissed the flowers. At that moment the room-door opened, and a whole crowd of beautiful flowers came dancing in—Ida had not the least idea where they had come from, though she felt certain they were the flowers from the king's palace. First of all came two lovely roses wearing little golden crowns—they were king and queen; then came the prettiest stocks and pinks bowing to all sides. They had a band with them—large poppies and peonies were blowing on pea-pods until they were quite red in the face. The bluebells and the little white snowdrops tinkled as if they had bells on them. The band was fun. Then came many other flowers and they all danced together, blue violets, red and white daisies and lilies-of-the-valley. And all the flowers kissed one another—it was quite delightful to watch them.

At last the flowers said good night to one another; then little Ida crept back to bed, too, and there she dreamed of all that she had seen.

When she got up the next morning, she went straight to the little table to see if the flowers were still there. She drew back the curtains from the little bed—yes, there they lay all together, but they were quite withered, much more so than the day before. Sophie was lying in the drawer where she had laid her and she looked quite sleepy.

'Can you remember what you have to tell me?' little Ida asked, but Sophie looked completely stupid and did not say a single word.

'You're very naughty,' said Ida, 'and they did all dance with you.' Then she took a little cardboard box with pretty birds painted on it, opened it and laid the dead flowers inside. 'This shall be your nice little coffin,' she said, 'and when my cousins from Norway come to see me, they shall help to bury you out in the garden so that you can grow up again in the summer and be even more beautiful!'

The cousins from Norway were two lively boys called Jonas and Adolph. Their father had made them a present of two new cross-bows, and they had brought them to show Ida. She told them about the poor flowers that had died, and then they got leave to bury them. The two boys walked in front with their cross-bows on their shoulders, and little Ida followed them with the dead flowers in their pretty box. Out in the garden a little grave was dug. First Ida kissed the flowers, then she put them with their box into the ground, and Adolph and Jonas fired their cross-bows over the grave, for they had no guns nor cannon either.

Thumbelina

ONCE upon a time, there was a woman who longed for a little child of her own, but she had no idea where she could get one. So off she went to see an old witch, and she said to her, 'I'd so much like to have a little child! Won't you please tell me where I can get one from?'

'Why, yes, that's no trouble at all!' said the witch. 'You must take this grain of barley—it's not the kind that grows in the farmer's field or that hens eat, either— put it in a flower-pot, and then wait and see what happens!'

'Oh, thank you kindly!' said the woman. She gave the witch a shilling, and then went home and planted the grain of barley. A beautiful big flower sprang up at once —it looked very much like a tulip, but the petals were tightly closed as though it were still in bud.

'What a pretty flower it is!' said the woman, kissing its beautiful red and yellow petals, but just as she kissed it, the flower suddenly burst open. You could see it was a real tulip now, but right in the middle of the flower, on a green stool, sat a tiny little girl, delicate and lovely: she was not above an inch tall, and so she was called Thumbelina.

She was given a splendid lacquered walnut-shell as her cradle, blue violet-petals formed her mattress, and a rose-petal her eiderdown. There she slept at night, but during the day she played on the table where the woman had set a plate with a wreath of flowers arranged round the edge so that the stalks lay in the water. On the surface, a large tulip-petal floated, and Thumbelina could sit in it and sail from one side of the plate to the other—she had two white horsehairs to row with. It looked very pretty indeed. She could sing, too—so daintily and charmingly that no one had ever heard the like.

One night, as she lay in her beautiful bed, an ugly old toad came hopping in through the window, where there was a broken pane of glass. The toad looked very big and wet and ugly as she hopped straight down on to the table where Thumbelina lay asleep under her red rose-petal.

'She'd make a nice wife for my son!' said the toad, and so she took hold of the walnut-shell where Thumbelina was sleeping, and hopped off with her through the broken pane down into the garden.

Down at the bottom flowed a big broad stream, and close by the bank the ground was marshy and muddy: here the toad lived with her son. Ugh! he was ugly and repulsive, too, and looked exactly like his mother. 'Croak, croak, cro-ak-ak!' was all he could say when he saw the charming little girl in the walnut-shell.

'Don't talk so loud, or she'll wake!' said the old toad. 'She could still run away from us, for she's as light as swansdown! We'll put her out in the stream on one of the broad water-lily leaves—she's so light and small, it'll seem like an island to her! She won't be able to run away from there, and in the meantime we'll spring-clean the best room down under the mud, and you shall settle down and live there together!'

Out in the stream grew a mass of water-lilies with broad green leaves that looked as if they were floating on top of

the water; the leaf that lay farthest out was also the biggest, and the old toad swam out to it and there she put down the walnut-shell with Thumbelina inside.

The poor little thing woke quite early in the morning, and when she saw where she was, she began to cry bitterly, for there was water all round the big green leaf, and she had no way at all of getting to land.

The old toad sat down below in the mud, decorating her room with rushes and yellow water-flowers to make it neat and pretty for her new daughter-in-law. Then she swam out with her ugly son to the leaf where Thumbelina was standing. They had come to fetch her pretty bed which they wanted to have ready in the bride's bedroom before she came. The old toad bowed deeply in the water to her and said, 'This is my son you see with me: he's going to be your husband, and the two of you shall have a very nice place to live in down below in the mud!'

But all the son could say was, 'Croak, croak! Cro-ak-ak!'

So they took her pretty little bed and swam away with it, but Thumbelina sat quite alone on the green leaf and wept, for she had no wish to go and live with the horrid old toad, nor to have her ugly son for a husband. The little fishes, swimming down below in the water, had seen the toad and heard what she said, and so they popped their heads up to take a look at the little girl. As soon as they set eyes on her, they saw how lovely she was, and they were very upset that she had to go and live in the mud with the ugly toad. No, that should never happen! Down in the water, they swarmed round the green stalk that held the leaf she was standing on and gnawed it through with their teeth. And so the leaf floated away down the stream with Thumbelina, far away where the toad could not reach her.

Thumbelina sailed along past a great many places, and the little birds sitting in the bushes saw her and sang, 'What a charming little maiden!' The leaf floated farther and farther away with her, and so at last Thumbelina journeyed into a strange country.

A pretty little white butterfly fluttered round her for some time and at last settled on the leaf, for it had taken quite a liking to Thumbelina, and she was very happy now, for the toad could no longer reach her and everything was so lovely as she sailed along. The sun was shining upon the water and it looked like gleaming gold. Then she took her sash and tied one end of it round the butterfly and made the other end fast in the leaf so that it now sped along much more swiftly and, of course, took her with it.

Just then a great cockchafer came flying by; he caught sight of her, and in a flash fastened his claws about her slender waist and flew up into a tree with her. But the green leaf floated away down the stream, and the butterfly flew with it, for it was tied to the leaf and could not free itself.

Heavens, how terrified poor Thumbelina was when the

cockchafer flew up into the tree with her! But she was most sorry for the beautiful white butterfly she had tied fast to the leaf: if it could not free itself, it would certainly die of hunger. But the cockchafer cared nothing for that. He sat down with her on the largest green leaf in the tree, gave her honeydew from the flowers to eat, and told her she was very pretty, although she was not at all like a cockchafer. Then all the other cockchafers that lived in the tree came to visit her. They looked at Thumbelina, and the young lady cockchafers shrugged their feelers and said, 'But she's only two legs—what a pitiful-looking thing she is!' 'She hasn't any feelers!' 'Her waist is so thin—pooh, she looks just like a human! How ugly she is!' said all the lady cockchafers—and yet Thumbelina was really very pretty! And that's what the cockchafer who had carried her off thought, too, but when all the others said she was ugly, he believed so as well in the end, and would have nothing more to do with her—she could go wherever she would. They flew down from the tree with her and set her upon a daisy; there she wept because she was so ugly that the cockchafers would have nothing to do with her, and yet she was the loveliest little thing you could imagine, as bright and dainty as the most beautiful of rose-petals.

The whole summer through, poor Thumbelina lived quite alone in the great forest. She plaited herself a bed of grasses and hung it under a large dock-leaf to keep the rain off her; she gathered the pollen from the flowers to eat, and she drank the dew that formed every morning on the leaves. And so summer and autumn passed, and winter came—a long, cold winter. All the birds that had sung so beautifully for her flew away, the trees and the flowers withered, and the large dock-leaf she had lived under curled up and nothing was left of it but a shrivelled yellow stalk. She was dreadfully cold, for her clothes were in tatters, and she herself was so delicate and small, poor Thumbelina, that she might have frozen to death. It began to snow, and every snow-flake that fell upon her felt as a whole shovelful might do if it were thrown at one of us, for we are big and she was only an inch tall. So she wrapped herself up in a withered leaf, but it did not warm her, and she shivered with cold.

Just beyond the edge of the forest which she had now come to lay a great corn-field, but the corn had long since been carted, and now only the dry bare stubble stood up out of the frozen ground. But it was like a forest for her to go through, and oh, she shivered so much with the cold! And so she came to the field-mouse's door. It was a little hole under the stubble. There the field-mouse lived snug and comfortable with a whole store-room full of corn and a fine kitchen and dining-room. Poor Thumbelina stopped just inside the doorway like a wretched beggar-girl, and asked for a little bit of a grain of barley, for she had had nothing at all to eat for the last two days.

'You poor little thing!' said the field-mouse, for she was a good-natured old field-mouse at heart. 'Come into my warm room and have something to eat with me!'

She liked the look of Thumbelina, and so she said, 'You're welcome to stay with me for the winter, but you must keep my room nice and

clean, and tell me stories, for I'm very fond of stories.'
And Thumbelina did what the good old field-mouse asked
of her, and lived very comfortably.

'We shall soon have a visitor!' said the field-mouse.
'My neighbour comes to visit me every weekday. His
house is even more comfortable than mine: he has fine
large rooms, and he wears such a lovely black velvet fur—
if you could only get him for a husband, you'd be well
provided for. But he can't see. You must tell him all the
most beautiful stories you know!'

But Thumbelina did not like that idea at all: she had
no wish to marry the neighbour, for he was a mole. He
came visiting in his black velvet fur—he was very rich
and very learned, said the field-mouse. His house was
twenty times as spacious as the field-mouse's, and learning he had, too; but he did not care for the sun and the
beautiful flowers, and he spoke contemptuously of them
because he had never seen them. Thumbelina had to sing
for him, and she sang both 'Ladybird, ladybird, fly away
home!' and 'The monk is walking in the meadow'. The
mole fell in love with her on account of her beautiful
voice, but he said nothing, for he was always a very
cautious man.

He had recently dug himself a long passage through
the earth from his own house to theirs, and he gave the
field-mouse and Thumbelina leave to walk there whenever
they wished. But he told them not to be afraid of the dead
bird that lay in the passage. The bird was quite whole,
with its feathers and beak intact: it must have died quite
recently at the beginning of the winter, and it now lay
buried just where he had made his passage.

The mole took in his mouth a bit of rotten wood which
shines just like fire in the dark, and then went in front to
light the long dark passage for them. When they came to

the place where the dead bird lay, the mole set his broad nose against the roof of the passage and pushed the earth up, thus making a big hole which the light could shine through. In the middle of the floor lay a dead swallow with its beautiful wings pressed close against its sides and its legs and head tucked in under its feathers: the poor bird had obviously died of cold. Thumbelina was so sorry for it: she loved all the little birds that had sung and twittered so beautifully for her the whole summer through. But the mole kicked it with his short legs and said, 'That's one that won't whistle any more! It must be wretched to be born a little bird! Thank Heaven none of my children will ever be one! They've nothing to say for themselves but "tweet-tweet", and in the winter they die of hunger!'

'Yes, as a sensible man, you may well say so!' said the field-mouse. 'What does a bird get for all its "tweet-tweet" when winter comes? It dies of hunger and cold—and yet it's thought so much of!'

Thumbelina said nothing, but when the others had turned their backs upon the bird, she bent down, gently moved aside the feathers that lay over its head, and kissed its closed eyes. 'Perhaps this is the one that sang so beautifully for me during the summer,' she thought. 'What a lot of happiness it brought me, dear, beautiful bird!'

Then the mole stopped up the hole he had made to let the daylight shine through, and went home with the ladies. But that night Thumbelina could not sleep at all: so she got out of bed and plaited a fine large rug of hay. She carried it down and spread it over the dead bird. She tucked some soft cotton-wool she had found in the field-mouse's living-room round the bird's body so that it should lie warm in the cold earth.

'Good-bye, beautiful little bird!' she said. 'Good-bye,

and thank you for the lovely song you sang in the
summer-time, when all the trees were green and the sun
shone warmly on us!' Then she laid her head upon the
bird's breast, but as she did so, she was quite startled, for
it felt just as if something were knocking inside. It was
the bird's heart. The bird was not dead: it lay numb with
cold, and now that warmth was returning to it, it showed
signs of life again.

In the autumn the swallows all fly away to warmer
lands, but if one of them should be delayed, it is so overcome with cold that it falls quite lifeless to the ground.
There it remains, and the cold snow covers it over.

Thumbelina had had such a fright that she was actually
trembling, for she was only an inch tall and compared
with her the bird was a great big creature. But she plucked
up her courage, tucked the cotton-wool more closely
round the poor swallow, and fetched a mint-leaf which she
herself used as a bedspread and laid it over the bird's head.

The next night she crept down to the bird again. It was
unmistakably alive, but so weak that it could barely open
its eyes for a moment to look at Thumbelina who was
standing there with a bit of rotten wood in her hand—for
other light had she none.

'Thank you, thank you, pretty little child!' the sick
swallow said to her. 'I'm so nice and warm now, I shall
soon get my strength back and be able to fly out again
into the warm sunshine!'

'Oh,' she said, 'it's so cold outside! It's snowing and
freezing! Stay in your warm bed, and I'll look after you!'

Then she brought the swallow some water in a petal,
and it drank and told her how it had torn one of its wings
on a thorn-bush, and so was unable to fly as fast as the
other swallows, who had flown far, far away to warmer
lands. At length it had fallen to the ground, but more

than that it could not remember and had no idea how it came to be where it was.

The swallow stayed down there all winter, and Thumbelina was kind to it and grew very fond of it, but neither the mole nor the field-mouse was told the least thing about it, for they did not like the poor forlorn swallow.

As soon as spring came and the sun's warmth began to penetrate the earth, the swallow said good-bye to Thumbelina and opened the hole which the mole had made just above its head. It was lovely to feel the sun shining in upon them, and the swallow asked her if she would not go with it: she could sit on its back and they would fly far away into the green forest. But Thumbelina knew it would make the old field-mouse very sad if she left her like that.

'No, I can't do that!' said Thumbelina.

'Good-bye, good-bye, you kind pretty girl!' said the swallow, as it flew out into the sunshine. Thumbelina watched it go, and tears came into her eyes, for she had grown very fond of the poor swallow.

'Tweet, tweet!' sang the bird, and flew off into the green forest.

Thumbelina was very sad. She was never allowed to go out into the warm sunshine; and the corn which had been sown in the field above the field-mouse's house grew up so high that it was like a great dense forest for the poor little girl who was only an inch tall.

'Now during the summer you must get your trousseau ready!' the field-mouse said to her, for their neighbour, the tiresome mole in the black velvet fur, had now asked her to marry him. 'You must have both woollens and linens! You must have something to sit on and lie on when you're the mole's wife!'

Thumbelina had to work hard with her spindle, and

the field-mouse hired four spiders to spin and weave for her night and day. Every evening the mole would pay them a visit, and his talk was always the same: when summer came to an end and the sun was no longer shining so dreadfully hot—it was baking the earth as hard as a rock—yes, when summer was over, he would marry Thumbelina. But she was very unhappy about it, for she did not like the tiresome old mole at all. Every morning when the sun rose, and every evening when it set, she would creep out-of-doors, and whenever the wind parted the corn so that she could see the blue sky, she would think how pleasant and beautiful it was outside, and she would wish so hard that she could see her dear swallow again: but it would never come back, for it had flown far away into the beautiful green forest.

When autumn came, Thumbelina had the whole of her trousseau finished.

'In four weeks' time you'll be having your wedding!' the field-mouse said to her. But Thumbelina wept and said she would not have the tiresome old mole.

'Fiddle-de-dee!' said the field-mouse. 'Don't be so obstinate, or I shall bite you with my white teeth! You're going to get a very nice husband indeed! Why, the queen herself has nothing to match his black velvet fur! And he has both a kitchen and a cellar. You should thank God for him!'

And so their wedding-day arrived. The mole had already come to take Thumbelina away; she would have to live with him deep down under the earth, and she would never be able to go out into the warm sunshine because he disliked it. The poor child was very unhappy because she had now to say good-bye to the beautiful sun, which she had still been allowed to look at from the doorway while she was living with the field-mouse.

'Good-bye, bright sun!' she said, stretching her arms up towards it, and she walked a little way from where the field-mouse lived, for the corn was now harvested and there was only the dry stubble left. 'Good-bye, good-bye!' she said, as she threw her small arms round a little red flower that was growing there. 'Give my love to the swallow if you should ever see him again!'

At that very same moment she heard, 'Tweet, tweet!' just above her: she looked up, and there was the swallow flying overhead. It caught sight of Thumbelina and was delighted to see her. She told it how she was being forced to marry the nasty old mole, and how she would then have to live right under the earth where the sun never shone. She could not help weeping at the thought of it.

'The cold winter is coming on now,' said the swallow, 'and I'm flying far away to a warmer land. Will you come with me? You can sit on my back and bind yourself fast with your sash: then we shall fly away from the nasty mole and his dark home, far away over the mountains to warm lands where the sun shines more beautifully than it does here, where there is always summer and lovely flowers. Do fly away with me, dear little Thumbelina— you saved my life when I lay frozen in the dark cellar under the earth!'

'Yes, I'll go with you,' said Thumbelina, and she seated herself upon the bird's back, with her feet resting on its outstretched wings, and tied her belt firmly to one of its strongest feathers. And so the swallow flew high up into the air, over forest and lake, high up over the great mountains where snow always lies. Thumbelina froze in the cold air, but she crept under the bird's warm feathers, and only popped her little head out to see all the beautiful scenery below her.

So they came to the warm lands where the sun shines

much more brightly than it does here. The sky seemed twice as high, and along the ditches and hedges grew the loveliest green and blue grapes. Oranges and lemons hung in woods scented with myrtle and mint, and along the country lanes lovely children ran and played with great brightly coloured butterflies. But the swallow flew farther still, and everything grew more and more beautiful. Under magnificent green trees, by a blue lake, stood a palace built in ancient times of shining white marble, with vines entwined round its tall pillars. Right on top of the pillars were many swallows' nests, and in one of them lived the swallow that carried Thumbelina.

'Here's my house!' said the swallow. 'But if you will choose yourself one of those lovely flowers growing down there, I will set you down on it, and you will live as happily there as you could wish!'

'That would be lovely!' she said, clapping her little hands.

A great white marble column lay fallen on the ground: it was broken into three pieces, and between them grew the most beautiful white flowers. The swallow flew down with Thumbelina and set her upon one of the broad petals: but what a surprise she had!—there, in the middle of the flower, sat a little man, clear and transparent like glass; he had the prettiest golden crown upon his head and the loveliest bright wings on his shoulders; and he himself was no bigger than Thumbelina. He was the guardian-spirit of the flower. In every flower there lived a little man or woman just like him, but he was king over them all.

'Oh, how beautiful he is!' whispered Thumbelina to the swallow. The little prince was quite frightened of the swallow, for it was such an enormous bird by the side of this dainty little creature, but when he saw Thumbelina he was overjoyed, for she was quite the most beautiful girl he had ever seen. And so he took the golden crown off his own head and placed it upon hers. He asked her what she was called, and he said that if she would be his wife, she should be queen over all the flowers! Well, that was a husband indeed!—quite a different matter from the toad's son and the mole with the black velvet fur! And so she said yes to the handsome prince. From every flower appeared a little lady or gentleman, so beautiful and dainty it was a joy to look at them; and every one brought Thumbelina a present, but the best of all was a pair of beautiful wings from a large white fly. They were fastened upon Thumbelina's shoulders, and then she, too, could fly from flower to flower. They were all so full of joy, and the swallow sat up above in its nest and sang for them as well as it could, but it was very sad at heart, for it was so fond of Thumbelina that it wanted never to be parted from her.

'You cannot be called Thumbelina!' the flower-sprite

said to her. 'It's an ugly name, and you are so beautiful. We shall call you Maia!'

'Good-bye, good-bye!' said the swallow, and flew away from the warm lands once more, far away back to Denmark. There it had a little nest by the window of the room where the man who can tell tales lives, and it sang its 'tweet, tweet!' for him, and that's how we come to know the whole story.

The Little Mermaid

FAR out to sea the water is as blue as the petals of
the loveliest cornflower, and as clear as the purest
glass, but it is very deep, deeper than any anchor-
chain can reach, and many church towers would have to
be put one on top of another to reach from the bottom
to the surface of the water. Down there live the merfolk.

Now you must not think that there is nothing there but
the bare white sandy bottom; oh no, the most wonderful
trees and plants grow there, and their stems and leaves
are so supple that with the least movement of the water
they stir like living things. All kinds of fish, large and
small, flit among the branches just as birds do in the air
up here. In the very deepest place of all lies the merking's
palace. Its walls are coral, and its long pointed windows
the clearest amber, and its roof is made of mussel-shells
that open and shut with the movement of the water—it
looks most beautiful, for in each shell lies a shining pearl,

E

and a single one of them would be the chief beauty in a queen's crown.

The merking down there had been a widower for many years, and his old mother kept house for him; she was a wise woman, but proud of her royal rank, and so she always went about with twelve oysters on her tail, while other high-born merfolk might have only six. Otherwise she deserved high praise, especially because she was so fond of the little merprincesses, her granddaughters. They were six lovely children, and the youngest was the most beautiful of them all—her skin was as clear and pure as a rose-petal, her eyes as blue as the deepest lake, but like all the rest, she had no feet and her body ended in a fish's tail.

All day long they could play down there in the palace, in the great halls where living flowers grew out of the walls. When the great amber windows were opened, the fish would swim in to them, just as the swallows will fly in when we open our windows, but the fish would swim right up to the little princesses, eat out of their hands and let themselves be stroked.

Outside the palace there was a great garden with fiery-red and dark-blue trees, their fruit shining like gold and their flowers like burning fire, with ever-moving stems and leaves. The soil itself was the finest sand, but blue like sulphur-flames. Over everything down there lay a wonderful blue glow; you would think that, instead of being on the bottom of the sea, you were standing high up in the air with nothing but sky above and below you. In clear calm weather you could see the sun looking like a purple flower with all that light streaming out from its centre.

Each of the little princesses had her own little plot in the garden, where she could dig and plant whatever she liked. One gave her flower-bed the shape of a whale, another thought hers would look better in the form of a little mermaid, but the youngest made hers quite round and would only have flowers that shone red like the sun. She was a strange child, quiet and thoughtful, and when the other sisters decorated their gardens with the most wonderful things they had got from wrecked ships, she would only have, apart from the rose-red flowers which looked like the sun high up above her, a beautiful marble statue, a handsome boy carved out of clear white stone and come down to the bottom of the sea with the wreck of a ship. She planted by it a rose-red weeping-willow which grew magnificently and hung its fresh branches right over the statue down to the blue sand of the ground, where its shadow showed violet and was in constant motion like its branches—its top and its roots seemed always to be playing at kissing one another.

She found her greatest delight in hearing about the world of men up above; her old grandmother had to tell her all she knew about ships and cities, men and beasts. What she thought especially wonderful and beautiful was that up on earth the flowers had a sweet scent, for that they did not have on the bottom of the sea, and the woods were green and the fish you could see there among the branches could sing so loudly and beautifully it was a joy to hear them—grandmother called the little birds fish, for otherwise they would not have been able to understand her, for they had never seen a bird.

'When you reach your fifteenth birthday,' said grandmother, 'you shall be allowed to go up out of the sea and sit in the moonshine on the rocks and watch the great ships sailing by, and you shall see woods and cities, too!'

During that year one of the sisters was fifteen, but the others—well, each was a year younger than the next, and

so the youngest of them all still had five whole years to
wait before she dared swim up from the bottom of the sea
and see what it looks like where we live. But each one
promised to tell the next what she had seen and found
most lovely during her first day on earth, for their grandmother had not told them nearly enough—there was so
much they wanted to know about.

None of them was so full of longing as the youngest,
and she was the very one that had the longest to wait and
was so quiet and thoughtful. Many a night she stood by
the open window and looked up through the dark-blue
water where the fish were waving their fins and tails. She
could see the moon and the stars, and though they shone
quite palely, they looked much larger through the water
than they do to our eyes; and when it looked as if a black
cloud were gliding across below them, she knew it was
either a whale swimming over her or else a ship with many
men on board—men who, of course, had no idea that a
lovely little mermaid was standing down below and
stretching her white hands up towards their keel.

And now the eldest princess was fifteen years old and
could rise up above the surface of the sea.

When she came back, she had hundreds of things to tell
them, but the loveliest of all, she said, was to lie in the
moonshine on a sandbank in the quiet of the sea, and see,
close by the coast, the great city where the lights were
winking like a hundred stars, hear the music and the
noise and bustle of carts and people, see the towers and
spires of the many churches and listen to the ringing of
their bells. And just because she could not go up into the
city, that was what she longed to do more than anything
else.

Oh, how intently her youngest sister listened to her!
And whenever, after that, she stood in the evening by the

open window, looking up through the dark-blue sea, she thought of the great city with all its noise and bustle, and then she seemed to hear the church-bells ringing down to her.

The next year the second sister was allowed to rise up through the water and swim wherever she wished. She popped her head up just as the sun was going down, and that sight she found the most beautiful. The whole sky had looked like gold, she said, and the clouds—she just could not describe their loveliness! Red and violet, they had sailed away over her head, but far swifter than they, flew a flock of wild swans, like a long white ribbon, away over the water to where the sun stood; she swam off towards it, but it sank, and the rosy gleam disappeared from the surface of the sea and the clouds.

The year after, the third sister went up above—she was the most venturesome of them all, and so she swam up a broad river which flowed into the sea. She saw lovely green hills with vineyards upon them, and castles and farms peeped out from the magnificent forest. She heard all the birds singing, and the sun shone so warmly, she often had to duck under the water to cool her burning face. In a little bay she came across a crowd of little children running about quite naked and splashing in the water. She wanted to play with them, but they ran off in fright. Then a little black animal came along—it was a dog, but she had never seen a dog before. It barked at her so terrifyingly that she became alarmed and made off for the open sea, but she could never forget the magnificent forest, the green hills, and the pretty children who could swim in the water, even though they had no fishes' tails.

The fourth sister was not so venturesome. She stayed out in the middle of the wild sea, and told them that was quite the loveliest place; you could see for many miles all round you, and the sky stood overhead like a huge glass bell. She had seen ships, but far away, looking like gulls; playful dolphins had turned somersaults, and great whales had spouted water up from their nostrils so that it looked as if there were hundreds of fountains round about.

Now came the turn of the fifth sister. Her birthday happened to fall in winter, and so she saw what the others, during their first visits, had not seen. The sea looked quite green, and great icebergs were swimming round about, each one looking like a pearl, she said, and yet they were far larger than the church towers built by men. They appeared in the strangest shapes, glittering like diamonds. She had seated herself on one of the largest, and, in terror, ships sailed wide of the ice where she sat, her long hair streaming in the blast. Late in the evening the sky became overcast with cloud, and it thundered and lightened, while the dark sea lifted the great ice-floes high up and made them shine in the strong flashes of lightning. On all ships, sails were taken in, and there was alarm and fear, but she sat peacefully on her floating iceberg, and watched the blue flashes of lightning strike zig-zagging down upon the shining sea.

The first time the sisters, each in her turn, came to the surface of the sea, they were always delighted with the new and beautiful sights they saw, but now that they were grown girls and had leave to go up there whenever they wished, they were quite indifferent about it and longed for home again, and at the end of a month they said that the bottom of the sea was the most beautiful place of all, the place where they felt most comfortable and most at home.

Many an evening the five sisters would take one another by the arm and swim in a row up to the surface of the water. They had lovely voices, more beautiful than any human voice, and when the wind was blowing up to a gale and they thought ships might be lost, they would swim in front of the ships and sing so beautifully how lovely it was on the bottom of the sea and bid the sailors not to be afraid of coming down there. But the men could not understand their words: they thought it was the gale they heard. Nor did they ever see the beauty down below them, for when their ship sank, the men were drowned, and only as dead men did they ever come to the merking's palace.

On those evenings when the sisters rose arm-in-arm like this high up through the sea, their little sister was left behind quite alone, gazing after them, and she looked as though she would weep, but a mermaid has no tears and so she suffers all the more.

'Oh, if only I were fifteen!' she said. 'I know that I shall really grow to love that world above the sea and all the people that live and dwell there!'

And then at last she was fifteen.

'Well, we've got you off our hands now!' said her grandmother, the old queen-dowager. 'Come along now, let me dress you up like your sisters!' And she placed a wreath of white lilies on her hair, but every petal of the flowers was half a pearl. Then the old lady fastened eight large oysters firmly on the princess's tail to show her high rank.

'But it hurts so!' said the little mermaid.

'We must all suffer a little to look smart!' said the old lady.

Oh, she would have loved to shake off all that finery and put down that heavy wreath! The red flowers in her garden suited her much better, but she dared not change them now. 'Good-bye!' she said, and then she rose, lightly and clearly like a bubble, up through the water.

The sun had just gone down as she raised her head up above the water, but the clouds were all still gleaming with rose and gold, and in the middle of the pale-pink

sky the evening-star shone clear and lovely, the air was mild and fresh and the sea a glassy calm. A great three-masted ship lay there with only a single sail set, for there was not a breath of wind, and the sailors were sitting about in the rigging and on the spars. There was music and song, and as the evening grew darker, hundreds of coloured lights were lit—it looked as if the flags of all the countries in the world were waving in the air. The little mermaid swam right up to the cabin window, and every time she rose with the swell of the water, she could see through the crystal-clear panes where a large number of well-dressed people were standing, but the most handsome of them was the young prince with the large black eyes. He was certainly not much more than sixteen; it was his birthday, and that was why there was all this celebration. The sailors were dancing on deck, and as the young prince stepped out, over a hundred rockets shot up in the air, shining as brightly as daylight, so that the little mermaid was quite terrified and ducked under the water, but she soon popped her head up again, and it looked just as if all the stars of heaven were falling down on her. She had never seen fireworks before. Great suns were whirling round, magnificent firefish were soaring up into the blue sky, and it was all reflected back from the clear, still sea. On the ship itself, there was so much light, you could see every little rope, let alone the people. Oh, how handsome the young prince was, shaking everyone by the hand, laughing and smiling, while the music rang out into the lovely night!

It grew late, but the little mermaid could not turn her eyes away from the ship and the handsome prince. The coloured lights were put out, no more rockets rose into the air, nor was there any more cannon-fire to be heard either, but deep down in the sea there was a murmuring and a rumbling. Meanwhile, she sat on the water, rocking up and down, so that she could look into the cabin. But the ship gathered speed as one sail was spread after another. Then the waves ran higher, great clouds closed in, and far away there were flashes of lightning. Oh, there was going to be a dreadful storm! And so the sailors took in sail. The great ship sped rolling and swaying through the wild sea, the waves rose like great black mountains about to break over the mast, but the ship dived like a swan down among the high billows and was lifted up again on the piled-up waters. To the little mermaid their speed was pleasant and amusing enough, but the sailors did not think so. The ship creaked and cracked, the stout planks bent under the heavy blows dealt by the sea, the mast snapped in the middle like a reed, and the ship heeled over on her side as the water rushed into her hold. Then the little mermaid saw that they were in danger— she herself had to look out for beams and broken ship's timbers driving on the water. At one moment it was so pitch-black that she could see nothing at all; then when the lightning flashed, it was so bright again she could make out all those on board, each man staggering about as best he could. She was searching especially for the young prince, and as the ship parted, she saw him sink down in the deep sea. For the moment she was overjoyed, for now he was coming down to her, but then she remembered that men could not live in the water, and that he could go down to her father's palace only as a dead man. No, die he must not! And so she swam off among the beams and planks driving on the sea, completely forgetting that they could have crushed her, dived deep under the water and rose again high up among the waves, and then at last she reached the young prince who could scarcely swim any farther in that stormy sea. His arms and legs were beginning to tire, his beautiful eyes had shut, and he would have been left to die had the little mermaid not come to him. She held his head up above the water and let the waves drive her with him wherever they would.

When morning came the storm had passed, but of the ship there was not a stick to be seen. The sun rose out of the water so red and bright, the prince's cheeks seemed to gain life from it, but his eyes remained shut. The mermaid kissed his beautiful high forehead and stroked his wet hair back; she thought he looked like the marble statue down in her little garden; she kissed him again and wished that he might yet live.

Then she saw dry land in front of her, high blue mountains with snow shining white upon their summits as if it were swans that lay there; down by the coast were lovely green woods and before them lay a church or an abbey—she did not rightly know what, but at least a building. Oranges and lemons grew there in the garden, and in front of the gate tall palm-trees stood. The sea made a little bay there, dead still but very deep right up to the rocks where the fine white sand was washed up. She swam over to that point with the handsome prince, laid him upon the sand and took particular care that his head lay well up in the warmth of the sun.

Then the bells rang in the great white building, and many young girls came out through the garden. The little mermaid then swam farther out behind some high rocks that jutted out of the water, covered her hair and her breast in sea-foam so that no one could see her little face, and then watched to see who would come down to the poor prince.

It was not long before a young girl came down there; she seemed quite frightened, but only for a moment, and then she went and fetched some more people. And the mermaid saw the prince revive and smile at everybody round about him, but he did not turn and smile at her, for of course he did not even know that she had rescued him. She felt so sad that when he was carried into the great building, she dived sorrowfully down into the water and made her way home to her father's palace.

She had always been quiet and thoughtful, but now she became even more so. Her sisters asked her what she had seen the first time she had been above the sea, but she told them nothing.

Many an evening and morning she rose up where she had left the prince. She watched the fruit in the garden ripen and she saw it gathered in; she saw the snow melt on the high mountains, but the prince she did not see, and so, every time, she turned home even more sorrowful than before. Her one comfort was to sit in her little garden and throw her arms round the beautiful marble statue that looked so like the prince. But she no longer looked after her flowers, and they grew, as if in a wilderness, out over the paths, and twisted their long stems and their leaves in among the branches of the trees until it was quite dark there.

At last she could bear it no longer, and told one of her sisters all about it, and so all the others got to know about it, too, right away, but no one else beyond them and a couple of other mermaids, who, of course, told no one, except their closest friends. One of them knew who the prince was—she, too, had seen the party on board the ship, and she knew where he was from and where his kingdom lay.

'Come, little sister!' said the other princesses, and with their arms about each others' shoulders they rose up out of the sea in a long row in front of the spot where they knew the prince's palace lay.

It was built of a gleaming pale-yellow stone, with great marble steps, some leading right down into the sea. Magnificent gilt domes rose above the roof, and between the pillars which surrounded the whole building stood marble statues that looked as if they were alive. Through the clear glass of the tall windows, you could see into the splendid halls where costly silk curtains and tapestries were hung and all the walls were adorned with great paintings that it was a real joy to look upon. In the middle of the largest hall splashed a great fountain, its jets of water mounting high up towards the glass dome in the ceiling through which the sun shone upon the water and the lovely plants that grew in the great basin.

Now she knew where he lived, and there she came to the surface of the sea many an evening and night. She would swim much closer to the shore than any of the others had ever dared to do, yes, she would go right up the narrow canal below the magnificent marble balcony which cast its long shadow out over the water. There she would sit and look at the young prince who thought he was quite alone in the clear moonlight.

She saw him many an evening sailing to music in the fine boat where the flags were flying. She would peep out from among the green rushes, and if the wind caught her long silver-white veil and anyone saw it, he thought it was a swan spreading its wings.

Many a night, when the fishermen lay with their lights upon the water, she heard them speaking so well of the young prince, and that made her glad she had saved his life when he had driven half-dead upon the waves, and she would remember how closely his head had rested upon her breast and how deeply she had kissed him—and he knew nothing at all about it, and could not even dream of her.

She came to like people more and more, more and more she wished she could go up among them; their world seemed to her far greater than her own, for they could sail away over the sea in ships and climb upon the high mountains high above the clouds, and the lands they owned stretched farther, with forests and fields, than her eye could reach. There was so much she wanted to know, but her sisters were not able to give answers to every-thing, and so she questioned their old grandmother, and she knew the upper world, as she very rightly called the lands above the sea, very well indeed.

'If they are not drowned, can people live for ever?' asked the little mermaid. 'Don't they die, as we do down here in the sea?'

'Yes, of course they do!' the old lady said. 'They have to die, too, and their lifetime is even shorter than ours. We can live until we are three hundred years old, but then when our life is finished here, we are only foam upon the water, we do not even have a grave down here among our dear ones. We have no immortal soul, we never again come to life, we are like the green rushes—once they are cut through, they cannot grow green again! But people on the other hand have a soul which lives for ever, which goes on living after the body has become dust; it rises up through the bright sky, up to all the shining stars! Just as we dive up out of the sea to look at the lands where people live, so they dive up to lovely unknown places that we shall never come to see.'

'Why were we not given an immortal soul?' asked the little mermaid sadly. 'I would give all the hundreds of years I have to live to be a human girl for just one day and then to receive my part in the Kingdom of Heaven!'

'You must not go thinking about such things!' said the old lady. 'We have a much happier and better time than the people up there do!'

'Then I must die and float like foam upon the sea, and not hear the music of the waves or see the lovely flowers and the red sun! Can't I do anything at all to gain an eternal soul?'

'No!' said the old lady. 'Only if a human man should fall in love with you so deeply that you would be more to him than father and mother; only if he should cling to you with all his thought and all his love, and let the priest place his right hand in yours with a vow of faith here and for all eternity: then his soul would overflow into your body, and you, too, would have your share in human fortune. He would give you a soul and yet keep his own. But that can never happen! What is especially delightful here in the sea—your fishtail—they find ugly up there on earth: they won't think any the better of you for it— there you must have two clumsy props they call legs to be thought beautiful!'

Then the little mermaid sighed and looked sadly at her fishtail.

'Let us be joyful!' said the old lady. 'We'll skip and dance through the three hundred years we have to live. It's a good long time really, and afterwards we shall be able the more contentedly to rest. We'll hold a court ball this evening!'

There was a splendour such as you would never see on earth. The walls and the ceiling of the great ballroom were of thick but clear glass. Several hundred huge mussel-shells, rose-red and grass-green, stood in rows on either side with burning blue flames in them, lighting up the whole room and shining out through the walls, so that the sea outside was quite brightly lit. You could see the countless fish, great and small, that came swimming towards the glass walls: on some shone scales of purple-red, on others they seemed to be of silver and gold. Through the middle of the hall flowed a broad running current, and on this the mermen and women danced to their own lovely singing. Such beautiful voices are not to be found among the people on earth. The little mermaid sang the most beautifully of them all, and they all applauded her. And, for the moment, she felt joy in her heart, for she knew she had the most beautiful voice of all who live upon the earth or in the sea. But she very soon found herself thinking once more of the world above her: she could not forget the handsome prince and her own sorrow at not having, like him, an immortal soul. And so she stole out of her father's palace, and while all was song and merriment inside, she sat sadly in her little garden. Then she heard the sound of a French horn ring down through the water, and she thought, 'He must be sailing up there now, him I hold dearer than father and mother, him my thoughts cling to, and into whose hands I would put my life's happiness. I would risk everything to win him and an immortal soul! While my sisters are dancing there in my father's palace, I will go and see the sea-witch—I have always been so frightened of her, but perhaps she can advise and help me!'

Then the little mermaid went out of her garden, away towards the roaring whirlpools behind which the witch dwelt. She had never been that way before. No flowers grew there, no sea-grass—only the naked grey sand of the sea-bed stretched away towards the whirlpools that whirled round like roaring mill-wheels and bore away everything that came within their grasp down with them into their depths. Right through the midst of these tremendous whirlpools she had to go to reach the sea-witch's district, and there, for a long stretch, there was no other way but over the warm bubbling mud the witch called her peat-bog. Beyond this lay her house in the middle of a lonely forest. The trees and bushes were all polyps, half beast, half plant, that looked like hundred-headed snakes growing out of the earth. All the branches were long slimy arms with fingers like supple worms, and limb by limb they were in constant motion from their roots to their topmost tips. Everything they could seize upon in the ocean they twined themselves fast about and never more let go. The little mermaid grew quite terrified as she stood just outside the forest. Her heart beat with fear and she very nearly turned back, but then she thought of the prince and the soul of man, and so she found courage. She bound her long streaming hair firmly about her head so that the polyps should not be able to seize her by it, and placed both her hands together over her breast, and in this way she flew through the water like a fish in among the grisly polyps that stretched their supple arms and fingers after her. She saw that each of them had something it had seized, and hundreds of small arms held it like strong bands of iron. Men who had perished at sea and had sunk deep down below peeped out like white skeletons from the polyps' arms. Ships' rudders and sea-chests they held in their grip, and the skeletons of land animals and a little mermaid they had seized and strangled—that made her more afraid than almost anything else.

Then she came to a great slimy opening in the forest where great fat water-snakes were frisking about and showing their ugly yellow-white bellies. In the middle of the opening, a house had been built from the bones of shipwrecked men. There the sea-witch sat letting a toad eat out of her mouth, just as people will let a little canary eat sugar. The ugly fat water-snakes she called her little chickens, and she let them roll about on her great spongy breasts.

'I know well enough what it is you want!' said the sea-witch. 'You're acting like a fool! However, you shall have your way, for it will bring you misfortune, my lovely princess! You'd like to get rid of your fishtail and have two stumps in place of it so that you can walk like a human! Then the young prince will fall in love with you, and you'll be able to get him and an immortal soul as well!' At the same time the witch laughed so loudly and unpleasantly that the toad and the snakes fell rolling on to the ground. 'You've come just at the right time,' said the witch. 'If it had been after sunrise tomorrow morning, I

F

could not have helped you until another year had passed. I shall make you a drink: before the sun rises, you must swim to land with it, sit yourself down upon the shore, and drink it. Then your tail will divide and shrink into what men call a lovely pair of legs. But it will hurt: it will

be like a sharp sword going through you. Everybody who sees you will say you are the loveliest human child they have ever seen! You will keep your gliding motion: no dancer will be able to glide along like you, but every step you take will be like treading on a sharp knife that cuts you and makes your blood flow. If you are willing to suffer all this, then I will help you.'

'Yes!' the little mermaid said in a trembling voice, and she thought of the prince and of winning an immortal soul.

'But remember,' said the witch, 'once you have taken human form, you can never become a mermaid again! You will never be able to go down through the water to see your sisters or your father's palace. And if you do not win the prince's love so that he will forget father and mother for your sake, cling to you with all his mind and let the priest place your hands in one another's so that you become man and wife, you will not get an immortal soul! The very first morning after he weds another, your heart will break, and you will become foam upon the water.'

'I am willing!' said the little mermaid, and she was as pale as death.

'But you must pay me, too!' said the witch. 'And it is no small thing I am asking for. You have the loveliest voice of all down here upon the bottom of the sea, and no doubt you think you will be able to bewitch him with it, but that voice you must give to me. The best thing you possess will I have in return for my precious drink! For I must give you my own blood in it to make the drink sharp like a two-edged sword!'

'But if you take my voice,' said the little mermaid, 'what shall I have left?'

'Your lovely figure,' said the witch, 'your gliding walk and your speaking eyes—with them you will be able to charm a man's heart, never you fear! Well, have you lost your courage? Put out your little tongue so that I can cut it off in payment, and you shall have your powerful drink!'

'It shall be done!' said the little mermaid, and the witch put her cauldron on to boil the magic potion. 'Cleanliness is a good thing!' she said, and scoured the cauldron out with the snakes which she had tied into a knot. Then she scratched herself on the breast and let her black blood drip into it. The steam formed shapes so strange and wonderful that they would have filled you with fear and dread. Every second the witch put something new into the cauldron, and when the brew was properly boiling it sounded like a crocodile weeping. At last the drink was ready—and it looked like the clearest water!

'There it is!' said the witch, and cut out the tongue of the little mermaid, who was now dumb and could neither sing nor speak.

'If the polyps should catch hold of you as you go back through my woods,' said the witch, 'you have only to throw one single drop of this potion over them and their arms and fingers will burst into a thousand pieces!' But the little mermaid had no need to do it, for the polyps drew back in fear of her when they saw the shining drink glistening in her hand like a sparkling star. And so she soon returned through the forest, the bog, and the roaring whirlpools.

She could see her father's palace: the lights were out in the great ballroom; no doubt they were all asleep in there, but yet she dared not go and look at them—she was dumb now and had made up her mind to go right away from them for ever. It seemed as if her heart would break with sorrow. She slipped into the garden, took one flower from each of her sisters' flower-beds, blew a thousand kisses towards the palace, and rose up through the dark-blue sea.

The sun had not yet risen when she saw the prince's palace and clambered on to the stately marble steps. The moon was shining lovely and clear. The little mermaid drank the sharp burning drink, and it felt as if a two-edged sword went through her delicate body. She fainted with the pain of it and lay as if she were dead. When the sun shone over the sea, she woke up and she felt a stinging

pain, but right in front of her stood the handsome young
prince, his coal-black eyes fastened upon her so that she
dropped her own and saw that her fishtail had gone and
that she had the nicest little white legs any young girl
could have, but she was quite naked and so she wrapped
her long thick hair about her. The prince asked who she
was and how she had come there, and she looked gently
yet sadly at him with her dark-blue eyes, for speak she
could not. Then he took her by the hand and led her into
the palace. Every step she took was, as the witch had told
her it would be, like treading on pointed tools and sharp
knives, but she bore it all willingly: the prince's hand on
hers, she stepped as light as a bubble, and he and everyone
there marvelled at her graceful gliding walk.

She was given costly clothes of silk and muslin to wear,
and she was the most beautiful girl in the palace, but she
was dumb and could neither sing nor talk. Beautiful
slave-girls, clad in silk and gold, appeared and sang for the
prince and his royal parents: one sang more beautifully
than all the rest, and the prince clapped his hands and

smiled at her. And then the little mermaid grew sad for she knew that she herself had sung far more beautifully. She thought, 'Oh, if only he could know that, to be near him, I have given my voice away for ever!'

Then the slave-girls danced graceful swaying dances to the noblest music, and the little mermaid raised her beautiful white arms, rose upon the tips of her toes and glided away over the floor, dancing as no one had ever danced before. With every movement her loveliness grew even more apparent, and her eyes spoke more deeply to the heart than the slave-girls' song.

Everyone was enraptured by it, and especially the prince, who called her his little foundling, and she danced on and on, although every time her foot touched the ground it was like treading on sharp knives. The prince said that she should remain with him always, and she was given permission to sleep outside his door on a velvet cushion.

He had a man's suit made for her so that she could go riding with him. They rode through the scented forest where the green branches brushed her shoulders and the little birds sang among the fresh leaves. She went climbing with the prince on the high mountains, and although her delicate feet bled so that all could see, she laughed at it and went with him until they saw the clouds sailing down below them like a flock of birds making their way to distant lands.

At home at the prince's palace, when the others were asleep at night, she would go out on to the broad marble steps, and standing in the cold sea-water would cool her burning feet, and then she would think of those down below in the deep.

One night her sisters came arm-in-arm, singing so sorrowfully as they swam over the water, and she waved to them and they recognized her and told her how sad she had made them all. After that they came to see her every night, and one night she saw, far out, her old grandmother, who had not been to the surface of the sea for many years, and the merking with his crown upon his head. They stretched their hands out towards her, but they dared not come as near the land as her sisters.

Day by day she grew dearer to the prince: he was fond of her as one might be fond of a dear good child, but it never occurred to him to make her his queen, and his wife she had to be, or else she would not find an immortal soul but on the morning of his wedding would become foam upon the sea.

'You are fonder of me than of all the others?' the little mermaid's eyes seemed to say when he took her in his arms and kissed her fair brow.

'Yes, of course you are dearest to me,' said the prince, 'because you have the best heart of all of them. You are the one I am most fond of, and you are like a young girl I once saw but shall never find again, no doubt. I was on board a ship which was wrecked, and the waves drove me to land near a holy temple served by several young maidens. The youngest of them found me there by the seashore and saved my life. I saw her only twice: she is the only one I could love in all the world, but you are like her —you have almost taken the place of her picture in my soul. She belongs to the holy temple, and so good fortune has sent me you—never will we part from one another!'

'Ah, he does not know that I saved his life!' thought the little mermaid. 'I bore him over the sea away to the woods where the temple stands, I hid behind the foam and watched to see if anyone would come. I saw the pretty maiden he loves more than me!' And the mermaid sighed deeply—weep she could not. 'The maiden belongs to the holy temple, he said. She will never come out into the world, they will not meet again, and I am here with him, I see him every day—I will look after him and love him and give up my life to him!'

But now everybody was saying that the prince was to marry and have the neighbouring king's lovely daughter, and it was for that purpose he was fitting out such a splendid ship. 'The prince is travelling to see the neighbouring king's land. That's what they're saying, of course, but it's really to see the neighbouring king's daughter! And he's taking a great following with him!' But the little mermaid shook her head and laughed; she knew the prince's thoughts much better than the rest of them. 'I have to make a journey,' he had told her. 'I have to go and see this lovely princess! It's my parents' wish—but they won't force me to bring her home as my bride: I cannot love her! She will not look like the lovely maiden in the temple, as you do. If I should ever choose a bride, then it would sooner be you, my dumb foundling with the speaking eyes!' And he kissed her red mouth, played with her long hair, and laid his head against her heart so that it dreamed of human happiness and an immortal soul.

'You do not seem a bit afraid of the sea, my dumb child!' he said, as they stood on the splendid ship which was to carry him to the land of the neighbouring king. And he told her of storm and calm, of rare fish in the deep and of what divers had seen. And she smiled at what he told her, for, of course, she knew more than anyone about the bottom of the sea.

In the moon-clear night when they were all asleep except the helmsman standing by the wheel, she sat by the ship's rail and gazed down through the clear water, and she thought she could see her father's palace: on the very top of it her old grandmother was standing with her silver crown upon her head, and gazing up through the swift currents towards the ship's keel. Then her sisters came up to the surface; they gazed sorrowfully at her and wrung their white hands. She waved to them and smiled and wanted to tell them that all was going well and happily with her, but the ship's boy drew near her and her sisters dived below so that he was left believing that the whiteness he had seen was only foam upon the water.

The next morning the ship sailed into the harbour of the neighbouring king's fine city. All the church bells were ringing, and trumpets blared from the high towers while the soldiers stood to attention with waving flags and glinting bayonets. Every day there was merrymaking: balls and parties followed one upon another. But the princess was not there yet: she was being brought up far away in a holy temple, they said, where she was learning all the royal virtues. At last she arrived.

The little mermaid stood there eager to see her beauty, and, she had to admit it, a more graceful figure she had never seen. Her skin was so delicate and pure, and behind her long dark lashes smiled a pair of steadfast dark-blue eyes.

'It is you!' said the prince. 'You who saved me when I lay like a corpse on the shore!' And he held his blushing bride tightly in his arms. 'Oh, I am all too happy!' he said to the little mermaid. 'The best thing I could ever hope for but never dared to, has happened to me. You will be glad I am happy, for you are fonder of me than the rest of them!' And the little mermaid kissed his hand, and she thought she felt her heart breaking. His wedding morning would be her death and change her into foam upon the sea.

All the church bells rang, the heralds rode through the

streets and proclaimed the betrothal. Upon all the altars burned sweet-scented oil in precious silver lamps. The priests swung their censers, and bride and bridegroom took one another by the hand and received the bishop's blessing. The little mermaid stood in silk and gold holding the bride's train, but her ears did not hear the festive music, her eyes did not see the holy ceremony, her thoughts were upon the night of her death, upon all she had lost in this world.

That very same evening the bride and bridegroom went on board their ship. The cannon were fired and all the flags were streaming, and amidships a royal tent of gold and purple had been raised and furnished with the loveliest cushions. And there the bridal pair were to sleep in the still cool night.

The sails bellied in the wind, and the ship glided away lightly and smoothly over the clear sea.

When it grew dark many-coloured lamps were lit, and the sailors danced merry dances on deck. The little mermaid could not help thinking of the first time she had dived up to the surface of the sea and had seen the same splendour and rejoicing, and she whirled in the dance with the rest, swerving as a swallow swerves when it is pursued, and they all applauded her in admiration, for never before had she danced so brilliantly. Sharp knives seemed to cut into her delicate feet, but she did not feel it, for the pain in her heart cut yet more sharply. She knew this was the last evening she would ever see him for whom she had forsaken her kindred and her home, given up her lovely voice, and daily suffered unending torment—and he had no idea of it. This was the last night she would breathe the same air as he, or look upon the deep sea and the starry blue sky; an everlasting night without thoughts or dreams awaited her, for she had no soul and could not gain one. And all was rejoicing and merry-making on board until well gone midnight. She laughed and danced with the thought of death in her heart. The prince kissed his lovely bride, and she played with his black hair, and arm-in-arm they went to rest in the splendid tent.

The ship grew still and quiet: only the helmsman stood by the wheel. The little mermaid laid her white arms upon the rail and looked towards the east for the first red of morning—the first ray of the sun, she knew, would kill her. Then she saw her sisters rise up to the surface of the sea: they were pale like her; their beautiful long hair no longer fluttered in the breeze—it had been cut off.

'We have given it to the witch so that she would help us and you would not have to die this night! She has given us a knife—here it is! Can you see how sharp it is? Before the sun rises, you must thrust it into the prince's heart, and as his warm blood splashes on to your feet, they will grow together into a fishtail and you will be a mermaid again, and then you can come down to us in the water and live your three hundred years before you turn into the dead salt foam of the sea. Hurry! Either he or you must die before the sun rises! Our old grandmother is so overcome with sorrow that her white hair has fallen out just as ours fell before the witch's scissors. Kill the prince and come back to us! Hurry!—Do you see that red streak in the sky? In a few minutes the sun will rise, and then you must die!' And they gave a strange deep sigh and sank beneath the waves.

The little mermaid drew aside the purple hangings of the tent, and she saw the lovely bride sleeping with her head upon the prince's breast, and she bent down and kissed his fair forehead. She looked at the sky where the red of morning was shining more and more brightly; she looked at the sharp knife and gazed once again upon the prince who murmured his bride's name in his dreams. She alone was in his thoughts, and the knife quivered in the mermaid's hand—but she flung it far out into the waves which shone red where it fell and looked as if drops of blood had spurted up out of the water. Once more she looked with half-glazed eyes upon the prince, threw herself from the ship down into the sea, and felt her body dissolving into foam.

Then the sun rose out of the sea and its rays fell gently and warmly on the death-cold sea-foam; and the little mermaid had no feeling of death upon her. She looked at the bright sun, and up above her floated hundreds of lovely transparent forms; through them she could see the ship's white sails and the red clouds in the sky. Their voices were music, but so ethereal were their tones that no human ear could hear them, just as no earthly eye could see them. Their own lightness bore them without wings through the air. The little mermaid noticed that she had a body like theirs that rose higher and higher out of the foam.

'To whom am I coming?' she asked, and her voice sounded like those of the other beings, so ethereal that no earthly music could echo its tones.

'To the daughters of the air!' answered the others. 'A mermaid has no immortal soul, and she can never gain one unless she wins the love of a mortal man: her immortality depends upon the power of another. The daughters of the air have no eternal soul either, but they can by good deeds create one for themselves. We are flying to the hot climates, where the warm pestilence-laden atmosphere kills people. There we waft cool breezes, we spread the sweet scent of flowers through the air and send freshness and healing. When we have striven to do what good we can for three hundred years, we gain our immortal soul and are given a share in the eternal happiness of mankind. You, poor little mermaid, have striven with your whole heart for the same thing as we strive for. You have suffered and endured, and raised yourself into the world of the spirits of the air. And now you, too, through your good deeds can create an immortal soul for yourself in three hundred years.'

And the little mermaid lifted her bright arms up towards God's sun, and for the first time she felt tears coming. On the ship there was bustle and life again: she saw the prince with his beautiful bride looking for her—they were staring sadly into the bubbling foam as if they knew she had thrown herself into the waves. Unseen, she kissed the bride's brow, smiled upon the prince, and with the other children of the air she soared up upon a rose-red cloud sailing through the air.

'In three hundred years we shall float just like this into the Kingdom of God!'

'We might come there even sooner!' whispered one. 'Unseen we float into people's homes where there are children, and for every day we find a good child that makes its parents happy and deserves their love, so God shortens our period of trial. The child does not know when we are flying through the room, and then when we smile upon it in happiness, a year is taken from our three hundred. But if we see a bad, naughty child, then we must weep tears of sorrow, and every tear adds a day to the time of our trial!'

The Emperor's New Clothes

MANY years ago there lived an Emperor who was so uncommonly fond of gay new clothes that he spent all his money on finery. He cared nothing for his soldiers; nor did he care about going to the theatre or riding in the woods, except for one thing—it gave him a chance to show off his new clothes. He had a different suit for every hour of the day, and since he spent so much time changing, instead of saying, as one does of a king, 'He is in his council chamber,' they said, 'The Emperor is in his wardrobe.'

Life was very entertaining in the big city where he had his court. Strangers arrived every day, and one day there appeared two rogues who spread the story that they were weavers who had mastered the art of weaving the most beautiful cloth you can imagine. Not only were the colours and patterns outstandingly lovely, but the clothes made from the cloth had the wonderful property of remaining invisible to anyone who was not fit for his job or who was particularly stupid.

'They would indeed be fine clothes to have!' thought the Emperor. 'With those on, I could find out what men in my kingdom are unfit for the jobs they have. And I should be able to tell the wise men from the fools! Yes, I must have some of that cloth made up for me at once!' And he handed over a large sum of money to the two rogues to enable them to begin the work.

So they set their two looms up and looked as if they were hard at work, but there was nothing at all on the looms. They boldly demanded the finest silk and gold thread, which they put in their haversacks, and went on pretending to work at the empty looms until far into the night.

'I should like to know how far they've got with my cloth,' thought the Emperor. But when he remembered that no one who was stupid or unfit for his job could see it, he felt somewhat hesitant about going to see for himself. Now, of course, he was quite certain that, as far as he was concerned, there were no grounds for fear, but nevertheless he felt he would rather send someone else first to see how they were getting on. Everybody in the city knew what wonderful powers the cloth had, and they were all very anxious to see how incompetent and stupid their neighbours were.

'I'll send my honest old minister to the weavers,' thought the Emperor. 'He's the best one to see how the cloth's coming on, for he's sense enough, and no one's fitter for his job than he is.'

So the good-natured old minister entered the room where the two rogues sat pretending to work at the empty looms. 'God help us!' thought the old minister, his eyes wide open. 'I can't see a thing!' But, of course, he was careful not to say so out loud.

Both rogues requested him very politely to take a step nearer, and asked him whether he didn't think the pattern beautiful and the colours charming. As they pointed to the empty loom, the poor old minister stared and stared, but he still could not see anything, for the simple reason that there was nothing to see. 'Heavens above,' he thought, 'surely I am not a stupid person! I must say such an idea has never occurred to me, and it must not occur to anyone else either! Am I really unfit for my job? No, it certainly won't do for me to say I can't see the cloth!'

'Well, you don't say anything,' said the one who was still weaving. 'Don't you like it?'

'Oh, er—it's delightful, quite the finest thing I've ever seen!' said the old minister, peering through his glasses. 'The design and the colours—oh, yes, I shall tell the Emperor they please me immensely!'

'Well, it's very kind of you to say so!' said the two weavers, and they went on to describe the colours and the unusual nature of the pattern. The old minister listened very carefully so that he could say the same thing when he returned to the Emperor. And that is just what he did.

The rogues now demanded a further supply of money, silk, and gold, which they said they must have for their work. But they put it all in their own pockets, and not a single thread ever appeared on the loom. However, they continued, as before, to weave away at the empty loom.

Soon afterwards the Emperor sent another unsuspecting official to see how the weaving was going on and whether the cloth would soon be finished. The same thing happened to him that happened to the minister: he stared and stared, but as there was nothing but the empty loom, he could not see a thing.

'Yes, it's a lovely piece of stuff, isn't it?' said the two rogues. And they showed him the cloth, and explained the charming pattern that was not there.

'Stupid I most certainly am not!' thought the official. 'Then the answer must be that I am not fit for my job, I suppose. That would be a very odd thing, and I really can't believe it. I shall have to see that no one else suspects it.' And then he praised the cloth he could not see, and assured them how happy he was with the beautiful colours and the charming pattern. 'Yes,' he told the Emperor, 'it's quite the finest thing I've ever seen!'

The story of the magnificent cloth was now on everybody's lips.

And now the Emperor wanted to see it himself while it was still on the loom.

With a large number of carefully chosen courtiers—among them the two good old men who had been there before—he paid a visit to the two crafty rogues, who were weaving away with all their might, but with neither weft nor warp.

'Isn't it really magnificent?' asked the two officials. 'Will Your Majesty be pleased to examine it? What a pattern! What colours!' And they pointed to the empty loom, fully believing that the others could undoubtedly see the cloth.

'What's this!' thought the Emperor. 'I don't see a thing! This is really awful! Am I stupid? Am I not fit to be Emperor? That would be the most shocking thing

G

that could happen to me!—Oh, it's very beautiful,' he said aloud. 'It has my very highest approval.' He nodded in a satisfied manner, and looked at the empty loom: on no account would he tell anyone that he could not see anything. All the courtiers who had come with him stared and stared, but none of them could make out any more than the others. But they all repeated after the Emperor, 'Oh, it's very beautiful!' And they advised him to have a suit made of the wonderful new cloth so that he could wear it for the first time for the great procession that had been arranged. 'It's magnificent! Delightful, excellent!' was repeated from mouth to mouth, and they all appeared to be deeply impressed and delighted with it. The Emperor gave each of the rogues an Order of Knighthood to hang in his buttonhole and the title of Knight of the Loom.

The two rogues sat up the whole night before the morning when the procession was to take place, and they had sixteen candles burning. Everyone could see that they had a job on to get the Emperor's new clothes ready in time. They pretended to take the cloth off the loom, they cut out large pieces of air with their big tailor's scissors, they sewed away with needles that had no thread in them, and at last they said, 'Look, the clothes are ready!'

The Emperor with the most distinguished of his gentlemen came to see for himself, and the rogues both held one arm up as if they were holding something, and they said, 'Look, here are the trousers. Here's the jacket. This is the cap.' And so on and so on. 'They are as light as gossamer! You'd think you'd nothing on your body, and that, of course, is the whole point of it!'

'Yes,' said all the gentlemen, but they couldn't see anything, because there was nothing there.

'Will Your Imperial Majesty most graciously be pleased to take your clothes off?' said the rogues. 'Then we shall put the new ones on Your Majesty over here in front of the big mirror.'

The Emperor laid aside all his clothes, and the two rogues pretended to hand him his new clothes, one at a time. They put their arms round his waist, and appeared to fasten something that was obviously his train, and the Emperor turned himself round in front of the mirror.

'My, how well it suits His Majesty! What a perfect fit!' they all said. 'What a pattern! What colours! It must be worth a fortune!'

'The canopy which is

to be borne over Your Majesty in the procession is waiting outside,' said the Chief Master of Ceremonies.

'Right,' said the Emperor, 'I'm quite ready. Doesn't it fit well?' And he turned round once more in front of the mirror and pretended to take a good look at his fine suit.

The gentlemen of the chamber, whose job it was to bear the train, fumbled on the floor with their hands as if they were picking it up, and then they held their hands up in the air. They dared not let anyone notice that they couldn't see anything.

And so the Emperor walked in the procession under his fine canopy, and everybody in the streets and at their windows said, 'My, look at the Emperor's new clothes! There's never been anything like them! Look at the beautiful train he has to his coat! Doesn't it hang marvellously!' No one would let anyone else see that he couldn't see anything, for if he did, they would have thought that he was not fit for his job, or else that he was very stupid. None of the Emperor's clothes had ever had such a success before.

'But, Daddy, he's got nothing on!' piped up a small child.

'Heavens, listen to the voice of innocence!' said his father. And what the child had said was whispered from one to another.

'He's nothing on! A little child said so. He's nothing on!'

At last, everybody who was there was shouting, 'He's nothing on!' And it gradually dawned upon the Emperor that they were probably right. But he thought to himself, 'I must carry on, or I shall ruin the procession.' And so he held himself up even more proudly than before, and the gentlemen of the chamber walked along carrying a train that was most definitely not there.

The Daisy

YOU must listen carefully now!

Out in the country, close by the roadside, lay a charming little cottage—you must have seen it yourself some time or other: there's a little garden in front with flowers and a painted fence, and close by, in the ditch, right in the middle of the loveliest green grass, grew a little daisy. The sun shone just as warmly and beautifully upon it as it did upon the large, rich, magnificent blooms inside the garden, and so the daisy grew hour by hour. One morning it stood fully open with shining white petals, small and fine, like rays of light round the little golden sun in the centre. The thought never entered its head that no one saw it down there in the grass or that it was a poor, common little flower— no, indeed, it was so full of joy, it turned straight towards the warm sun, looked up at it, and listened to the lark singing in the sky.

The little daisy was as happy as if it were a holiday, and yet it was only Monday: all the children were in school, and while they sat upon their seats and learnt their lessons, the daisy sat upon its little green stalk and learnt its lesson, too—it learnt from the warm sun and from everything round about it how good God is, and the little lark seemed to sing so clearly and beautifully everything which the daisy itself felt in silence. And the daisy looked up with a kind of respect at the happy bird that could sing and fly, but it was not at all sad that it could not do these things itself. 'I can see and listen!' it thought. 'The sun shines upon me and the wind kisses me! Oh, what gifts are given me!'

Inside the fence stood many stiff, grand flowers: the less scent they had, the more proudly they held up their heads. The peonies puffed themselves out, trying to be bigger than the roses—but it isn't size that matters! The tulips had the most beautiful colours, and they knew it, too, and held themselves upright so that you could see them even better. They took no notice at all of the little daisy outside, but it looked at them and thought, 'How rich and lovely they are! Yes, that beautiful bird is sure to fly down and visit them! Praise God I stand so near that I can see what a fine show they make!' And just as it was thinking that, down flew the lark with a twitter, but not to the peonies and tulips—oh, no, but down into the grass to the poor little daisy, that was so taken aback with pure joy that it no longer knew what to think.

The little bird hopped all round it and sang, 'Oh, how soft the grass is! And look what a sweet little flower there is with a golden heart and a silver dress!' For the daisy's yellow centre looked just like gold and the small petals round it were shining white.

How happy the little daisy was! No one could possibly understand how happy. The bird kissed it with its beak, sang for it, and then flew away again into the blue sky. It was quite a quarter of an hour before the flower was fully itself again. Half-ashamed, and yet inwardly full of joy, it looked at the flowers inside the garden: they must have seen the honour and happiness that had befallen it, they could not help understanding the joy it felt; but the tulips stood twice as stiffly as before, and they were so put out they looked quite sharp and red in the face. The peonies were quite thick-headed, and it was a good thing they couldn't speak, else the daisy would have got a regular talking-to. The poor little flower could see well enough that they were not in a very good humour, and that pained it deeply. At that very moment, a girl came into the garden with a large knife, sharp and shining; she went straight over to the tulips and cut them off, one after the other. 'Oh!' sighed the little daisy. 'That was really dreadful! It's all over with them now!' Then the little girl went away with the tulips, and the daisy was very glad it stood outside in the grass and was only a little flower of no account. It was very thankful indeed; and when the sun went down, it closed its petals, fell asleep and dreamed all night long of the sun and the little bird.

The next morning when the flower once again stretched out all its white petals, like so many little arms, happily towards the air and the light, it recognized the bird's voice, but its song was full of sadness. Yes, the poor lark had good cause for sorrow: it had been caught, and it was now sitting in a cage close by the open window. It sang of flying free and happy over the countryside, it sang of the young green corn in the field, and the delightful journeys it could make upon the wing high up in the air. The poor bird was not in a happy mood—there it sat, a prisoner in its cage.

The little daisy wanted so much to help, but what could it do? Yes, it was very difficult to hit upon anything. It completely forgot how lovely everything round it was, how warmly the sun shone, and how beautifully white its petals looked: it could think only of the captive bird it was quite unable to do anything for.

At that moment two small boys came out of the garden: one of them had a knife in his hand, as big and sharp as the one the girl had to cut the tulips with. They went straight towards the little daisy, who couldn't in the least imagine what they were after.

'We can cut a nice turf here for the lark!' said one of the boys, and began to make a deep square cut all round the daisy, so that it ended up in the middle of the turf.

'Pull the flower up!' said the other boy, and the daisy trembled all over with fear, because if it were pulled up, it would be sure to die, and it wanted so much to live now that it was going to be put into the cage with the turf for the captive lark.

'No, let it be!' said the first boy. 'It makes the turf look pretty!' And so it was left where it was and put into the cage for the lark.

But the poor bird loudly lamented the loss of its freedom, and beat the iron bars of its cage with its wings. The little daisy could not speak, could not say one word of comfort, though it wanted to so much. And so the whole morning went by.

'There's no water here!' said the captive lark. 'They are all out, and they've left me without a drop to drink! My throat is dry and burning! It's like fire and ice inside me, and the air feels so heavy! Oh, I must die, away from the warm sunshine, the fresh green, and all the loveliness God has made!' And then it buried its little beak deep in the cool turf to refresh itself a little: its eyes fell upon the daisy, and the bird nodded to it, kissed it with its beak, and said, 'You will wither here, too, poor little flower! They've given me you and this little green patch of grass in place of the whole world I had outside: every little blade of grass must be a green tree for me, and every one of your white petals a sweet-smelling flower! Oh, you only tell me how much I've lost!'

'Who could possibly comfort him!' thought the daisy, but it couldn't move a leaf; though the fragrance which its delicate white petals breathed out was far stronger than is usually found among daisies. The bird noticed it, too, and although it was in an agony of thirst and tore off the green blades of grass, it didn't touch the flower at all.

It was evening, and still no one came to bring the poor bird a drop of water. Then it stretched out its beautiful wings and fluttered them convulsively. Its song was a mournful peep. Its little head sank down towards the flower, and the bird's heart broke from want and longing: the flower could not close its petals together and sleep as it did the evening before—it hung down sick and sad towards the earth.

First thing the next morning the boys came, and when they saw the bird was dead, they wept; they wept many tears and dug it a nice grave which they decorated with flower petals. The bird's body was brought out in a pretty red box—the poor bird should be given a royal funeral! While it lived and sang, they forgot it and left it in its cage to suffer want; now it was buried in state with many tears.

But the turf the daisy grew in was thrown out in the dust on the roadway. No one gave it a thought, though it had felt most for the little bird and wanted so much to comfort it!

The Steadfast Tin-Soldier

THERE were once five and twenty tin-soldiers: they were all brothers, because they had all been born from one old tin spoon. They carried rifles on their shoulders, and they held their heads up and looked straight in front of them. Their uniform was red and blue and very fine indeed. The very first thing they heard in this world, when the lid of the box in which they lay was taken off, was the word 'Tin-soldiers!' shouted by a small boy as he clapped his hands. He had been given them because it was his birthday, and he now set them out on the table. One soldier looked exactly like another—only a single one of them was a little different: he had one leg because he had been cast the last, and there wasn't enough tin left. Yet he stood just as firm on his one leg as the others did on their two, and he's the one the story is really about.

On the table where they were set out were many other

toys, but the one that caught the eye most was a fine cardboard castle. Through the little windows you could see right into the rooms. Outside stood little trees round a little mirror which was meant to look like a lake. Wax swans swam on it and were reflected there. It was altogether charming, but the most charming thing about it was undoubtedly a little young lady who stood in the middle of the open castle door: she was cut out of cardboard, too, but she wore a skirt of the finest linen and a narrow blue ribbon draped round her shoulders. This was fastened in the middle by a shining spangle, as big as the whole of her face. This little lady stretched both her arms out, for she was a dancer, and raised one leg so high in the air that the tin-soldier could not find it at all, and believed that she had only one leg like himself.

'She'd be the wife for me!' he thought. 'But she's of very high birth: she lives in a castle, and I have only a box—besides, there are five and twenty of us, and there isn't room for her! But I can try to make her acquaintance!' And so he lay down full-length behind a snuff-box which stood on the table, and from there he had a good view of the fine little lady, who continued to stand on one leg without losing her balance.

When it was late in the evening, all the tin-soldiers were put in their box and the people of the house went to bed. And now the toys began to play—they played at visiting and soldiers and going to fine balls. The tin-soldiers rattled in their box, for they wanted to join in, but they couldn't get the lid off. The nut-crackers jumped head-over-heels, and the slate-pencil made a dreadful noise on the slate: there was such a row that the canary woke up and began to chat with them—in verse, too! There were only two who didn't move from their places, and they were the tin-soldier and the little dancer: she held herself so upright upon the tip of her toes, with both arms stretched out; he stood just as firmly on his one leg, and his eyes didn't leave her for one second.

Now the clock struck twelve, and with a clatter the lid sprang off the snuff-box: there was no snuff in it, no, but a little black goblin popped up—it was a sort of trick.

'Tin-soldier!' said the goblin. 'Will you keep your eyes to yourself!'

But the tin-soldier pretended he hadn't heard.

'Just you wait till tomorrow!' said the goblin.

When morning came and the children were up, the tin-soldier was put over on the window-ledge, and whether it was the goblin or a draught that did it, the window suddenly swung open and out fell the tin-soldier head-first from the third storey. He fell at a dreadful pace, his leg in the air, and ended up upon his head, with his bayonet stuck between the paving-stones.

The maid and the small boy went down at once to look for him, but although they came very near to treading on him, they still couldn't see him. If the tin-soldier had shouted, 'Here I am!' they would have found him right enough, but he considered it wasn't done to cry out when he was in uniform.

Now it began to rain, and the drops fell thicker and thicker until it was a regular shower. When it was over, a couple of street-urchins came by.

'Look!' said one of them. 'There's a tin-soldier! He must go for a sail!'

And so they made a boat from a newspaper, put the tin-soldier in the middle, and away he sailed down the gutter. Both the boys ran along by his side, clapping their hands. Heavens above, what waves there were in the gutter, and what a current there was! It had been a real downpour. The paper boat tossed up and down, and every now and then whirled round so quickly that the tin-soldier became quite giddy. But he remained steadfast, and without moving a muscle, he looked straight in front of him and kept his rifle on his shoulder.

All at once the boat was driven into a long stretch of gutter that was boarded over, and here it was quite as dark as it was in his box at home.

'I wonder where I shall get to now,' he thought. 'Yes, yes, it's all the goblin's fault! Ah, if only the young lady were here in the boat, it might be twice as dark for all I'd care!'

At that very moment there appeared a great water-rat that lived under the gutter-boarding.

'Have you got your passport?' asked the rat. 'This way with your passport!'

But the tin-soldier said nothing, and held his rifle even more tightly. The boat was carried along and the rat followed. Ooh, how it ground its teeth, and shouted to sticks and straws, 'Stop him! Stop him! He's not paid his toll! He's not shown his passport!'

But the current grew stronger and stronger. The tin-soldier could already catch a glimpse of daylight ahead where the boarding left off, but he also heard a roaring which was quite enough to terrify a bolder man than he: just imagine, where the boarding ended, the gutter emptied straight out into a big canal! It would be just as dangerous for him to be swept into that, as it would be for us to go sailing over a great waterfall.

He was already so close to it now that he could not stop himself. The boat swept out. The poor tin-soldier held himself as stiffly as he could—no one should say of him that he as much as blinked an eyelid. The boat spun round three or four times and filled with water right to the brim, so that nothing could stop it from sinking. The tin-soldier stood up to the neck in water, and the boat sank deeper and deeper. The paper became looser and looser, and now the water flowed over the soldier's head. Then he thought of the pretty little dancer whom he would never see again, and these words rang in the tin-soldier's ears:

> Onward, onward, warrior!
> Death's what you must suffer!

Now the paper parted, and the tin-soldier fell through —and he was at once swallowed by a big fish.

Oh, how dark it was inside! It was even worse than it was under the gutter-boarding, and it was so cramped, too! But the tin-soldier remained steadfast, and lay full-length with his rifle on his shoulder.

The fish twisted and turned about in the most frightening manner. At last it became quite still, and a flash of lightning seemed to pass right through it. Daylight shone quite brightly, and someone cried out, 'The tin-soldier!' The fish had been caught, taken to market, sold and brought up to the kitchen, where the maid had cut it open with a big knife. She picked the soldier up by the waist with two fingers and took him into the living-room, where they all wanted to see the remarkable man who had travelled about in the inside of a fish; but the tin-soldier's head was not a bit turned by their admiration. They stood him up on the table, and there—well, what wonderful things can happen in the world!—the tin-soldier was in

the very same room he had been in before, he saw the very same children, and the toys were standing on the table—there was the fine castle with the lovely little dancer: she was still standing on one leg with the other raised high in the air—she, too, was steadfast. The tin-soldier was deeply moved—he was ready to weep tin tears, but that was hardly the thing to do. He looked at her and she looked at him, but they said nothing.

At that very moment one of the small boys took the tin-soldier and threw him right into the stove—he gave no reason at all for doing it: the goblin in the box must have been to blame.

The tin-soldier stood in a blaze of light and felt terribly hot, but whether it was really the heat of the fire or the heat of love, he didn't know. His bright colours had completely gone—no one could say whether this had happened on his travels or whether it was the result of his sorrow. He looked at the little dancer, and she looked at him: he felt himself melting, but he still stood steadfast with his rifle on his shoulder. A door opened and the wind caught the dancer: she flew like a sylph right into the stove to the tin-soldier, burst into flame and vanished. Then the soldier melted to a blob of tin, and the next day, when the maid cleared the ashes out, she found him in the shape of a little heart. Nothing remained of the dancer but her spangle, and that was burnt coal-black.

H

The Wild Swans

FAR away from here, where the swallows fly when we have winter, there lived a king who had eleven sons and one daughter, Elisa. The eleven brothers—they were princes, of course—went to school with stars upon their breasts and swords by their sides: they wrote upon golden slates with diamond slate-pencils, and said their lessons off by heart just as well as they could read them from a book—you could see at once that they were princes. Their sister Elisa sat on a little stool made of looking-glass, and had a picture-book which had cost half a kingdom.

Oh, yes, the children had a very good time, but it was not always to be so.

Their father, who was king over the whole land, married a wicked queen, who was not at all kind to the poor children. This was made clear to them from the very first day: a great celebration was held throughout the palace, and so the children played at visiting, but instead of getting all the cakes and baked apples that were left over, as they used to do, they were given nothing but sand in a tea-cup, and told to make believe with that.

The week after, the queen sent the little sister, Elisa, away to the country to live with a peasant family, and it was not long before she turned the king so much against the poor princes that he would have nothing more to do with them.

'Fly out into the world and shift for yourselves!' said the wicked queen. 'Fly away like great birds without voices!' She had not the power, however, to do them all the evil she would, and they became eleven beautiful wild swans. With a strange harsh cry, they flew out of the palace windows away over the park and the woods.

It was still quite early in the morning when they passed by the peasant's cottage where their sister Elisa lay asleep; they hovered over the roof, craned their long necks this way and that, and beat their wings, but no one heard them or saw them. Off they had to go again, high up towards the clouds, far away into the wide world, where they flew over a great dark forest which stretched right down to the sea-shore.

Poor little Elisa stood in the peasant's living-room and played with a green leaf—she had no other toys. She stuck a hole in the leaf, peeped through it up at the sun, and it was just as if she saw her brothers' clear eyes; and every time the warm sun-beams shone upon her cheeks, she thought of her brothers' kisses.

One day went by just like another. Whenever the wind blew through the great rose-hedge outside the cottage, it would whisper to the roses, 'Who could be more beautiful than you?' But the roses would shake their heads and say, 'Elisa!' And whenever the old woman sat in the doorway on Sundays reading her hymn-book, the wind would turn the pages over and say to the book, 'Who could be more pious than you?' 'Elisa!' the hymn-book would answer. And what the roses and the hymn-book said was the pure truth.

When she was fifteen she had to return home, and when the queen saw how beautiful she was she grew angry and spiteful. She would willingly have changed her into a wild swan like her brothers, but she dared not do that right away, because the king would want to see his daughter.

In the early morning the queen went into the bath-room, which was built of marble and decorated with soft cushions and beautiful rugs, and she took three toads with her, kissed them, and said to the first, 'When Elisa gets into the bath, sit upon her head and make her dull and lazy like you! You sit on her forehead,' she said to the second, 'and make her ugly like you, so that her father will not recognize her! Rest upon her heart,' she whispered to the third, 'and give her evil thoughts to torment her!' So she put the toads in the clear water, which immediately took on a greenish tinge, called Elisa, undressed her, and made her step into the water. As soon as she lay down, the first toad settled in her hair, the second on her forehead, and the third upon her breast, but Elisa did not seem to notice anything at all. When she stood up there were three red poppies floating on the water—if the creatures had not been poisonous and kissed by the witch, they would have changed into red roses. They became flowers, even so, just from resting upon her head and her heart: she was too pious and innocent for witchcraft to have any power over her.

When the wicked queen saw that, she rubbed her with walnut juice so that she became quite dark brown, she smeared her lovely face with an evil-smelling ointment and matted her beautiful hair: it was impossible to recognize the lovely Elisa any longer.

And so when her father saw her he was quite alarmed and said it was not his daughter. No one else would own her, either, except the watch-dog and the swallows, and they were only humble beasts, and there was nothing they could say.

Then poor Elisa wept and thought of her eleven brothers who were all far away. Sadly she stole out of the palace, and all day long she wandered over field and bog until she entered the great forest. She had no idea where she would go, but she felt so sad and longed so much for her brothers, who had been driven out into the world like herself, that she made up her mind to try to find them.

She had been in the forest only a short while when night fell: she had left path and roadway far behind. Then she lay down on the soft moss, said her evening prayers, and leaned her head against the stump of a tree. It was all so still, the air was mild, and round about her in the grass and on the moss hundreds of glow-worms shone like a green fire, and when she touched one of the branches gently with her hand, the glowing insects fell about her like star-dust.

All night long she dreamed of her brothers: they played again as children, they wrote with their diamond slate-pencils upon their golden slates and they looked at that beautiful picture-book which had cost half a kingdom. But they did not, as they had done before, write nothing but noughts and straight lines upon their slates—

no, they wrote of the bold deeds they had done, of all they had seen and been through: and everything in the picture-book came alive—the birds sang, and the people stepped out of the book and talked to Elisa and her brothers, but when she turned over the page, they jumped straight back again so that the pictures should not get muddled.

When she woke the sun was already high: she could not see it, of course, for the high trees spread out their branches thick and fast, but the sunbeams played upon them like a fluttering golden gauze. There was a fresh smell of green leaves, and the birds almost settled on her shoulders. She heard water splashing from many large springs which all fell into a pool with a lovely sandy bottom. True, bushes grew thickly round it, but there was one place where the deer had trodden a large opening, and through this Elisa made her way down to the water. It was so clear that if the trees and bushes had not moved with the wind, she might have thought they were painted on the bottom, so clearly was reflected every leaf, whether it caught the rays of the sun or was quite hidden in the shade.

As soon as she saw her own face she had quite a fright, it was so brown and dreadful, but when she had wetted her little hand and rubbed her eyes and forehead, the white skin shone through again. Then she put aside all her clothes and stepped into the fresh water, and there was not a lovelier king's daughter in the whole world than she was.

When she had once more dressed and plaited her long hair, she went to the gushing spring, drank from the hollow of her hand, and wandered farther into the forest without knowing where she was going. She thought upon her brothers; she thought upon the goodness of God who would surely not forsake her: He made the wild crab-apples grow to satisfy the hungry; He showed her a tree, the branches bowed with fruit, and from it she made her midday meal. She set props under its branches, and then entered the darkest part of the forest. It was so still, she heard her own footsteps, she heard every little withered leaf she trod upon. There was not a bird to be seen; not a sunbeam could penetrate the great thick branches of the trees; the tall trunks stood so close together that when she looked straight ahead, it seemed that one great trellis of timber after another shut her in. Yes, here was a loneliness she had never known before.

The night was so dark, too: not a single little glow-worm shone in the moss. Sadly she lay down to sleep: then the branches over her head seemed to part, and Our Lord looked down upon her with gentle eyes, and little angels peeped out over His head and under His arms.

When she woke in the morning she did not know whether she had dreamed it or whether it had really been so.

She had gone some steps forward when she met an old woman with berries in her basket, and the old woman gave her some of them. Elisa asked her if she had not seen eleven princes riding through the forest.

'No,' said the old woman, 'but yesterday I saw eleven swans with golden crowns upon their heads swimming down the stream close by here!'

And she led Elisa a little farther forward to a steep bank: at the bottom of the slope a stream wound its way: the trees upon its banks stretched their long leafy branches over towards each other, and where their natural growth was not sufficient for them to touch, they had torn their roots loose from the earth and leaned out over the water with their branches intertwined.

Elisa said good-bye to the old woman, and went along

down the stream to where it flowed out upon the great open beach.

The beautiful sea lay open before the young girl's eyes, but not a ship appeared upon it, not a boat was to be seen, nothing to carry her farther. She looked at the countless pebbles on the shore: the water had worn them all to a round form—glass, iron, stone, everything that lay washed up on the beach had been moulded by the water, and yet it was far softer than her delicate hand. 'It goes on rolling untiringly, and so all these hard stones are made smooth and even. I will be just as tireless! Thank you for your lesson, clear, rolling waves! Some day, my heart tells me, you will bear me to my dear brothers!'

On the seaweed washed up by the tide lay eleven white swan feathers: she gathered them together like a bunch of flowers. Drops of water lay upon them, but no one could see whether they were dew or tears. It was lonely on the seashore, but she did not notice it, for the sea changed everlastingly—yes, it changed more in a few hours than fresh inland waters in a whole year. When a great black cloud passed over it, the sea seemed to answer, 'I can look dark, too.' And then the wind would blow strong and the waves turn to white foam. But when the clouds shone brightly tinged with red and the wind slept, then the sea was like a rose-leaf. It was now green, now white, but however peacefully it rested, there was still a slight movement on the shore, the water lifting lightly like the breast of a sleeping child.

When the sun was on the point of setting, Elisa saw eleven white swans with golden crowns upon their heads flying towards the land. They came gliding one behind the other, looking like a long white ribbon. Then Elisa climbed the slope and hid behind a bush: the swans settled near her and beat their great white wings.

As the sun sank below the water, the swan-forms suddenly fell away and there stood eleven handsome princes, Elisa's brothers. She uttered a loud cry, for although they had changed much, she knew they were her brothers, she felt they must be: and she sprang into their arms, calling them by their names, and they were very, very happy when they saw and recognized their little sister who was now so grown-up and beautiful. They laughed and they cried, and they soon understood how wicked their step-mother had been to them all.

'We brothers,' said the eldest, 'fly in the likeness of wild swans as long as the sun is in the sky: when it sets we appear as men again. And so, about sunset, we always have to be careful to have a resting-place for our feet, for if we were flying high up in the clouds, we might find ourselves in human form hurtling down into the deep. We do not live here: there lies a land just as beautiful as this on the farther side of the sea; but the way is long from here—we have to cross the great ocean, and there is not a single island on our way where we could spend the night, only a lonely little rock which rises steeply half-way across. It is only just big enough for us to rest upon it standing side by side: when the seas are heavy, the spray flies high over us. But yet we thank God for it. There we spend the night in our human form, and without it we could never visit the dear land of our birth, because we have to spend two of the longest days of the year on our flight here. Only once a year do we get the chance of visiting the home of our fathers and we dare not stay longer than eleven days, time enough to fly over this great forest to where we can catch a glimpse of the palace where we were born and where father still lives, and see the high tower of the church where mother is buried. Here we have the feeling that even the trees and the bushes are akin to us; here the wild horses race away over the plains just as we used to see them in our childhood; here the charcoal-burner sings the old songs we used to dance to as children—here, in short, is the land of our birth, the land that draws us back, and where we have found you, our dear little sister. We dare not stay here longer than two days now, and then we must away over the sea to a land that is beautiful but not our mother-land. How can we take you with us?—We've neither ship nor boat!'

'How can I free you from the spell?' asked their sister.

And they talked together nearly the whole night through, and dozed but a few hours.

Elisa awoke to the sound of swans' wings swishing over her. Her brothers had been transformed again, and they flew round in great circles and at last far away, but one of them, the youngest, stayed behind: and the swan laid its head in her lap and she patted its white wings: they were together the whole day. Towards evening the others came back, and when the sun set they stood in their natural form.

'Tomorrow we fly away from here, and we dare not return for a whole year, but we can't leave you like this! Have you the courage to come with us? My arm is strong enough to carry you through the forest, so should not all our wings together be strong enough to fly with you over the sea?'

'Yes, take me with you!' said Elisa.

They spent the whole night plaiting a net of supple willow bark and tough rushes, and they made it big and strong: Elisa lay down in it, and when the sun rose and the brothers had changed back to wild swans, they seized the net in their beaks and flew high up towards the clouds with their dear sister who lay still sleeping. The sunbeams fell right upon her face, and so one of the swans flew above her head shading her with its broad wings.

They were far from land when Elisa woke: she thought she was still dreaming, so strange did it seem to her to be carried over the sea, high up through the sky. By her side lay a branch of lovely ripe berries and a bundle of tasty roots: the youngest of her brothers had gathered them and put them there for her, and she smiled her thanks to him, for she knew that he was the one who was flying just over her head and shading her with his wings.

They were so high up that the first ship they saw below them looked like a white sea-gull resting upon the water. A cloud lay behind them, a great mountain of a cloud, and Elisa saw her own gigantic shadow and those of the eleven swans flying on it: it was a finer picture than she had ever seen before, but as the sun rose higher and the cloud was left farther behind them, the drifting shadow-picture disappeared from view.

All day long they flew on like an arrow whistling through the air, but now they had their sister to carry, it was taking them longer than usual. Bad weather was blowing up and evening was drawing near: anxiously Elisa watched the sun sinking, and she was still unable to spot the lonely rock in the sea; the swans seemed to her to be beating their wings more strongly. Ah, it was her fault they were not going quickly enough: when the sun set they would change into men, fall into the sea and drown. Then she prayed earnestly in her heart to God, but she still saw no sign of the rock: the black cloud was drawing nearer, strong gusts of wind proclaimed an approaching gale, the clouds stood banked in one great threatening wave and shot forward in a solid leaden mass: lightning followed, flash upon flash.

The sun was now right upon the rim of the sea. Elisa's heart trembled: then the swans shot downwards so swiftly that she thought she would fall, but just then they straightened out again. The sun was half below the water when she first caught sight of the little rock beneath her: it looked no bigger than the head of a seal stuck up out of the water. The sun was sinking rapidly: it was now only the size of a star. As her foot touched the solid ground the sun went out like the last spark in a piece of burning paper. She saw her brothers standing round her arm in arm, but there was only just enough room for them and her. The sea beat against the rock and flung its spray like a shower of rain over the top of them. The sky was brightly lit by repeated flashes of lightning and the thunder rolled clap upon clap; but the brothers and sister held hands and sang a hymn, and that gave them comfort and courage.

At daybreak the air was clean and still, and as soon as the sun rose the swans flew away from the island with Elisa. The seas were still running high, and when she was high in the air it looked as if the white foam upon the dark-green sea were millions of swans floating on the water.

As the sun rose higher Elisa saw in front of her, half swimming in the air, a land of mountains with shining ice-masses upon the mountain-sides, and in the middle a palace stretched quite a mile in length, with one bold colonnade on top of another. In front waved woods of palm-trees and magnificent flowers as big as mill-wheels. She asked if this were the land she was bound for, but the swans shook their heads, for what she saw was the cloud-palace of Morgan le Fay, ever-changing in its loveliness, and they dared not take any human person there. As Elisa was gazing upon it, woods and palace collapsed and faded, and in their place stood twenty proud churches, all alike, with high towers and pointed windows. She thought she heard the organ play, but it was the sea she heard. Then when she was quite near the churches, they turned into a whole fleet of ships sailing down below her; she looked down, and it was only a sea-mist swirling over the water. Yes, there was an everlasting change before her eyes, and then she saw the real land she was bound for; the loveliest blue mountains rose up with forests of cedar, towns and castles. Long before the sun went down she was sitting on the hill-side in front of a great cave over-grown with delicate green creepers that looked like an embroidered carpet.

'Now we shall see what you'll dream here tonight!' said the youngest brother and showed her her bedchamber.

'If only I might dream how I could set you free!' she said; and her mind was so filled with this thought, she prayed earnestly to God to help her, and even when she had fallen asleep, she went on with her prayer. Then she appeared to be flying high up in the sky to the cloud-palace of Morgan le Fay, and the fairy came to meet her, beautiful and radiant, and yet looking quite like the old woman who had given her the berries in the forest and told her of the swans with the golden crowns.

'Your brothers can be freed!' she said. 'But have you enough courage and endurance? It's true the sea is softer than your delicate hands and yet shapes hard stones, but it doesn't feel the pain your fingers will feel, and it has no heart and doesn't suffer the anxiety and torment you must endure. Do you see this stinging-nettle I am holding in my hand? Many of the same kind grow round about the cave where you are sleeping; only those and the ones that spring up from the graves in the churchyard can be used —mark that!—You must pick them—though they will sting you and raise blisters on your skin—tread the nettles with your feet and get a yarn like flax from them, and with that twist a thread and make eleven shirts like coats of mail with long sleeves. Throw these over the eleven wild swans and the spell will be broken. But you must take care to remember that from the moment you begin your task right up to the time it is finished, even though it take years, you must not speak: the first word you utter will pierce your brothers' hearts like a dagger— their lives hang upon your tongue. Remember all I have told you!'

And at the same time she touched Elisa's hand with the nettle; it was like a burning fire. Elisa woke with the pain. It was bright daylight, and close by where she had slept lay a nettle like the one she had seen in her dream. Then she fell upon her knees, thanked Our Lord, and left the cave to begin her task.

She plunged her delicate hands down among the ugly nettles that stung like fire; they burnt great blisters on her hands and arms, but she would suffer gladly if she could free her dear brothers. She trod every nettle with her naked feet, and twisted the green flax into a thread.

When the sun had set, her brothers came back, and they were alarmed to find her so silent; they thought it was a new spell their wicked step-mother had put upon her. But when they saw her hands, they realized what she was doing for their sake, and the youngest brother wept, and where his tears fell she felt no more pain and the burning blisters disappeared.

She spent the night at her task, because she could not rest until she had freed her dear brothers. The whole of the following day, while the swans were away, she sat in solitude, but never had time flown so quickly. One shirt was completely finished, and she began upon the next.

Then a hunting-horn sounded through the mountains; she grew quite frightened as the sound came nearer; she heard the hounds baying, and in terror she fled into the cave, tied together in a bundle the nettles she had gathered and combed, and sat upon it.

At the same moment a great hound sprang out of the bushes, followed immediately by another and still another; they bayed loudly, retreated and sprang forward again. A few minutes later the huntsmen were all standing before the cave, and the most handsome among them was the king of the land: he stepped towards Elisa, for he had never seen a more beautiful girl.

'How do you come to be here, sweet child?' he asked. Elisa shook her head; she dared not speak, for that would cost her brothers' lives and freedom; and she hid her hands under her apron so that the king should not see what she had to suffer.

'Come with me!' he said, 'You cannot stay here! If you are as good as you are beautiful, I will clothe you in silk and velvet and put a golden crown upon your head, and you shall live in my finest castle!' And then he lifted her up upon his horse; she wept and wrung her hands, but the king said, 'I want only your happiness! One day you

will thank me for this!' And so, holding her in front of him on his horse, he rode off between the mountains, and the huntsmen followed behind.

When the sun set, the magnificent royal city with its churches and domes lay before them, and the king led her into the palace, where great fountains splashed in high marble halls, their walls and ceilings resplendent with paintings. But she had no eyes for it. She wept and grieved; listlessly, she let the women attire her in royal garments, plait pearls in her hair, and draw fine gloves over her blistered fingers.

When she stood there in all her finery, she was so dazzlingly beautiful that the court bowed even more deeply before her and the king chose her to be his bride, although the archbishop shook his head and whispered that the beautiful girl of the woods was undoubtedly a witch who had blinded their eyes and infatuated the king's heart.

But the king did not listen to him: he commanded the music to strike up, the richest dishes to be brought in, and the loveliest girls to dance about her. She was led through sweet-smelling gardens into magnificent halls; but not a smile passed over her lips or shone from her eyes—sorrow stood there as her inheritance and everlasting possession. Then the king opened a little chamber close by, where she was to sleep: it was decorated with costly green tapestries, and looked quite like the cave where she had been found; on the floor lay the bundle of yarn she had spun from the nettles, and from the ceiling hung the shirt she had finished knitting—one of the huntsmen had brought all this along with him as something of a curiosity.

'In here you can dream you are back in your old home!' said the king. 'And here is the work you were occupied with. It will amuse you now in all your splendour to think on times gone by.'

When Elisa saw what lay so near her heart, a smile played about her mouth and the blood returned to her cheeks: she thought upon her brothers' release and kissed the king's hand, and he pressed her to his heart, and commanded all the church bells to proclaim their wedding-feast. The beautiful dumb girl from the woods would be queen of the land.

Then the archbishop whispered evil words in the king's ear, but they made no impression upon his heart: the wedding must stand, the archbishop himself had to place the crown upon her head, and he pressed the narrow ring

I

firmly down over her forehead with such ill-will that it hurt. And yet there lay a heavier ring about her heart in her sorrow for her brothers, so that she did not feel the physical pain. Her mouth was dumb—one single word would cost her brothers their lives—but in her eyes lay a deep love for the good and handsome king, who did all he could to make her happy. Day by day she loved him more and more. Oh, if only she dare open her heart to him and tell him of her sufferings, but silent she had to be, and in silence must she complete her task. And so, at night, she would slip from his side, go to the little room that was decorated to look like the cave, and finish knitting one shirt after another. But when she began upon the seventh she ran out of yarn.

She knew that the nettles she must use grew in the churchyard, but she had to pick them herself—how could she get out to do it?

'Oh, what is the pain in my fingers to the agony my heart suffers!' she thought. 'I must risk it! Our Lord will not take his hand from me!' With fear in her heart, as if it were an evil deed she had to do, she crept down into the garden in the moon-bright night, and made her way down the long avenues, and out into the lonely streets that led to the churchyard. There she saw a coven of ugly witches sitting in a circle on one of the broadest tombstones: they took their rags off as if they were going to bathe, and then with their long skinny fingers they dug down into the fresh graves, pulled out the dead bodies, and fed upon the flesh. Elisa had to pass close by them, and they fastened their evil eyes upon her, but she said her prayers, gathered the stinging-nettles, and carried them home to the palace.

Only one single person had seen her, and that was the archbishop: he was up while the others were asleep. He was now sure he had been right in his opinion that all was not as it should be with the queen: she was a witch and had used her powers to infatuate the king and all the people.

During confession he told the king what he had seen and what he feared, and as the harsh words fell from his tongue, the carven images of the saints shook their heads as if to say, 'It is not so—Elisa is innocent!' But the archbishop took it the wrong way, and thought that they were bearing witness against her, that they were shaking their heads over her sin. Then two heavy tears rolled down the king's cheeks, and he went home with doubt in his heart. He pretended to sleep at night, but no sleep would come to close his eyes in peace: he noticed Elisa get up. Every night she did the same thing, and every time he followed her softly and watched her disappear into her little room.

Day by day his face grew darker: Elisa noticed it, but could not understand why, though it troubled her and added to the suffering she felt in her heart for her brothers. Her salt tears ran down her royal velvet and purple, and lay there like glistening diamonds; and all who saw her splendour wished they were queen, too. She would soon reach the end of her task, however, for only one shirt still remained to be done, but she had no more yarn left and not a single nettle. And so once more, though this would be the last time, she would have to go to the churchyard and pick a few handfuls. She thought anxiously of the lonely walk and the frightful witches, but her will was as firm as her trust in the Lord.

And so she went, but the king and the archbishop followed her. They saw her disappear by the iron gate that led into the churchyard, and when they drew near, the witches were sitting on the grave-stones just as Elisa had seen them, and the king turned away for he imagined her among them—only that very evening had she laid her head upon his breast.

'I shall let the people judge her!' he said, and the people passed judgement that she should burn in the red flames.

She was borne away from the splendour of the royal halls into a dark damp hole where the wind whistled in through the iron bars of the window. Instead of velvet and silk, they gave her the bundle of nettles she had gathered, to lay her head on, and she had to use the hard stinging shirts she had knitted, as bedding and blankets. But they could have given her nothing she would sooner have—she turned to her task again, and prayed to God. Outside, the street urchins sang mocking songs about her: not a soul comforted her with a loving word.

Towards evening came the swish of a swan's wing close by the window-bars—it was the youngest of the brothers: he had found their sister. She sobbed aloud with joy, although she knew that the coming night was probably the last she had to live: but now her work was nearly finished and her brothers were there.

The archbishop came to spend her last hour with her,

as he had promised the king he would, but she shook her head, and asked him with looks and gestures to go: that night she had to finish her task, or everything—pain and tears and sleepless nights—everything would have been to no purpose. The archbishop went away speaking hard words against her, but poor Elisa knew she was innocent, and went on with her work.

There were little mice running over the floor, and they dragged the nettles over to her feet, to help a little at any rate, and a thrush settled by the iron window-bars and sang the whole night through as joyfully as it could so that she should not lose heart.

It was still no more than day-break, an hour before sunrise, when the eleven brothers stood at the palace gate and demanded to be taken before the king; but they were told that could not be done—it was still night, the king was asleep and they dared not wake him. They prayed, they threatened; the guard came—yes, even the king himself stepped out to ask what it all meant; at that very moment the sun rose and the brothers were no longer there, but away over the palace flew eleven wild swans.

Everybody streamed out of the city gate to see the witch burnt. A wretched horse dragged the cart she sat in; she had been given a smock of coarse sackcloth; her lovely long hair hung loose about her beautiful head, her cheeks were deathly pale, and her lips moved softly while her fingers wove the green yarn—even on her way to death, she did not give up the task she had begun: the ten shirts lay at her feet, and she was knitting away at the eleventh, while the rabble scoffed at her.

'Look at the witch, see the way she mutters! There's no hymn-book in her hand, you bet! Look at her sitting there with her beastly witchcraft! Tear it away from her! Tear it into a thousand pieces!'

And they all pressed in upon her and would have torn it apart, when the eleven white swans came flying towards her: they settled round her on the cart and beat their great wings. The mob drew back in alarm.

'It's a sign from heaven! She must be innocent!' many whispered, but they did not risk saying so aloud.

As the executioner seized her by the hand, she hastily threw the eleven shirts over the swans, and there stood eleven handsome princes, but the youngest had a swan's wing in place of one arm because a sleeve was missing from his shirt which she had not completely finished.

'Now I can speak!' she said. 'I am innocent!'

And the people who saw what had happened bowed before her as if she were a saint, but she sank lifeless in her brothers' arms, overcome by excitement, fear, and pain.

'Yes, she is innocent!' said the eldest brother, and then

he told them everything that had happened, and while he was speaking, a perfume like that of a million roses spread about them, for every stick of wood heaped about the stake had taken root and put out branches: there stood a great tall hedge fragrant with red roses. Right at the top was one flower, white and gleaming, which shone like a star; the king plucked it and placed it on Elisa's breast, and then she woke with peace and happiness in her heart.

And all the church bells rang by themselves, and the birds came in great flocks. The way back to the palace became a wedding procession such as no king had yet seen.

The Flying Trunk

THERE was once a merchant who was so rich he could have paved the whole street with silver coins —and have had nearly enough over for a little alley-way as well. But that's not what he did: he had another use for his money. Every time he laid out a shilling, he got five shillings back. That's the sort of merchant he was— and then he died.

All his money now went to his son, and he lived a life of pleasure. He went to dances every night, he made paper kites out of ten-shilling notes, and played ducks and drakes on the lake with golden sovereigns instead of pebbles. That was a sure way of getting rid of his money, and get rid of it he did. At last he had no more than five shillings left, and all the clothes he had were a pair of slippers and an old dressing-gown. His friends no longer cared for him now that they could not go out with him any more, but one of them, a good-hearted young man, sent him an old trunk, and said, 'Pack up!' Now that was all very well, but he had nothing to pack. And so he got into the trunk himself.

It was a queer kind of trunk; as soon as you pressed the lock, up would fly the trunk and away it would go. Now it so happened that that was just what he did, and— whoosh!—up the chimney it flew with him, high up over the clouds, farther and farther away. The bottom creaked and he was afraid it would fall to pieces, and then he would have performed a very fine somersault! At last he came to the land of the Turks. He hid the trunk in the woods under the withered leaves, and then made his way into the town. This he could do easily enough, for among the

Turks everybody walked about just as he was, in dressing-gown and slippers. He met a nurse with a small child. 'Just a minute, Turkish nurse!' he called out. 'What's that great palace close by the town here with the windows so high up in the wall?'

'That's where the king's daughter lives!' she said. 'A fortune-teller once said that she would be made very unhappy over a love-affair, and so no one is allowed to visit her unless the king and queen are there!'

'Thanks!' said the merchant's son, and then he made his way back to the woods, sat down in his trunk, flew up over the roof-tops, and crept in through the window to the princess.

She was lying on the sofa asleep: she looked so lovely that the merchant's son couldn't help kissing her. She woke up and was really quite frightened, but he told her he was the Turkish god who had come down through the sky to visit her, and she thought that sounded rather nice.

So they sat down beside one another, and he told her stories about her eyes: they were the loveliest dark lakes and thoughts swam about in them like mermaids. He told

her about her forehead: it was a snow-covered mountain
which had the most magnificent halls with beautiful
pictures in them. And then he told her about the stork
that brings sweet little babies.

Yes, indeed, they were very charming stories! Then he
asked the princess to marry him, and she said, 'Yes,' right
away.

'But you must come here on Saturday,' she said. 'The
king and queen are coming to tea. They'll be very proud
when they know I'm going to marry the Turkish god.
But see that you know a really good story, for that's what
my parents are especially fond of. My mother likes them
to have a moral and a distinguished air about them; my
father likes them jolly with something to laugh at.'

'Very well,' he said, 'I shall bring no wedding-gift but
a story!' Then they parted, and the princess gave him a
sword. It was set with gold coins, and those he could
most certainly make use of.

He now flew away, bought himself a new dressing-
gown, and then sat down in the woods to compose a
story. It had to be finished by Saturday, and that wasn't
so easy after all.

But at last the story was finished and Saturday came.

The king and the queen and the whole court were
waiting to have tea with the princess, and they all received him in such a very pleasant way!

'Will you tell us a story?' asked the queen. 'Something
instructive that one has to think about.'

'But something one can laugh at as well!' put in the
king.

'Certainly!' he said, and so he began. This is the story
he told, and you must listen to it carefully.

'There was once a bundle of sulphur-matches who

were quite insupportably proud because of their high ancestry. Their family-tree—that is to say, the great pine-tree they were all little chips of—had been a great old tree in the forest. The matches now lay upon the mantelshelf between a tinder-box and an old iron saucepan, and they were telling them about their young days. "Yes," they said, "when we were on the green bough, we were in clover right enough![1] Every morning and evening there was diamond-tea left by the dew, all day long we had sunshine, whenever the sun shone, and all the little birds would tell us stories. We couldn't help noticing how well off we were when we looked at the hardwoods, for they were clothed only in the summer-time, while our family could afford green clothing both summer and winter. But then the wood-cutters came along and caused a great social upheaval. Our family was split up: the head of the family got a job as main-mast on a fine ship which could sail wherever it wished right round the world; the other branches ended up in other places; and we have now the task of striking a light for the common herd. That's how it is that people of good family like us find themselves here in the kitchen."

'"Hm, my story's quite different from that!" said the iron saucepan that lay by the side of the matches. "Right from the very first moment I came into the world, I've been scoured and boiled time and time again! I'm all for solid respectability, I am, and, strictly speaking, I'm the most important person in the house here. My one real pleasure in life is to lie like this after dinner, clean and spruce upon the mantelshelf, and have a little sensible conversation with my friends. Except for the water-bucket, which goes down into the yard from time to time,

[1] In Danish the phrase 'to be on a green bough' is an idiom meaning 'to be in clover'. L. W. K.

it's true to say that we spend all our lives indoors. Our only newsmonger is the shopping-basket, but she's always so full of disturbing talk about the Government and the People—yes, not so long ago there was an old pot here who was so shocked by it all that he fell down and cracked himself to pieces! She's quite irresponsible, I tell you!"

'"You talk too much!" said the tinder-box, and the steel struck the flint and made the sparks fly. "Now what about a pleasant evening?"

'"Yes, let's discuss which of us is of the most consequence!" said the matches.

'"No, I don't like talking about myself," said the earthenware pot. "Let's have an evening's entertainment. I'll begin. I shall describe something everyone has experienced: that'll be something we can all enter into with pleasure, and it will be very amusing. 'Near the Baltic, by the Danish beeches—'"

'"That's a good beginning!" said all the plates together. "It's going to be the sort of story I like!"

'"Yes, I spent my youth there in a very quiet family. The furniture was polished, the floor washed, and clean curtains put up every fortnight."

'"What an interesting way you have of telling a story!" said the broom. "You can tell at once it's a woman speaking: there's a kind of theme of cleanliness running through it!"

'"Yes, I noticed that!" said the water-bucket, and gave a little hop of pleasure, so that it said, "Plonk!" on the floor.

'And the pot went on telling her story, and the end was just as good as the beginning.

'The plates all clattered with pleasure, and the broom took some green parsley from the sand-hole and made a crown for the pot, for he knew that would annoy the others. "If I crown her today," he thought, "she'll have to crown me tomorrow."

' "I'm going to dance!" said the fire-tongs, and dance she did. My, how she could stand on one leg and kick the other up in the air! The old chair-cover over there in the corner split himself just looking at her! "Can I be crowned, too?" asked the tongs. And so she was.

' "What a common lot they are!" thought the matches.

'They now called upon the tea-urn to sing, but she said she had a cold and could only sing when she was on the boil. She was, of course, standing on her dignity, and refused to sing anywhere but on the dining-room table with the master and mistress.

'Over there in the window sat an old quill-pen which the maid used to write with. There was nothing remarkable about her, except that she had been dipped far too deeply in the ink-bottle. But she was rather proud of that. "If the tea-urn doesn't want to sing," she said, "she needn't! There's a nightingale hanging in a cage outside: he can sing—though, to be sure, he never had lessons, but we won't speak harshly of him this evening!"

' "I find it most unbecoming," said the kettle, who was the prima donna of the kitchen and half-sister to the tea-urn, "that anyone should listen to such a foreign bird! I ask you, is it patriotic? I leave it to the shopping-basket to judge the matter!"

' "I'm too upset!" said the shopping-basket. "No one can imagine how deeply upset I am. Is this a proper way of passing the evening? Would it not be better to set the house to rights? Then everyone would be in his own place, and I could direct the whole thing. That would be something worth doing!"

' "Yes, let's turn the place upside-down!" they all

cried together. But at that very moment the door opened. It was the maid. They stood quite still, and no one spoke a word. But there was not a pot there who did not know for certain what he could have done and how distinguished a person he was. "Yes, if I'd wanted to," they thought, "I could have made it an amusing evening all right!"

'The maid picked up the matches and struck them. My, how they spluttered and burst into flame!

'"Now," they thought, "everyone can see that we're the most important people here! What radiance we have! What enlightenment!" And then they burnt out.'

'That was a charming story!' said the queen. 'I quite felt I was in the kitchen with those sulphur-matches. Yes, you shall certainly have our daughter.'

'Yes, rather!' said the king. 'You shall have her on Monday!' And now they spoke to him like one of the family.

So the wedding was arranged, and the evening before, the whole city was illuminated; cakes and buns were thrown to the children to scramble for; the street urchins stood on their toes, cheering and whistling through their fingers; everybody had a gorgeous time.

'I must see about doing something, too,' thought the merchant's son. And so he bought rockets and crackers and every sort of firework he could think of, put them in his trunk, and flew up in the air with them.

Whoosh, how they went! How they banged away!

The Turks were all jumping up in the air with excitement, so that their slippers were flying about their ears: they had never seen such an aerial display before. Now they fully realized that it was indeed the Turkish god himself who was going to marry their princess.

As soon as the merchant's son descended into the wood again with his trunk, he thought, 'I'll take a walk into town, and then I shall get to hear how it went off.' And it was of course quite reasonable that he should want to do so.

My, how people talked! Every single person he spoke to about it had seen it after his own particular fashion, but they all thought it beautiful.

'I saw the Turkish god himself!' said one of them. 'He had eyes like shining stars and a beard like foaming water!'

'He was flying in a cloak of fire!' said another. 'And the loveliest little cherubs were peeping out from under its folds!'

Indeed, he heard the most charming things about himself, and the next day was to be his wedding-day.

And now he made his way back to the woods to sit down and rest in his trunk—but where was it? The trunk was burnt up. A spark from the fireworks had been left behind: it had caught fire, and the trunk was in ashes. He could fly no more: no more could he come to his bride.

She stood the whole day upon the roof and waited for him. And there she is, waiting still; but he wanders round the world telling stories. But they are no longer as delightful as the one he told about the sulphur-matches.

The Storks

ON top of the last house of a little town stood a stork's nest. Mother-stork was sitting in the nest with her four small young ones, who poked out their heads and their little black beaks which had not yet turned red. A little way off upon the roof-top, father-stork was standing, very stiff and upright; he had tucked one leg up underneath him in order to stop himself from falling asleep while he was keeping watch. You might have thought he was carved out of wood, he stood so still. 'It certainly looks well for my wife to have someone on guard by the nest!' he thought. 'They can't possibly know I'm her husband: they'll think I've been ordered to stand here. It looks very fine!' And so he went on standing on one leg.

Down in the street a whole crowd of children were playing, and when they saw the storks, one of the boldest of the boys began singing the old rhyme about them, and then they all joined in and sang what they could remember of it:

> 'Storky, storky, stop, stop!
> Fly home to your roof-top!
> Your wife is sitting upon her nest
> With four enormous youngsters.
> By hanging the first dies;
> Iron bars round the next rise;
> The third in the fire fries;
> The fourth upside-down lies!'

'Just hear what those boys are singing!' said the baby storks. 'They say we shall be hanged and burnt!'

'You mustn't take any notice of that!' said mother-stork. 'Don't listen to them and they'll do you no harm!'

But the boys went on singing, and they pointed with their fingers at the storks. Only one boy, called Peter, said it was a shame to make fun of dumb creatures and refused to take part in it. Mother-stork tried to soothe her young ones. 'Take no notice,' she said. 'Just see how quietly your father's standing, and on one leg, too!'

'We're so frightened!' said the young ones, and tucked their heads deep down into the nest.

The next day, when the children met again to play, they began their rhyme as soon as they saw the storks:

'By hanging the first dies;
The next in the fire fries!'

'Shall we really be hanged and burnt?' asked the young storks.

'No, of course not!' said their mother. 'But it's time you learnt to fly; I must see that you get some practice! Then we'll go over to the meadow and pay a visit to the frogs: they'll curtsey to us in the water and sing, "Croak, croak!" and then we shall eat them up—that'll be a great treat!'

'And what will happen then?' asked the young storks.

'Then all the storks in the land will gather together and the autumn manœuvres will begin. It's very important to fly well by then, because the general will stab to death with his beak anyone that can't. So see that you learn something when we begin our exercises!'

'Then we shall be killed just as the boys said—and listen, they're saying it again now!'

'Listen to me and not to them,' said mother-stork. 'After the great manœuvres, we fly to warm lands, oh, ever so far away, over mountains and forests. We fly to Egypt where there are three-cornered houses of stone that go up to a point right above the clouds: they are called pyramids and they are older than any stork can imagine. There's a great river that overflows and turns the land to mud, and we walk in the mud and eat frogs.'

'Oh!' said all the young ones.

'Yes, it really is lovely! There's nothing to do but eat the whole day long, and while we are having such a good time, there's not one green leaf left on the trees in this country: it's so cold here that the clouds freeze to bits and fall down in little white pieces!' It was snow she meant, of course, but she could not explain it any more clearly.

'Will the naughty boys freeze to bits, too?' asked the young storks.

'No, they won't freeze to bits, but they'll get very near it and will have to sit and mope inside their dark living-rooms. But you will be able to fly about in strange lands where there are flowers and warm sunshine!'

Time passed by, and now the young ones had already grown so big they could stand up in the nest and see a long way all round them, and father-stork came flying home every day with fine frogs, small grass-snakes and all the other stork tit-bits he could find. And it was great fun to see him do his tricks for them: he would lay his head on his tail, clacking his beak, and tell them stories, all of them about the marsh.

'Listen now, you must learn to fly!' said mother-stork one day, and so all four young ones had to step out on to the roof-top. Oh, how they staggered and tried to keep their balance with their wings, and in spite of their efforts came very near to falling off!

'Now look at me!' said their mother. 'You must hold your heads this way, and you must place your feet like this! Left, right! Left, right! That's the way to get on in the world!' Then she flew a little way: the young ones gave a clumsy little hop, and bump! there they lay, for their bodies were much too heavy.

'I don't want to fly!' said one of the young ones as he crept into the nest again. 'I don't care if I don't go to the warm lands!'

'Do you want to freeze to death, then, when winter

comes? Shall the boys come and hang you and burn you and roast you? I'll call them right now!'

'Oh, no!' said the young stork, hopping on to the roof again like the others. On the third day they really could fly a little, and so they thought they could sit and rest on the air, too, but when they tried it, bump! down they tumbled, and they had to take to their wings again. And now, down in the street, the boys came and sang their rhyme:

'Storky, storky, stop, stop!'

'Shall we fly down and peck their eyes out?' said the young ones.

'No, let them alone!' said their mother. 'Now just pay attention to me—that's much more important! One, two, three! Now we'll fly to the right! One, two, three! Now left round the chimney-stack!—That was really very good! That last wing-beat was so neat and well-timed that I'll let you come to the marsh with me tomorrow! There are several very nice stork families that go there with their children. Just show me that mine are the best now, and remember to hold your heads up—it looks well and makes a good impression!'

'But aren't we going to have our revenge on those rude boys then?' asked the young storks.

'Let them scream as much as they like! Remember, you'll be flying with the clouds to the land of the pyramids, while they'll have to freeze without one green leaf or one sweet apple to comfort them.'

'Yes, we'll be revenged!' they whispered to one another, and then it was time for their exercises again.

Of all the boys in the street, none sang that mocking rhyme more persistently than the one who had begun it, and he was quite small, certainly not more than six years

old—of course, the young storks thought he was a
hundred for he was so much bigger than their mother
and father, and how could they tell how old children
and grown-up people were! All their revenge should be
concentrated on this boy—he had been the first to mock
them and he was always there. The young storks were
becoming more and more irritated, and the older they
grew, the less willing they were to put up with it. At last
their mother had to promise them that they should
definitely have their revenge, but she would leave it until
the last day before they left the country.

'We must first see how well you do at the big manœuvres.
If you do badly, the general will thrust his beak into
your breasts, and then the boys will be right—at any rate,
after a fashion! Let's see if you do well!'

'Yes, we will!' the young ones said, and the pains they
took after that! They practised every day and flew so
beautifully and lightly it was a pleasure to see them.

And now autumn came. The storks all began to gather
together before they flew away to warmer lands while we
had winter. What a manœuvre that was! Over woods and
towns they had to go just to see how well they could fly,
for it was undoubtedly a great journey that lay in front of
them. The young storks did so well that they got an
'excellent' and a prize of frogs and snakes. That was the
highest mark they could get, and the frogs and snakes
they could eat—and they did, too.

'Now we'll be revenged!' they said.

'Yes, that you shall!' said mother-stork. 'And I've
thought of the very thing! I know the pond where all the
little human babies lie waiting for the stork to come and
take them to their parents. There the dear little babies
sleep and dream such sweet dreams as they will never
know again. All parents love to have a little child like

that, and all children want to have a sister or a brother. Now we'll fly over to the pond and take one to each of the children who've not sung that wicked rhyme and not made fun of the storks, and the other children shan't have one!'

'But what about that bad ugly-looking boy who began the singing!' cried the young storks. 'What shall we do to him?'

'There's a little dead child lying in the pond. It's dreamed itself to death. We'll take it to him, and then he'll cry because we've brought him a dead little brother. But you haven't forgotten the good boy—the one who said, "It's a shame to make fun of dumb creatures!"— have you? We'll bring him a brother and a sister, and as the boy's name is Peter, you shall all be called Peter, too!'

And it happened as she said: all the storks were named Peter, and that's what they are called still.

Willy Winky

THERE is no one in the whole world who knows so many stories as Willy Winky!—He is a wonderful story-teller!

He comes late in the evening when children are sitting quietly at the table or on their stools; he comes very softly up the stairs, for he walks in his stockinged feet; he opens the door gently; and then, puff!—he sprays sweet milk very, very lightly into the children's eyes, always just enough to stop them keeping their eyes open, and so they never see him. Then he slips behind them and blows softly on their necks, and they grow heavy-eyed. But it does no harm, for Willy Winky means well: he only wants the children to be quiet, and they are most quiet when they have gone to bed. They have to be quite still before he can tell them stories.

When the children are asleep, Willy Winky seats himself upon the bed. He is beautifully dressed: his jacket is of silk, but it is impossible to say what colour it is, for, as he turns himself about, it shines now green, now red, now blue. Under each arm he carries an umbrella: he has one with pictures on it, and that he holds over good children and then they dream the loveliest stories the whole night through; and he has one with nothing on it at all, and that he holds over naughty children and they sleep so heavily that when they wake in the morning they have not dreamed a thing.

Now we must hear how Willy Winky came every evening for a whole week to a little boy called Hjalmar, and we shall listen to the stories he told him! There are seven stories in all, because there are seven days in a week.

Monday

'Now just listen!' said Willy Winky in the evening when he had got Hjalmar to bed. 'I'm going to brighten your room up!' And as he spoke, all the plants in the flower-pots grew into big trees which stretched their long branches under the ceiling and along the walls, so that the whole room looked like a beautiful summer-house. All the branches were full of flowers, and every flower was lovelier than a rose. It had a beautiful scent and, if you ate it, it was sweeter than jam. The fruit glimmered like gold and there were buns, too, bursting with sultanas—it was marvellous! But just then there began a frightful wailing over in the table-drawer where Hjalmar's school-books lay.

'What's the matter now!' said Willy Winky, going over to the table and opening the drawer. There was such a pushing and a squeezing going on on Hjalmar's slate because a wrong figure had got into his sum, that the slate was on the point of falling to pieces. The slate-pencil was hopping and skipping about on the end of its string just like a little dog—it wanted to help with the sum, but it could not!—And then the wailing came from Hjalmar's writing-book, and it was really dreadful to listen to! Along the bottom of every page stood all the capital letters, each with a little one by its side, a whole row of them meant to be copied. And near them stood several other letters that thought they looked like them: Hjalmar had written these, and they were lying about as if they had tripped over the pencil-line they should have been standing on.

'Look, you should stand like this!' said the copy. 'See, sloping this way, with a fine flourish!'

'Oh, we'd love to,' said Hjalmar's letters, 'but we can't, we're so poorly made!'

'Then you must have some medicine!' said Willy Winky.

'Oh, no!' they cried, standing so straight it was a pleasure to see them.

'Well, we shan't get any stories told now!' said Willy Winky. 'I shall have to drill them! Left, right! Left, right!' And so he drilled the letters, and they stood as upright and well-formed as any copy could be. But when Willy Winky had gone and Hjalmar looked at them in the morning, they were just as wretched-looking as before.

Tuesday

As soon as Hjalmar was in bed, Willy Winky touched all the pieces of furniture in the room with his little magic spray, and they at once began to talk. They all talked about themselves, except the spittoon who stood there in silence. He was annoyed with their conceit: there they were, all talking only of themselves, thinking only of themselves, without sparing a single thought for one who stood so humbly in the corner and let himself be spat upon.

Over the chest-of-drawers hung a large painting in a gilt frame: it was a landscape where you could see lofty old trees, flowers among the grass and a great water with a river flowing through the forest, past many castles, far away into the wild sea.

Willy Winky touched the painting with his magic spray, and as he did so, the birds began to sing, the branches of the trees waved and even the clouds moved—you could see their shadows crossing the landscape.

Willy Winky now lifted little Hjalmar up to the frame, and Hjalmar put his legs into the picture, right into the tall grass, and there he stood. The sun shone down upon him between the branches of the trees. He ran over to the water and seated himself in a little boat that lay there. It was painted red and white, its sails shone like silver, and six swans, with golden crowns about their necks and dazzling blue stars upon their heads, drew the boat past the green forests where the trees spoke of robbers and witches, and the flowers of dainty little elves and the stories the butterflies had told them.

The prettiest fish, with scales like silver and gold, swam after the boat; now and again they would leap up and there would be a splash in the water. Birds, red and blue, great and small, flew in two long rows behind him, midges danced and the cockchafer said, 'Boom, boom!'—They all wanted to go with Hjalmar, and every one of them had a story to tell.

What a pleasure-cruise that was! The forest was now thick and dark, now like the loveliest of gardens with sunshine and flowers; great palaces of glass and marble rose from it, with princesses standing on the balconies— and they were all little girls Hjalmar knew well and had often played with. They held their hands out, and each one offered him the loveliest sugar-pig you could buy anywhere, and as he sailed by, Hjalmar took hold of one end of the sugar-pig while the princess held fast to the other, and so each got a piece—she the smaller and Hjalmar the bigger! At every palace little princes stood on guard with golden swords upon their shoulders and rained down raisins and tin-soldiers—they were proper princes!

Hjalmar was now sailing through the forest, and now, it seemed, through great halls or the middle of a town. He sailed, too, through the town where his nurse lived: she had carried him about when he was quite a little boy and had been very fond of him, and there she was now, nodding and waving and singing the pretty verses she had written herself and sent him:

> 'Oh, many an hour I think of you,
> My own dear Hjalmar, my treasure!
> Your lips I've covered with kisses true,
> Your brow and your cheeks without measure.
>
> Your very first words I heard you say,
> And then had to wish you good-bye.
> The Lord God bless you from day to day—
> An angel you are from on high!'

And all the birds sang with her, the flowers danced upon their stalks, and the old trees nodded as if Willy Winky were telling them stories, too.

Wednesday

My, how the rain was pouring down outside! Hjalmar could hear it as he lay asleep, and when Willy Winky opened the window, the water came right up to the window-sill. There was quite a lake out there, and a magnificent ship lay moored against the house.

'Will you sail with me, little Hjalmar?' said Willy Winky. 'You can travel to foreign lands tonight and be back here again in the morning!'

And without more ado Hjalmar was standing in his Sunday best on board that fine ship. The weather at once cleared up, and they sailed through the streets, tacked about the church, and found themselves upon the wild open sea. They sailed so far that they lost all sight of land, and then they saw a flock of storks. They, too, had come from home and were on their way to warmer lands. The storks were flying one behind the other, and they had already flown a very, very long way. One of them was so tired that his wings could scarcely bear him any farther: he was the last in the line, and he was soon a good way behind the rest. At length he sank lower and lower upon his outstretched wings; he beat them once or twice, but it was no use; his feet touched the ship's ropes, he slid down the sail, and bump!—there he stood on deck.

Then the cabin-boy took him and put him in the hen-house with the hens, ducks and turkeys—the poor stork stood quite dismayed in the midst of them.

'What a sight!' said all the hens.

The turkey-cock puffed himself up as big as he could and asked who he was; and the ducks waddled backwards and nudged one another—'Quack to you! Quack to you!'

And the stork told them about the warm lands of Africa, and the pyramids and the ostrich that races over the desert like a wild horse. But the ducks did not understand a word of what he said, and so they nudged one another again—'He's daft!—Agreed?'

'Yes, of course he's daft!' said the turkey-cock,

gobbling away. Then the stork fell silent, thinking of his beloved Africa.

'That's a fine pair of thin legs you've got!' said the turkey. 'What do they cost a yard?'

'Quack, quack, quack!' tittered all the ducks, but the stork pretended he had not heard.

'You can laugh, too!' the turkey said to him. 'It was a very witty remark! Or perhaps it was too low for him. Ah, he's not broad-minded! Well, never mind him—we find ourselves interesting, so let's carry on!' And so the hens clucked and the ducks cackled, 'Quack, quack! Quack, quack!' It was odd how funny they themselves found it.

But Hjalmar went over to the hen-house, opened the door and called the stork, who hopped out to him on to the deck. He was now rested and he nodded to Hjalmar as if to thank him. Then he stretched his wings and off he flew to warmer lands. Meanwhile the hens clucked, the ducks quacked and the turkey-cock grew red in the face.

'Tomorrow we shall make soup out of you!' said Hjalmar, and then he woke up and found himself lying in his own little bed. But it was a wonderful journey that Willy Winky had taken him on that night.

Thursday

'I'll tell you something!' said Willy Winky. 'Don't be afraid now and you shall see a little mouse!' And with that, he held his hand out towards him and showed him the pretty little animal. 'She's come to invite you to a wedding. There are two little mice here who are entering into holy matrimony tonight. They live under the floor of mother's dining-room—they've a very nice flat there!'

'But how can I get through the little mouse-hole in the floor?' asked Hjalmar.

'Leave that to me!' said Willy Winky. 'Don't worry! I'll make you small!' Then he touched Hjalmar with his magic spray, and he at once grew smaller and smaller until at last he was no bigger than a finger. 'Now you can borrow the tin-soldier's clothes—I think they'll fit, and

it always looks well to wear uniform when you're in company!'

'Yes, it does!' said Hjalmar, and the next moment he was dressed like the smartest tin-soldier.

'Will you be good enough to seat yourself in your mother's thimble?' said the little mouse. 'Then I shall have the honour of pulling you along!'

'Fancy the young lady putting herself out like that!' said Hjalmar, and off they drove to the mouse-wedding.

They went down a long passage which led under the floor: it was only just high enough for them to drive the thimble through, and it was lit all the way with bits of rotten wood.

'Doesn't it smell lovely down here?' said the mouse who was pulling him along. 'The passage has all been smeared with bacon-rind! It couldn't be nicer, could it?'

And now they entered the room where the wedding was to take place. On the right stood all the little lady-mice putting their heads together and whispering as if they were making fun of one another; and all the little men-mice were standing on the left stroking their whiskers with their paws. In the middle of the floor were the bride and bridegroom, standing in a hollowed-out cheese-rind and kissing one another rapturously in front of everybody because they were betrothed and going to be married right away.

More and more guests were arriving all the time, and it was a wonder some of the mice were not trampled to death. The bridal pair had placed themselves right in the middle of the doorway, so that you could neither go out nor come in. The room, like the passage, had been smeared all over with bacon-rind, and that was all there was to eat, except for a pea which was brought in for dessert: a little mouse of the family had bitten the names of the bride and bridegroom in it—or rather, their initials—and that was something quite out of the ordinary.

The mice all said what a lovely wedding it was and how entertaining the conversation had been.

And so Hjalmar drove home again. There was no doubt he had been in distinguished company, but then he had had to make himself small and go in a tin-soldier's uniform.

Friday

'It's incredible how many grown-up people there are who want to get hold of me!' said Willy Winky. 'Especially those who have done something wrong. "Good little Willy," they say to me, "we can't close our eyes and we lie awake all night long and see all our evil deeds sitting on the edge of the bed like so many nasty little demons squirting hot water all over us. Do come and chase them away so that we can get a good sleep!" And then they sigh deeply. "We're quite willing to pay, you know. Good night, Willy! The money's lying on the window-sill!" But I don't do it for money,' said Willy Winky.

'Where are we going to tonight?' asked Hjalmar.

'Well, I don't know whether you'd like to go to a wedding again tonight. It'll be quite different from the one you went to yesterday. Your sister's big doll—the one that looks like a boy and is called Herman—is going to marry the doll Bertha. It's the doll's birthday as well, and so there'll be ever so many presents.'

'Yes, I know all about that!' said Hjalmar. 'Every time the dolls are in need of new clothes, my sister makes them have a birthday or a wedding! It's happened at least a hundred times!'

'Yes, but tonight's wedding is their hundred and first, and when they've been married a hundred and one times, that's the end of it! That's why this one's so different. Just look!'

Hjalmar looked towards the table: the little cardboard doll's-house was standing there with lights in the windows, and all the tin-soldiers were presenting arms outside. The bride and bridegroom were sitting on the floor leaning up against the table-leg: they were looking very thoughtful—and, no doubt, they had good reason to. But Willy Winky, dressed in grandmother's black skirt, married them, and when the service was over, all the furniture in the room joined in the following beautiful song which had been specially written by the pencil—it went to a tune like a drummer's tattoo:

> 'Our song shall come like windy weather
> To bride and groom at home together.
> They stand as stiff as a stick of heather,
> And both are made of gloving-leather!
> "Hurrah, hurrah, for heather and leather!"
> We loudly sing in wind and weather!'

L

And now they were given their presents, but they had requested that these should not include anything to eat because they had love to live on.

'Shall we go and stay in the country or travel abroad?' asked the bridegroom. And so they consulted the swallow who had travelled a great deal and the old backyard hen who had hatched out five broods of chickens. The swallow told them of lovely warm countries where grapes hang in big heavy clusters, where the air is mild and the mountains are tinted with colours quite unknown to us here.

'But they don't have our green cabbages!' said the hen. 'One summer I stayed in the country with all my chickens, and there was a gravel-pit there which we could go and scrape about in, and we had permission, too, to go into a garden where they grew green cabbages! Oh, how green they were! I can't imagine anything more beautiful!'

'But one cabbage-stalk looks just like another,' said the swallow, 'and besides we often get such wretched weather here!'

'Yes, but we're used to it!' said the hen.

'But it's cold here, freezing cold!'

'That's good for the cabbages!' said the hen. 'And we do get it hot, too, sometimes. Don't you remember a summer we had about four years ago that lasted five whole weeks and it was so hot you couldn't breathe! Then again, we don't have all the poisonous beasts they have in other places, and we're free from robbers! Anybody who doesn't think our country the most beautiful there is, is a low good-for-nothing creature that doesn't deserve to be here!' And the hen burst into tears. 'I've travelled, too! I've ridden fifty miles or so in a tub! There's no pleasure in travelling, I can assure you!'

'Well, the hen's a sensible woman!' said the doll Bertha. 'I don't like travelling over mountains either:

it's nothing but up and up and then down again! No, we'll go out to the gravel-pit and walk about in the garden where the cabbages grow.'

And so they did.

Saturday

'Am I going to have some stories now?' said little Hjalmar as soon as Willy Winky had got him to bed.

'We've no time for them this evening,' said Willy, as he opened his most beautiful umbrella over him. 'Just look at these Chinamen!' And the whole umbrella looked like a large Chinese bowl with blue trees and hump-backed bridges with little Chinamen standing on them and nodding their heads. 'We must have the whole world polished up spick-and-span for tomorrow,' said Willy. 'Don't forget it's a holy day—it's Sunday. I must go over to the church tower to see whether the little church-brownies are giving the bells a good shine to make them sound beautiful; I must go out into the fields to see if the winds are blowing the dust off the grass and the leaves; and—the biggest job of all—I must have all the stars down to polish! I put them in my apron as I take them down, but they have to be numbered first, and the holes they fit into must be numbered, too, so that they can be put back in their right places again, otherwise they wouldn't fit properly and we should have too many falling stars, one tumbling down after the other!'

'Listen, and I'll tell you something, Mr Winky!' said an old portrait hanging on the wall where Hjalmar was sleeping. 'I'm Hjalmar's great-grandfather: I want to thank you for telling the boy stories, but you mustn't confuse his ideas. The stars can't be taken down and polished! The stars are heavenly bodies like the earth, and that's just the beauty of it!'

'Thank you very much, old great-grandfather!' said Willy Winky. 'Thank you very much! You are indeed head of the family: you are old great-head! But I am older than you are! I'm an old heathen: the Greeks and Romans called me the god of dreams! I've visited the noblest houses, and I visit them still! I know how to mix with both great and small! Now you can tell your stories!'—And with that Willy Winky went and took his umbrella with him.

'So one daren't any longer say what one thinks!' said the old portrait.

And then Hjalmar woke up.

Sunday

'Good evening!' said Willy Winky, and Hjalmar nodded, but jumped up and turned great-grandfather's portrait round towards the wall so that it should not butt into the conversation as it had done the day before.

'Now you must tell me some stories—about "The Five Green Peas that Lived in a Pea-Pod", and about "The Oxlip that went a-Courting the Cowslip", and about "The Darning-Needle" who put on such airs that she fancied herself a sewing-needle!'

'Don't forget you can have too much of a good thing!' said Willy Winky. 'I'd rather show you something. I'll tell you what, I'll show you my brother! He's called Willy Winky, too, but he never comes more than once to anyone, and when he comes he takes you with him on his horse and tells you stories. He knows only two: one

that's so perfectly lovely that no one in the world could imagine anything like it, and one that's so dreadful and terrible—well, you just can't describe it!' And then Willy Winky lifted little Hjalmar up in front of the window and said, 'Now you can see my brother, the other Willy Winky! He's also called Death; but, you see, he doesn't look frightening, as he does in the picture-books where he's nothing but a skeleton. No, that's silver embroidery on his jacket and he wears the very finest of hussar uniforms with a cloak of black velvet flying out behind over his horse! And see how he gallops!'

And Hjalmar watched the other Willy Winky riding past and taking both old and young up upon his horse: some he sat in front of him, and others he sat behind, but he always asked first, 'What's your report-book like?' 'Good!' they all answered. 'Well, just let me have a look!' he would say. And so they had to show him their reports, and all those that had 'very good' or 'excellent' were put in front of him and were told the beautiful story; but those that had 'fair' or 'poor' had to get up behind and listen to the tale of terror. They trembled and wept, and wanted to jump off the horse, but that they could not do for they had grown fast to it the moment they touched it.

'But Death's the nicest Willy Winky!' said Hjalmar. 'I'm not a bit afraid of him!'

'And you shan't be either!' said Willy Winky. 'Just see to it that you get a good report!'

'Well, at least that's instructive!' muttered great-grandfather's portrait. 'Still, it helps if one can say what one thinks!' And so he was content.

And that's the story of Willy Winky! This evening perhaps he'll tell you something more himself.

The Swineherd

THERE was once a poor prince. He had a kingdom, which was quite small, yet nevertheless quite big enough to marry on—and that's what he'd set his heart on doing.

Now it would of course be somewhat bold of him to dare to say, 'Will you have me?' to the daughter of the Emperor. But dare he did, for his name was famous far and wide, and there were hundreds of princesses who would have said, 'Yes, please!' But did the Emperor's daughter?

Let's listen to the story and see.

On the grave of the prince's father there grew a rose-tree—oh, such a beautiful rose-tree it was!—which bloomed only once in every five years. And even then it bore only one flower, but that was a rose which smelled so sweetly that its scent would make one forget all one's sorrows and troubles. He had, too, a nightingale, which could sing as if all the beautiful melodies in the world were to be found in its little throat. The princess should have them both; and so the rose and the nightingale were placed in large silver caskets and sent to her.

The Emperor permitted them to be brought before him in the great hall where the princess was playing 'going a-visiting' with her ladies-in-waiting, for that was all they ever did. And when she saw the large caskets with the gifts inside them, she clapped her hands with joy.

'If only it's a little pussy-cat!' she said—but there lay the beautiful rose.

'Oh, but how nicely it's made!' said all the ladies-in-waiting.

'It's more than nice!' said the Emperor. 'It's lovely!'

But when the princess felt it, she was ready to weep.

'Oh, papa!' she said. 'It's not made at all—it's real!'

'Well!' said all the ladies-in-waiting. 'It's real!'

'Now before we get angry,' said the Emperor, 'let's first see what's in the other casket!' And there was the nightingale: it sang so beautifully that for the moment they were unable to say anything bad about it.

'*Superbe! Charmant!*' said the ladies-in-waiting, for they all spoke French, one worse than another.

'How that bird reminds me of her late majesty's musical-box!' said an old courtier. 'Yes, indeed, it has just the same tone, just the same delivery!'

'Yes!' said the Emperor, sobbing like a little child.

'I'll never believe that that's real!' said the princess.

'Indeed, it is—it's a real bird!' said those who had brought it.

'Oh,' said the princess. 'Well, then, let it fly away.' And nothing would induce her to give the prince permission to visit her.

But he would not let himself lose heart. He smeared his face black and brown, pushed his cap down on his head, and knocked at the door.

'Good day, Emperor!' he said. 'I couldn't get a job here in the palace, I suppose?'

'Hm, there are so many after them!' said the Emperor. 'But let me see—I do need someone who can look after the pigs, we've certainly enough of them!'

And so the prince was engaged as Imperial Swineherd. He was given a wretched little room down by the pig-sty, and there he had to stay. All day long he sat working, and when evening came he had made a beautiful little saucepan. It had bells all round it, and as soon as the saucepan came to the boil, they rang clear and sweet, and played the old melody:

> Alas, my dearest Augustin,
> All is now lost, lost, lost!

But the most wonderful thing of all was that, if you held your finger in the steam from the saucepan, you could immediately smell every dinner that was being cooked in every fire-place in the town. That was something very different from a rose!

Now the princess was out walking with all her ladies-in-waiting, and when she heard the melody, she stood quite still and listened with a look of pleasure, for she, too, could play 'Alas, my dearest Augustin!' In fact, it was the only thing she knew, and she played it with one finger.

'Why, that's the piece I know!' she said. 'He must be a very gifted swineherd! Listen, go in and ask him how much he wants for that instrument of his!'

And so one of the ladies-in-waiting had to run in and ask. But she put on her thick shoes first.

'What will you take for that saucepan?' said the lady-in-waiting.

'I'll take ten kisses from the princess!' said the swineherd.

'Heaven save us!' said the lady-in-waiting.

'Yes,' said the swineherd, 'but I couldn't take less!'

'Well, what does he say?' asked the princess.

'I really can't say it!' said the lady-in-waiting. 'It's quite dreadful!'

'Then you can whisper!' And so she whispered it.

'He's certainly very rude!' said the princess, and immediately walked away. But when she had walked a few steps the little bells rang out again clear and sweet:

> Alas, my dearest Augustin,
> All is now lost, lost, lost!

'Listen,' said the princess, 'ask him if he'll take ten kisses from my ladies-in-waiting!'

'No, thanks!' said the swineherd. 'Ten kisses from the princess, or else I keep the saucepan.'

'What a tiresome fellow it is!' said the princess. 'But you must all stand round me, so that no one can possibly see!'

And the ladies-in-waiting gathered round her and spread out their dresses; and so the swineherd got the ten kisses, and she got the saucepan.

Well, what pleasure it gave them! The whole of that evening and all the next day, the saucepan was kept boiling. There wasn't a fire-place in the whole town, from the court chamberlain's to the shoemaker's, but they knew what was cooking there. The ladies-in-waiting danced and clapped their hands.

'We know who's going to have sweet soup and pancakes! We know who's going to have porridge and chops! Isn't that interesting!'

'Most interesting!' said the Mistress of the Royal Household.

'Yes, but you must keep it a secret, because I'm the Emperor's daughter!'

'Heavens, of course we shall!' they all said together.

The swineherd—that's to say, the prince, but they knew no differently, of course, and thought he was a real swineherd—didn't let the day go by without busying himself with something. And so he made a rattle: when you swung it round you could hear all the waltzes, barn-dances, and polkas that have ever been known since the creation of the world.

'But that's superb!' said the princess as she was walking by. 'I've never heard a more beautiful piece of music!

Listen, go in and ask him the price of that instrument—but I will give no more kisses!'

'He wants a hundred kisses from the princess!' said the lady-in-waiting who had been in to ask.

'He must be mad!' said the princess, and walked away. But when she had gone a few yards she stopped and stood still. 'We must encourage art,' she said, 'and I am the Emperor's daughter! Tell him he may have ten kisses like yesterday; he can have the rest from my ladies-in-waiting!'

'Oh, but we shouldn't like that at all!' said the ladies-in-waiting.

'What nonsense!' said the princess. 'If I can kiss him, so can you! And remember, I provide your board and wages!' And so the lady-in-waiting had to go in and ask him again.

'A hundred kisses from the princess,' he said, 'or we each keep our own!'

'Stand round me!!!' she said. And so all the ladies-in-waiting gathered round her, and he began to kiss her.

'What on earth can that crowd be, down there by the pig-sty!' said the Emperor, as he stepped out on the balcony. He rubbed his eyes and put his glasses on. 'It's the ladies-in-waiting—up to some game, I'll be bound! I'd better go down and see!' And so he pulled his slippers up at the back—for they were really shoes which he had trodden down at the heels.

What a haste he was in, bless him!

As soon as he got down in the yard, he crept up to them very quietly, and the ladies-in-waiting had so much to do with counting the kisses—so that it should be fair, and he shouldn't take too many, nor yet too few—that they were quite unaware of the Emperor. He raised himself up on his toes.

'What on earth!' he said, when he saw them kissing each other. And he struck them both over the head with his slipper just as the swineherd was taking his eighty-sixth kiss. 'Out with you!' said the Emperor, for he was really angry, and both the princess and the swineherd were put outside his empire.

There she stood and wept, the swineherd scolded her, and the rain poured down.

'Oh, what a wretched girl I am!' said the princess. 'If only I'd taken that lovely prince! Oh, how unhappy I am!'

And the swineherd went behind a tree, wiped the black and brown off his face, cast aside his dirty old clothes, and stepped forth again dressed as a prince, so handsome that the princess curtsied as she saw him.

'I've grown to despise you!' he said. 'You wouldn't have an honest prince! You couldn't appreciate the rose and the nightingale, but you could kiss the swineherd for a plaything! Now I wish you well of it!'

And so he went into his kingdom, shut the door and shot the bolt home. So there was nothing for her but to stand outside and sing:

> 'Alas, my dearest Augustin,
> All is now lost, lost, lost!'

The Buckwheat

TIME and again, if you pass by a field of buckwheat after a thunder-storm, you will see that it has
been scorched quite black, just as if a flame of fire
had been over it. And then the countryman will tell
you, 'It's been struck by lightning.' But why has it? I will
tell you what the sparrow told me: the sparrow heard it
from an old willow-tree that stood by a field of buckwheat, and stands there yet. It's a big, venerable willow,
wrinkled and old, and it's split right to the middle. Grass
and bramble-runners grow out of the cleft: the tree leans
over and the branches hang right down to the ground just
like long green hair.

In all the fields round about, corn grew—rye, barley, and oats, beautiful oats that look, when they are ripe, like a whole flight of small yellow canaries on a bough. The corn stood well blest by heaven, and the heavier it grew, the lower it bowed down in humility.

But there was also a field of buckwheat, and that field lay straight on from the old willow-tree. The buckwheat did not bow down at all, like the other corn, but held its head up proud and stiff.

'I am quite as rich in the ear as the corn,' it said, 'and I'm more beautiful as well: my flowers are as lovely as the apple-tree's. It's a joy to look at me and mine: do you know anything finer than us, old willow-tree?'

And the willow-tree nodded its head as if it would say, 'Yes, that I do—well enough!' But the buckwheat was bursting with arrogance, and said, 'Stupid tree! It's so old, grass grows in its belly!'

And now a dreadful storm was gathering: all the flowers of the field closed their petals or bowed their delicate heads while the wind swept over them; but the buckwheat stood erect in its pride.

'Bow your head like us!' said the flowers.

'I'm sure I see no need for me to do that,' said the buckwheat.

'Bow your head like us!' cried the corn. 'The Angel of the Storm is flying over us! He has wings which stretch up to the clouds and right down to the earth, and he will slash you in two before you can pray him to have mercy on you.'

'I'm sure I shan't bow down!' said the buckwheat.

'Close your flowers and bow your leaves!' said the old willow-tree. 'Don't look up at the lightning when the cloud bursts. Even men dare not do that, because when you look at the lightning, you see into God's heaven.

And if the mere sight of it can make men blind, what would happen to us plants of the earth—we who are far humbler—if we dared to risk it!'

'Far humbler?' said the buckwheat. 'Now I will look into God's heaven, you see if I don't!' And so, in its presumption and pride, it did. It was just as if the whole world stood bathed in a flame of fire, so fiercely the lightning flashed.

Afterwards, when the storm had passed, the flowers and the corn stood refreshed by the rain in the still, clean air. But the buckwheat was burnt coal-black by the lightning—it was now a dead useless weed in the field.

And the old willow-tree moved its branches in the wind, and great drops of water fell from its green leaves, as if the tree were weeping, and the sparrows asked, 'What are you crying for? It's all so heavenly now! Look how the sun's shining, and how the clouds are moving, and just smell the perfume of the flowers and bushes! What are you crying for, old willow-tree?'

And the willow-tree told them about the pride and arrogance of the buckwheat, and about the punishment which followed—as it always does. I, who am telling you the story, heard it from the sparrows—they told it to me one evening when I asked them for a tale.

The Angel

'EVERY time a good child dies, an angel comes down to earth from God, takes the dead child in his arms and, spreading his great white wings, flies over all the places the child loved most. There he plucks a handful of flowers which they take up to God to bloom even more beautifully than they did upon earth. God in his goodness presses all the flowers to his heart, but the flower which is dearest to him he kisses, and then it receives a voice and can join in the chorus of heavenly bliss.'

All this an angel of God told a dead child as he was carrying him to heaven, and the child listened as if in a dream. And as they were passing over the places near home where the child had played, they went through gardens full of lovely flowers.

'Which ones shall we take with us to plant in heaven?' asked the angel.

There was a beautiful slender rose-tree standing there, but a careless hand had snapped its stem and so all its branches, full of big half-opened buds, hung down withered and trailing about its roots.

'The poor tree!' said the child. 'Take that one and then it will flower again up where God lives!'

So the angel took it and kissed the child for the thought, and the little one half-opened his eyes. They picked magnificent flowers, rich in colour, but they also took the humble marigold and the wild pansy.

'Now we have our flowers!' said the child, and the angel nodded, but they still did not fly up to God. It was night and everywhere was quite still. They remained in the great city, hovering over one of the narrowest streets where heaps of straw, ashes and rubbish were lying about; someone had been moving house; there were broken plates, bits of plaster, rags, old hats that had lost their brims—everything that did not look worth keeping.

And in the midst of all this confusion, the angel pointed to some broken pieces of a flower-pot and a lump of earth that had fallen out of it and was held together by the roots of a large withered wild flower—it was no good to anyone and so it had been thrown out into the street.

'We'll take that with us!' said the angel. 'I'll tell you about it as we fly!'

So off they flew, and the angel told his tale.

'Down there in that narrow street, in a low basement, there lived a poor sick boy. Ever since he was quite small he had been bed-ridden, and at his very fittest he could just manage to walk with his crutches a couple of times up and down the little room—that was all. On some days during the summer, the rays of the sun would fall for half an hour at a time into the basement entrance, and then the little boy would sit there, letting the warm sun shine

M

on him and watching the blood glow red between the delicate fingers he held up before his face, and he would say, "Yes, I've been out today!" All he knew of the woods in their lovely spring green was when the neighbour's son brought him the first branch of beech: he would hold it over his head and in a day-dream fancy he was under the beeches with the sun shining and the birds singing. One spring day the neighbour's son brought him some wild flowers, too, and among them there happened to be one with a root, and so it was planted in a flower-pot and put on the window-sill close by his bed. The flower had been planted by green fingers: it grew, sent out new shoots and bore flowers every year. For the sick boy it was the most beautiful of gardens, his little treasure on earth: he watered it and looked after it and saw to it that it got every ray of sunshine, right up to the last, that crept in through the low window. The flower became part of his dreams: the flowers opened and gave out their sweet scent for him and gladdened his eyes. He turned towards it as he lay dying and Our Lord called him.—He has been with God for a year now; for a year the flower stood forgotten in the window and withered, and so, when they moved house, it was thrown out with the sweepings into the street. And that's the flower, the poor withered flower, we've taken with us: that flower has given more joy than the richest bloom in a queen's garden!'

'But how do you know all this?' asked the child the angel was carrying up to heaven.

'How do I know it!' said the angel. 'I myself was that little sick boy who used to go on crutches! I know my own flower!'

And the child opened his eyes wide, and as he looked into the angel's lovely joyful face, they were in God's heaven, where all was joy and bliss. Then God pressed the dead child to his heart: he was given wings like the other angel and flew with him hand in hand. God pressed the flowers to his heart, too, but the poor withered wild flower he kissed, and, as he did so, it was given a voice and sang with all the angels gliding about God's throne —some quite near, others in great circles around them, stretching farther and farther away into infinity, but all equally happy. And they all sang, great and small, the good child and the poor wild flower that had lain withered and cast away with the sweepings, among the rubbish or moving, in the dark narrow street.

The Nightingale

IN China, as of course you know, the Emperor is a Chinaman, and all those he has about him are Chinese, too. It happened many years ago now, but for that very reason the story is worth listening to before it is forgotten. The Emperor's palace was the most magnificent in the world, completely and entirely made of fine porcelain, priceless but so brittle and fragile that you really had to watch your step. In the garden the most wonderful flowers were to be seen, and the most splendid of all had little silver bells tied to them and they tinkled so that no one should pass by without noticing them. Yes, everything was very cunningly contrived in the Emperor's garden, and it stretched so far that even the gardener did not know where it ended. If you went on walking, you would come to a lovely forest with lofty trees and deep lakes. The forest went right down to the sea, which was blue and so deep that great ships could sail right in under the branches of the trees. And in them there lived a nightingale that sang so beautifully that even the poor fisherman, who had so many other things to attend to when he was out at night drawing in his nets, would stop work and listen when he heard the nightingale. 'Lord, how beautiful it is!' he would say, but then he would have to attend to his job and the bird would be forgotten. But the next night when it sang again and the fisherman was out, he would say the same thing, 'Lord, how beautiful it really is!'

From all the corners of the world, travellers came to the Emperor's city, and they were filled with admiration for it, and for the palace and garden, too, but when they came to hear the nightingale, they all said, 'That's undoubtedly the best!'

And the travellers talked about it when they got home, and scholars wrote many books about the city, the palace and the garden, but they did not forget the nightingale—that was given first place. And those that could write poetry wrote the loveliest poems all about the nightingale in the forest by the deep sea.

These books went round the world, and one day some of them came to the Emperor, too. He sat in his golden chair and read and read, nodding his head with pleasure every moment at the splendid descriptions of the city, the palace and the garden. Then he came to, 'But the nightingale is undoubtedly the best of all!'

'What's this!' said the Emperor. 'The nightingale! I know nothing of it! Is there such a bird in my empire—and in my own garden of all places! I've never heard of it! What will one read of next!'

So he called for his gentleman-in-waiting, who was so distinguished a person that if anyone of inferior rank dared talk to him or ask him a question, he would answer nothing but, 'P!'—and that, of course, has very little meaning.

'It seems there's a most remarkable bird here called a nightingale!' said the Emperor. 'It's said to be the very finest thing throughout my great empire! Why have I never been told about it?'

'I've never before heard it mentioned!' said the gentleman-in-waiting. 'It's never been presented at court!'

'It's my wish it should come here this evening and sing for me!' said the Emperor. 'It's a fine thing when the whole world knows what I have and I don't!'

'I've never before heard it mentioned!' said the gentleman. 'But I shall search for it: I shall find it!'

But where was it to be found? The gentleman ran up and down all the stairs, through halls and corridors, but not one of all those he met had ever heard the nightingale spoken of. The gentleman ran back again to the Emperor and said it must undoubtedly be a tale invented by those who wrote books. 'Your Imperial Majesty mustn't believe everything that's written: it's all invention and something they call the Black Art!'

'But the book I read it in,' said the Emperor, 'was sent to me from the high and mighty Emperor of Japan, and so it can't be untrue! I will hear the nightingale! And it must be here this evening! It has my very highest favour! And if it doesn't come, the whole court shall be punched in the stomach after they've eaten their supper!'

'Tsing-pe!' said the gentleman and ran once more up and down all the stairs and through all the halls and corridors; and half the court ran with him, for they had no desire to be punched in the stomach. And there they all were, asking after this remarkable nightingale that the whole world knew about but no one at court had ever heard of.

At last they came across a poor little girl in the kitchen. She said, 'Oh, goodness, yes, the nightingale! Of course I know it! My, how it can sing! Every evening they let me take a few of the left-overs from the table home to my poor sick mother. She lives down by the sea-shore, and so when I'm on my way back and feel tired and take a rest in the woods, I hear the nightingale sing! It makes tears come into my eyes, just like mother kissing me!'

'My dear little kitchen-maid!' said the gentleman. 'I'll get her a permanent appointment in the kitchen and leave to see the Emperor eating if only she can take us to the nightingale! Its presence is commanded for this evening!'

So they all made their way out into the forest where the

nightingale was in the habit of singing. Half the court was there. And as they were putting their best foot forward, a cow began to low.

'Oh,' said the court page, 'now we've found it! It really has remarkable power for such a small creature! I'm quite certain I've heard it before!'

'No, that's the cows lowing!' said the little kitchen-maid. 'We're still a long way from the place!'

The frogs were now croaking in the pond.

'Lovely!' said the Chinese Master of the Imperial Household. 'Now I can hear her—it's just like tiny church bells!'

'No, that's the frogs!' said the little kitchen-maid. 'But I think we shall soon hear it now!'

And then the nightingale began to sing.

'That's it!' said the little girl. 'Listen! Listen! Look, it's sitting up there!' And she pointed to a little grey bird up in the branches.

'Is it possible!' said the gentleman. 'I never imagined it like that! How ordinary it looks! It's undoubtedly lost its colour at seeing so many distinguished people present!'

'Little nightingale,' cried the little kitchen-maid quite loudly, 'our gracious Emperor would very much like you to sing for him!'

'With the greatest of pleasure!' said the nightingale, and sang so beautifully it was a joy to hear it.

'It's just like glass bells!' said the gentleman. 'And look at the way its little throat works! It's remarkable we've never heard it before! It'll be a great success at court!'

'Shall I sing once again for the Emperor?' said the nightingale, thinking the Emperor was there.

'My excellent little nightingale,' said the gentleman, 'I have great pleasure in having to invite you this evening to a celebration at court, where you will charm His High Imperial Grace with your enchanting song!'

'It sounds best out in the green forest!' said the nightingale, but it went willingly with them when it heard that the Emperor wished it.

At the palace everything was properly polished up! The walls and floors, which were of porcelain, shone with the light of many thousand golden lamps! The loveliest flowers, which really could ring, were lined up along the corridors, and the running about and the draughts made all the bells ring so loudly you could not hear yourself speak.

Right in the middle of the great hall where the Emperor sat, a golden perch had been placed for the nightingale to sit upon. The whole court was there, and the little kitchen-maid had been given leave to stand behind the door since she now had the title of Real Kitchen-Maid. All were dressed in their very finest clothes, and they all looked at the little grey bird as the Emperor nodded to it.

Then the nightingale sang so sweetly that tears came into the Emperor's eyes and trickled down over his cheeks, and when the nightingale sang more beautifully still, it went right to his heart and the Emperor was so filled with joy that he said the nightingale should have his golden slipper to wear about its neck. But the nightingale thanked him and said it had already received reward enough.

'I have seen tears in the Emperor's eyes, and that to me is the richest of treasures! An Emperor's tears have a wonderful power! God knows I'm sufficiently rewarded!' And then it sang yet again in its sweet heavenly voice.

'That's the most charming way to flirt I've yet come across!' said all the ladies in the hall. So they put water in

their mouths to make them warble when they were spoken to—they thought they would be nightingales, too. Even the lackeys and the chambermaids let it be known that they were satisfied as well—and that's saying a great deal, for they are the most difficult of all people to please. Yes, indeed, the nightingale was a great success.

It was now to remain at court, where it was to have its own cage and be free to take the air twice during the day and once during the night. Twelve servants were to go with it, each holding fast to a silken cord tied round the bird's leg: there was, of course, no pleasure at all in going out like that.

The whole city talked about the remarkable bird, and whenever two people met, one would say to the other, 'Night!' and the other would reply, 'Gale!' And then they would sigh and understand one another. Yes, and eleven provision-dealers' children were named after it, but not one of them had a note in its body.

One day a large parcel came for the Emperor, and on the outside was written, 'Nightingale'.

'We've a new book here about our famous bird!' said the Emperor. But it was not a book: it was a little mechanical toy lying in a box, a clockwork nightingale made to look like the real one but studded all over with diamonds and rubies and sapphires. As soon as the clockwork bird was wound up, it would sing one of the pieces the real one sang, and its tail, glittering with silver and gold, would go up and down. Round its neck was hung a little ribbon on which was written, 'The Emperor of Japan's Nightingale is a poor thing compared with the Emperor of China's'.

'It's lovely!' they all cried, and the messenger who had brought the mechanical bird was at once given the title of Imperial Nightingale-Bringer-in-Chief.

'Now they can sing together—what a duet that'll be!'

And so they had to sing together, but it did not go right, for the real nightingale sang after its own fashion and the clockwork bird in waltz-time. 'It's not at fault,' said the Master of the Music. 'It keeps excellent time and is quite of my own school!' So the clockwork bird had to sing by itself—it was just as great a success as the real one, and it was so very much more pleasing to look at as well: it glittered like bracelets and brooches.

Three-and-thirty times it sang the selfsame piece, and it was not in the least tired. They would willingly have heard it through again, but the Emperor thought the real nightingale should now sing a little, too—but where was it? It had flown out of the open window away to its green forest, and no one had noticed.

'But what on earth can be the matter!' said the Emperor; and all the courtiers expressed their disapproval of the nightingale and decided that it was an extremely ungrateful creature. 'The one we still have is the better bird, however!' they said, and so the clockwork bird had to sing again, and that was the thirty-fourth time they heard the same piece, but they did not quite know it yet, for it was very difficult. The Master of the Music praised the bird beyond all measure and went so far as to assure them that it was better than the real nightingale not only in its plumage which sparkled with so many lovely diamonds, but in its internal mechanism, too.

'For you see, my lords—and, above all, Your Majesty! —with the real nightingale you can never tell what's going to come, but with the clockwork bird you can be absolutely certain! You know it will be thus and not otherwise! You can account for it: you can open it up and reveal the human mind at work; you can see how the waltzes are set, how they are made to play, and how one follows from another!'

'That's exactly what I think!' they all said, and the Master of the Music was given leave to show it to the people the next Sunday. They must hear it sing, too, said the Emperor. And hear it they did: they were all as pleased as if they had got merrily drunk on tea—a regular Chinese habit—and then they all said, 'Oh!', pointed their forefingers (you call them 'lickpots') in the air and nodded. But the poor fisherman who had heard the real nightingale said, 'It sounds pretty enough and there's a likeness, too, but something's missing—though I don't know what!'

The real nightingale was banished from the Emperor's dominions.

The clockwork bird had its own place on a silken cushion close by the Emperor's bed. All the gifts of gold and precious stones it had received lay round about it, and it had been raised to the rank of Singer-in-Chief to the Imperial Bedside-Table. It took precedence as Number One on the Left Side, for the Emperor considered the side where the heart lay the nobler one, and even in an Emperor the heart lies on the left. And the Master of the Music wrote a book in twenty-five volumes about the clockwork bird: it was very scholarly and very lengthy, and contained all the most difficult words in the Chinese language. Everybody said they had read it, for otherwise they would have been thought stupid and punched in the stomach.

And so it went on for a whole year. The Emperor, the court and all the rest of the Chinese people knew off by heart every little trill in the clockwork bird's song, and for that very reason they liked it all the better: they could now sing with it, and they did, too. The street urchins sang, 'Ti-ti-tee! Trill-trill-tri-i-ll!' and the Emperor sang it, too! Yes, there was no doubt about it, it was wonderful!

But one evening when the clockwork bird was singing its best and the Emperor was lying in bed listening to it,

something went 'ping!' inside the bird, and it was broken. 'Whir-r-r-r!' The wheels all whizzed round and the music stopped.

The Emperor leaped out of bed at once and called for his physician—but what could he do! So they sent for the clock-maker, and after a great deal of talking and poking about, he got the bird to go after a fashion. But he said it would have to be used very sparingly because the pins were very worn and it was impossible to replace them without upsetting the music. That was a great blow! Only once a year dared they let the bird sing, and even that was a strain on it. But then the Master of the Music made a little speech full of difficult words and said it was just as good as ever, and so, of course, after that it *was* just as good as ever.

Five years had now passed, and a great sorrow fell upon the whole land; they were all deeply attached to their Emperor, and now he was said to be seriously ill and not expected to live. A new Emperor had already been chosen, and people stood outside in the street and asked the gentleman-in-waiting how their Emperor was.

'P!' he said, shaking his head.

The Emperor lay cold and wan in his magnificent great bed. The whole court thought he was dead, and every one of them ran off to greet the new Emperor. The servants of the bedchamber ran out to gossip about it, and the palace maids were having a big coffee party. Cloth was laid down everywhere in all the halls and corridors so that you should not hear anyone walking about, and so it was very, very quiet. But the Emperor was not yet dead: he lay stiff and pale in his magnificent bed with its long velvet hangings and its heavy golden tassels. High up, a window stood open, and the moon shone in upon the Emperor and his clockwork bird.

The poor Emperor could hardly draw breath, and he felt just as if something were sitting on his chest. He opened his eyes, and then he saw that it was Death sitting there wearing his golden crown and holding the Emperor's golden sword in one hand and his splendid standard in the other. And all round him from the folds of the great velvet bed-curtains strange faces peeped out: some quite horrible, others beautiful and gentle. They were all the Emperor's good and evil deeds looking at him now that Death was sitting on his heart.

'Do you remember that?' whispered one after the other. 'Do you remember that?' And then they told him so many things that the sweat broke out on his brow.

'I never knew!' said the Emperor. 'Music, music! Bring the great Chinese drum!' he cried. 'So that I shan't hear all they're saying!'

But on and on they went, and Death nodded like a Chinaman at everything that was said.

'Music, music!' screamed the Emperor. 'Oh, beautiful little golden bird! Sing, do sing! I've given you gold and precious things; I hung my golden slipper about your neck with my own hands! Sing—do, do sing!'

But the bird stood silent: there was no one to wind it up, and without that it could not sing. But Death went on gazing at the Emperor with great empty eye-sockets, and everything was so still, so terribly still.

Then, at that moment, close by the window, the love-liest song rang out. It was the little live nightingale sitting on a branch outside: it had heard of its Emperor's dis-tress, and so had come to bring him comfort and hope. And as it sang, the ghostly forms grew paler and paler, the blood flowed more and more strongly through the Emperor's weak body, and even Death himself listened and said, 'Go on, little nightingale! Go on!'

'Yes, if you will give me that fine golden sword! Yes, if you will give me that rich standard! If you will give me the Emperor's crown!'

And Death gave up each of these treasures for a song, and the nightingale still went on singing: it sang of the quiet churchyard where white roses grow, where the elderberry-tree smells sweet and the fresh grass is damp with the tears of those who are left behind. Then Death was filled with longing for his garden, and drifted out through the window like a cold white mist.

'Thank you, thank you!' said the Emperor. 'You heavenly little bird, I know who you are! I drove you from my realm, and yet you've sung those evil visions

from my bed and driven Death from my heart! How shall
I reward you?'

'You have rewarded me!' said the nightingale. 'I drew
tears from your eyes the first time I sang to you, and I
shall never forget it! Those are the jewels that gladden a
singer's heart.—But now go to sleep and wake up fresh
and strong! I'll sing to you!'

And it sang—and the Emperor fell into a sweet sleep,
a sleep that was gentle and refreshing.

The sun was shining in upon him through the windows
when he woke up strengthened and in health again.
None of his servants had yet returned, for they all thought
he was dead, but the nightingale was still sitting there
and singing.

'You must stay with me always!' said the Emperor.
'You shall sing only when you want to, and I'll break
the clockwork bird into a thousand pieces!'

'No, don't do that!' said the nightingale. 'It's done its
best for you! Keep it as you did before! I cannot make
my home in the palace, but if you'll let me come when I
wish, then in the evening I'll sit outside upon the branch
by the window and sing for you to bring you happiness
and fill your mind with thoughts. I shall sing of the happy
and of those that suffer; I shall sing of the good and evil
round about that are hidden from you. The little song-
bird flies far and wide, to the poor fisherman, to the farm-
labourer's cottage, to everyone who is far away from you
and your court. I love your heart more than I do your
crown, and yet the crown has an air of something holy
about it!—I'll come and I'll sing for you!—But one thing
you must promise me—!'

'Everything!' said the Emperor, standing there in his
imperial robes which he had put on himself, and holding
the sword, heavy with gold, up to his heart.

'One thing I beg of you! Tell no one that you have a little bird that tells you everything—it will be better if you don't!'

And then the nightingale flew away.

The servants came in to look upon their dead Emperor—yes, there they stood, and the Emperor said, 'Good morning!'

The Sweethearts

THE Top and the Ball lay in a drawer together among the other playthings, and one day the Top said to the Ball, 'Couldn't we be sweethearts? After all, we lie in the same drawer together, don't we?' But the Ball, who was covered in morocco leather, and fancied herself like any other fine young lady, couldn't be expected to answer a question like that.

The next day the little boy who owned the toys came and painted the Top red and gold, and drove a brass nail right through it: when the Top spun round, it looked really magnificent.

'Just look at me!' it said to the Ball. 'Well, what do you say now? Don't you think we could be sweethearts? We're really very well suited to one another—you jump and I dance! No one could ever be happier than we two!'

'What an idea!' said the Ball. 'You obviously don't know that my mother and father were morocco-leather slippers and that I've a cork inside me!'

'Yes, but I'm made of mahogany!' said the Top. 'And the mayor himself turned me—he has a lathe of his own—and it gave him a great deal of pleasure, too!'

'Do you really expect me to believe that?' said the Ball.

'May I never be whipped again if I tell a lie!' answered the Top.

'You speak very well for yourself!' said the Ball. 'But it's quite impossible—I'm as good as half engaged to a swallow. Every time I go up in the air he bobs his head out of his nest and says, "Will you? Will you?" And now I've said, "Yes!" to myself—and that's as good as half an engagement! But I promise you I shall never forget you!'

'Well, that'll be a great help!' said the Top, and after that they spoke no more to one another.

The next day the Ball was taken out. The Top watched it flying high up in the air, just like a bird, until at last it was lost to sight. It came back again every time, but it always gave a high jump as it touched the ground, and that was either because it was restless and impatient or because it had a cork inside it. The ninth time, the Ball disappeared and did not come back any more. The boy searched and searched, but there was no doubt about it—it had disappeared.

'I know well enough where it is!' sighed the Top. 'It's in the swallow's nest and it's married to the swallow!'

The more the Top thought about the Ball, the deeper in love he fell. Just because he could not have her, his passion for her grew: but the really odd thing was that she had accepted someone else! And the Top danced round and spun, but his thoughts were always on the Ball, and in his fancy she grew ever more beautiful. And so, many years went by—and his love was a thing of the past.

The Top was no longer young. Then one day it was gilded all over—it had never looked so handsome before. It was now a gold Top, and it jumped about until it hummed again. Yes, that was something like! But all at once it jumped too high—and disappeared!

They looked and looked, even down in the cellar, but still they could not find it.

Where was it?

It had jumped into the dustbin where all sorts of things were lying—cabbage-stalks, sweepings, grit that had fallen down from the gutter.

'Well, this is a fine place to be in! My gilding will soon come off here! And what sort of outcasts have I got among?' And he looked out of the corner of his eye at a long cabbage-stalk that had been stripped far too closely, and at a curious round thing that looked like an old apple —but it was no apple, it was an old ball that had lain for many years up in the gutter and been soaked through with water.

'Thank heaven, here's someone of my own kind I can talk to!' said the Ball, looking at the gilt Top. 'I'm really made of morocco-leather, stitched by a young lady's own hands, and I have a cork inside me, though no one would think so to look at me! I was just going to be married to a swallow when I fell into the gutter, and there I lay, soaking wet, for five years! That's a long time for a young lady, believe me!'

But the Top said nothing. He thought of his old sweetheart, and the more he heard her say, the more certain he was that this was she.

Then the maid came along to turn out the dustbin. 'Hurrah,' she said, 'here's the gold top!'

And the Top went back to the living-room and was made much of, but nothing was heard of the Ball, and the Top never mentioned his old love again. Love dies when your sweetheart has lain soaking in a gutter for five years —in fact, you take care not to recognize her again when you meet her in the dustbin.

The Ugly Duckling

IT was so lovely out in the country! It was summer: the corn stood yellow and the oats green; down in the green meadows the hay had been stacked, and the stork was walking about there and chattering in Egyptian, for he had learnt that language from his mother. Round the fields and meadows there were vast woods, and in the midst of the woods were deep lakes—yes, it was really lovely out in the country! Right in the sunshine there lay an old manor-house with deep canals round it, and great dock-leaves grew from the wall down to the water—they were so tall that small children could stand upright under the biggest of them. They grew like a wild and tangled wood. A duck was sitting on her nest there: she was waiting for her little ducklings to hatch out, but she was rather tired of it now because it had lasted so long and she rarely had a visitor—the other ducks much preferred swimming round in the canals to running up and sitting under a dock-leaf to gossip with her.

At last, one after another, the eggs began to crack. 'Peep, peep!' they said—all the eggs had come alive, and the ducklings were poking their heads out.

'Quack, quack! Hurry up!' she said, and so they made as much haste as they could, and looked all round them under the green leaves, and their mother let them look as much as ever they wanted to, for green is good for the eyes.

'My, how big the world is!' said all the young ones, for they undoubtedly had much more room to move about in now than they had had inside their eggs.

'You don't think this is the whole world!' said their mother. 'Why, it stretches a long way on the other side of the garden, right into the parson's field! Though I have never been so far myself!—You're all here now, aren't you!' And so she got up. 'No, that you're not! The biggest egg is still there—however much longer is it going to be! I'm tired of it now, I can tell you!' And so she sat down again.

'Well, how is it going?' said an old duck who had come to pay her a visit.

'This one egg is taking such a long time!' said the mother-duck. 'It just won't hatch! But you must see the others now! They're the loveliest ducklings I've ever seen, all the image of their father—the wretch, he never comes to visit me!'

'Let me look at that egg that won't crack!' said the old duck. 'You can take it from me, that's a turkey's egg! I was once had, too, in the very same way, and the trouble and bother I had with the young ones! They're afraid of

water, I tell you! I could not get them in! I quacked and
snapped, but it was no use!—Let me see the egg! Yes, it's
a turkey's egg right enough! Let it be, and teach the other
children to swim!'

'No, I'll sit on it a little longer!' said the duck. 'I've
been sitting so long now, I can sit until the Deer Park
shuts for the winter!'

'Please yourself!' said the old duck, and off she went.

At last the big egg cracked. 'Peep, peep!' said the young
one, as he tumbled out; but oh, how big and ugly he was!
The duck looked at him. 'It's a terribly big duckling, that
one!' she said. 'None of the others looks like that! Surely
it's never a turkey-chick? Well, we shall soon find out!
Into the water he shall go, even if I have to kick him in
myself!'

The next day the weather was really heavenly, and the
sun was shining on all the green dock-leaves. The ducklings' mother came out with all her family and went down
to the canal. 'Splash!' She jumped into the water. 'Quack,
quack!' she said, and, one after another, the ducklings
plopped in; the water closed over their heads, but they
came up again at once and floated beautifully. Their legs
moved of their own accord, and there they all were, out
on the water—even the ugly grey one was swimming
with them.

'Well, that's no turkey!' she said. 'Look how beautifully he uses his legs and how straight he holds himself!
He's my own child and no mistake! He's really quite
handsome if you look at him properly! Quack, quack!—
Come with me now, and I'll take you into the world and
present you in the duck-yard; but mind you stay close by
me all the time in case you get trodden on, and keep a
sharp look-out for the cat!'

And so they went into the duck-yard. There was a

frightful noise in there, for there were two families fighting over the head of an eel, and then, after all, the cat got it.

'That's the way of the world, you see!' said the ducklings' mother, licking her beak, for she would have liked the eel's head, too. 'Use your legs now!' she said. 'Hurry yourselves along, and bow your heads to that old duck over there! She is the best bred of anyone here! She has Spanish blood—that's why she's so solid-looking, and you see, she has a piece of red cloth tied round her leg! That's something very special, the greatest distinction any duck can have. It means a very great deal indeed— so much that no one will ever get rid of her, and every- one—man and beast alike—treats her with respect! Hurry up now!—Don't turn your toes in! A well-brought-up duckling walks with feet well apart, like father and mother! Now then, bow your heads and say, "Quack!"'

And so they did; but the other ducks round about looked at them and said quite loudly, 'Look at that, we shall have to have that lot as well now, as if there weren't enough of us as it is! Lord, what a queer-looking duck- ling that one is! We won't put up with him!' And one of the ducks immediately flew at him and pecked him in the back of the neck.

'Let him alone!' said his mother. 'He's not harming anyone!'

'Yes, but he's too big and queer-looking!' said the duck that had pecked him. 'And so he's got to be put in his place!'

'They're pretty children mother has there!' said the old duck with the piece of red cloth round her leg. 'Every one of them pretty, except that one, and he's not turned out at all well! It's a pity she can't make him over again!'

'That can't be done, Your Grace!' said the ducklings'

mother. 'He's not good-looking, but he has a very nice disposition, and he swims just as beautifully as any of the others! And what's more, I dare say he'll grow quite handsome, and in time get a little smaller! He's lain too long in the egg, and so he's spoilt his figure!' Then she pecked at the down on the back of his neck and smoothed his body. 'Besides, he's a drake,' she said, 'and so it doesn't matter so much! He'll be strong, I'm sure of it— he'll get along all right!'

'The other ducklings are beautiful!' said the old duck. 'Make yourselves at home now—you can go and see if you can find an eel's head, and then you can bring it to me!'

And so they made themselves at home.

But the poor duckling that was the last to be hatched out of the egg and was so ugly-looking, was pecked and jostled and mocked by ducks and hens alike. 'He's too big!' they all said, and the turkey-cock, who had been born with spurs on and therefore thought he was an emperor, puffed himself up like a ship in full sail, went right up to him, and gobbled until he was quite red in the face. The poor duckling did not know where to stand or where to go, he was so miserable at being so ugly and being the laughing-stock of the whole duck-yard.

And so the first day passed, and afterwards it grew worse and worse. The poor duckling was chased about by everyone; even his brothers and sisters were unkind to him, and kept on saying, 'If only the cat would get you, you ugly thing!' And his mother would say, 'I wish you were far enough!' The ducks bit him, and the hens pecked him, and the girl who fed the poultry kicked him with her foot.

Then he ran off and flew away over the hedge; the little birds in the bushes rose terrified into the air. 'That's because I'm so ugly!' thought the duckling, shutting his eyes, but he ran on all the same. Then he came out into the great marsh where the wild ducks lived. There he lay the whole night, he was so tired and unhappy.

In the morning the wild ducks flew up and took a look at their new comrade. 'What kind of a fellow are you?' they asked. The duckling turned from one to another and greeted them as well as he could.

'You're ugly all right, and no mistake!' said the wild ducks. 'But that's all the same to us, as long as you don't marry into the family!'—Poor thing, getting married had never entered his head: all he wanted was leave to lie in the rushes and drink a little of the marsh water.

There he lay for two whole days, and then there came two wild geese, or, more properly, two wild ganders, for they were cocks. It was not many hours since they had been hatched, and so they were very pert and lively.

'Listen, comrade,' they said, 'you're so ugly we've taken quite a liking to you! Will you come along with us and be a bird of passage? Close by here, in another marsh, are some lovely sweet wild geese, young ladies every one of them, and they can say, "Quack!" with the best of them. You're so ugly, you're just the right fellow to try your luck with them!'

'Bang! Bang!' At that very moment there was a loud noise overhead, and both the wild ganders fell down dead in the rushes, and the water became red with blood. 'Bang! Bang!' It sounded again, and great flocks of wild geese flew up out of the rushes. Then the cracking noise was heard yet again. There was a great shoot in progress; the sportsmen lay all round the marsh, some even in the branches of the trees that stretched far out over the rushes. Blue smoke hung like clouds in among the dark trees and far out over the water. The dogs came splashing through the mud; rushes and reeds swayed on all sides. The poor duckling was terrified; just as he was ducking his head to hide it under his wing, a frightful great dog stood right in front of him, his tongue hanging right out of his mouth and his eyes shining wickedly. He thrust his muzzle right down towards the duckling and bared his sharp teeth—and then, splash! he had gone again without touching him.

'Oh, thank goodness!' sighed the duckling. 'I'm so ugly that even the dog will think twice before it bites me!'

And so he lay quite still while the duck-shot whistled in the rushes and shot after shot rang out.

It was far into the day before it was quiet again, but the poor young thing dared not move even then; he waited several hours yet before he looked round him, and then he took to his heels and left the marsh as far behind as he could; he ran over field and meadow, but the wind was blowing so sharply that he found it hard work to get along.

Towards evening he reached a poor little cottage; it was in such a wretched state that it could not make up its mind which side to fall down, and so it remained standing. The wind howled so strongly about the duckling that he had to sit down on his tail to withstand it; and it was growing worse and worse. Then he noticed that the door had fallen off one of its hinges and was hanging so askew that he could creep through the crack into the living-room; and that is what he did.

An old woman lived here with her cat and her hen. The cat, whom she called Sonny, could arch his back and purr; he could give out sparks, too, but he had to be stroked the wrong way first. The hen had little short legs, and so she was called Chicky Short-legs; she laid well, and the woman was as fond of her as if she had been her own child.

In the morning the strange duckling was spotted at once, and the cat began to purr and the hen to cluck.

'What's the matter?' said the woman, and looked all round her, but she could not see very well, and so she thought the duckling was a fat duck that had strayed away. 'Here's a fine catch, and no mistake!' she said. 'I can have duck-eggs now, if only it isn't a drake! Well, we shall see!'

And so the duckling was taken on trial for three weeks, but no eggs appeared. Now the cat was the master of the house and the hen was the mistress, and they always said, 'We and the world', for they considered themselves half the world, and the better half at that. The duckling thought there might be other opinions about that, but the hen would not hear of it.

'Can you lay eggs?' she asked.

'No!'

'Then you may hold your tongue!'

And the cat said, 'Can you arch your back and purr and give out sparks?'

'No!'

'Then you shouldn't express an opinion when sensible people are talking!'

And the duckling sat in the corner and felt very depressed. Then the thought of fresh air and sunshine came into his mind, and he was seized with such a strange desire to float upon the water that at last he could not help telling the hen about it.

'What's the matter with you?' she asked. 'You've nothing to do, and that's why these odd fancies come over you! Lay an egg or purr, and you'll get over them.'

'But it's so lovely floating on the water!' said the

duckling. 'So lovely ducking your head under and diving down to the bottom!'

'Yes, that must be a great pleasure!' said the hen. 'You must have lost your wits! Ask the cat—and he's the cleverest person I know—whether he likes floating on the water or diving to the bottom! I'll leave myself out of it. Ask our mistress, ask the old woman herself—there's no one in the world cleverer than she!—Do you suppose she's seized with a desire to float or duck her head under the water?'

'You don't understand!' said the duckling.

'Well, if we don't understand, then who could! It's certain you will never be cleverer than the cat and the old woman, not to mention myself! Don't show off, child! And thank your Maker for all the good things that have been done for you! Haven't you come into a warm room and found a social background you can learn something from? You talk a lot of nonsense, and your company is not at all amusing! You can believe me! I mean it for your good: I'm telling you a few home-truths about yourself, and that's how you can tell your true friends! Now just see that you lay some eggs and learn to purr or give out sparks!'

'I think I shall go out into the wide world!' said the duckling.

'Well, go on then!' said the hen.

And so the duckling went; he floated on the water and dived below the surface, but all the birds and beasts looked down on him on account of his ugliness.

Now autumn came: the leaves in the woods turned yellow and brown, the wind caught them and whirled them round in a dance; it looked cold up in the sky, the clouds hung heavy with hail and snow-flakes; and the raven, perched on the fence, screeched 'Caw! Caw!' from sheer cold—merely thinking about it was enough to make you feel regularly frozen: the poor duckling certainly did not have a very good time of it.

One evening, as the sun was setting wonderfully, a flock of lovely great birds came out of the bushes. The duckling had never seen anything so beautiful—they were shining white with long graceful necks: they were swans, and uttering a strange noise, they spread their splendid great wings and flew away from those cold parts to warmer lands and open lakes. They rose so high in the air, and the ugly little duckling felt so strange as he watched them; he turned round in the water like a wheel, craning his neck up after them and uttering a cry so loud and strange that it quite frightened him. Oh, he could not forget those lovely birds, those fortunate birds, and as soon as he lost sight of them, he dived right down to the bottom, and when he came up again, he seemed quite beside himself. He did not know what the birds were called nor where they were flying to, and yet he felt more deeply drawn to them than he had ever been to anything. He did not envy them in the slightest—how could it possibly enter his mind to wish himself so beautiful!—he would have been happy if even the ducks had let him stay with them, poor ugly creature that he was!

And the winter grew so very, very cold: the duckling had to swim round and round in the water to keep it from freezing right over; but every night the hole he swam in became smaller and smaller; it froze so hard that the ice-crust creaked; the duckling had to use his legs all the time to prevent the water from icing over; at last, he was tired out; he lay quite still and froze fast in the ice.

Early in the morning a farm-labourer came by, and seeing him, went out and broke the ice up with his wooden clogs, and then carried him home to his wife. There he recovered.

The children wanted to play with him, but the duckling thought they meant to hurt him, and in his fright he flew right into the milk-pan so that the milk splashed out into the room; the woman shrieked, clapping her hands over her head, and then he flew into the tub where the butter was, and then into the barrel of flour and out again.— My, what a sight he was! The woman shrieked and struck at him with the fire-tongs, and the children, laughing and screaming, pushed one another over in their efforts to catch the duckling. It was a good thing the door stood open—he rushed out into the bushes and the new-fallen snow—and there he lay as if in a swoon.

But it would be far too sad a business to describe all the hardship and misery he had to go through during that hard winter.—He was lying among the reeds in the marsh when the sun began to shine warm again; the larks were singing, and it was a lovely spring.

Then one day he stretched his wings; they rustled more strongly than before and bore him swiftly away; and before he was fully aware of it, he was in a great garden where the apple-trees stood in bloom and the lilac hung sweet-scented on its long green boughs right down to the winding canals. Oh, it was beautiful here in the fresh spring! And right in front of him, out of the thick hanging branches, came three lovely white swans, ruffling their feathers and floating lightly on the water. The duckling recognized the magnificent birds and a strange sadness came over him.

'I will fly over to those kingly birds, and they will peck me to death for daring to come near them, I'm so ugly! But it doesn't matter—better to be killed by them than snapped at by the ducks, pecked by the hens, kicked by the girl who looks after the poultry-yard, and suffer misery throughout the winter!' Then he flew out over the water and swam towards the splendid swans. They saw him and came shooting towards him with ruffling feathers. 'Only kill me!' said the poor creature, bowing his head down towards the water and awaiting his death— but what did he see in the clear water? He saw his own reflection beneath him, but he was no longer an awkward, dark-grey bird, ugly and repulsive—he was himself a swan.

It doesn't matter about being born in a duck-yard, as long as you're hatched from a swan's egg!

He felt really glad he had suffered all that hardship and adversity: he could now appreciate his good fortune and all the loveliness that greeted him.—And the great swans swam round him and stroked him with their beaks.

Some little children came into the garden and threw bread and corn out into the water, and the youngest cried, 'There's a new one!' And the other children shouted

joyfully, 'Yes, there's a new one come!' And, clapping their hands and dancing along, they ran to fetch their father and mother, and bread and cake were thrown into the water, and they all said, 'The new one is the most beautiful of them all! He is so young and lovely!' And the old swans bowed before him.

Then he felt quite shy and hid his head under his wing. He did not know what to do with himself, he was much too happy—but he was not at all proud, for a good heart is never proud. He thought of the time when he had been persecuted and despised, and now he heard them all say he was the loveliest of all those lovely birds. The lilacs bowed their branches right down to the water to him, and the sun was shining warm and fair: then he ruffled his feathers, lifted up his slender neck, and cried in the joy of his heart, 'I never dreamt I should find so much happiness when I was the ugly duckling!'

The Fir-Tree

OUT in the forest stood a pretty little fir-tree. It grew in a good place where the sun could get to it, and there was plenty of air and the companionship of many larger trees round about, both fir and pine. But the little fir-tree's one thought was to grow: it took no notice of the warm sunshine and the fresh air; it paid no attention to the country children who went by chattering when they were out gathering strawberries or raspberries. They would often pass that way with a whole crock full, or with strawberries threaded on straws, and then they would sit down by the little tree and say, 'Oh, what a pretty little baby tree it is!' But that wasn't at all the kind of thing the tree wanted to hear.

The year after, it was taller by a long new shoot, and the year after that by an even longer one, for you can always tell how many years a fir-tree has been growing by the number of spaces it has between its rings of branches.

'Oh, if only I were a big tree like the others!' sighed the little tree. 'Then I could spread my branches far out all round me and see the wide world from my top! The birds would build their nests among my branches, and when the wind blew I could nod gracefully like the others!'

It found no pleasure in the sunshine or the birds or the red clouds that, morning and evening, sailed overhead.

It was now winter and the snow lay round about white and sparkling, and when a hare came bounding along, it would often jump right over the little tree—and oh, how annoying that was! But two winters went by, and when the third came, the tree was so big that the hare had to go round it. Oh, to grow, to grow, to be big and old!—That, the tree thought, was the only pleasure in the world.

In the autumn the woodcutters came and felled some of the biggest trees. This happened every year, and the young fir-tree, well grown by now, shuddered as the magnificent great trees fell creaking and crashing to the ground. When the branches were hewn off, they looked quite naked as they lay there, long and slender and almost unrecognizable. Then they were laid on wagons, and horses dragged them away out of the forest.

Where were they going? What was in store for them?

In the spring when the swallows and storks returned, the tree asked them, 'Don't you know where they were taken to? Haven't you come across them?'

The swallows knew nothing, but the stork looked thoughtful, nodded his head and said, 'Yes, I think so! I met many new ships as I was flying from Egypt and they all had fine new masts—I dare say they were what you mean: they smelt of fir, and no matter how many times I greeted them, they kept their heads high, very high!'

'Oh, if only I were big enough to fly away over the sea, too!—What actually is the sea? What does it look like?'

'That would take far too long to explain!' said the stork, and off he went.

'Be happy in your youth!' said the sunbeams. 'Be

happy in your fresh growth, in the young life that's in you!'

And the wind kissed the tree and the dew wept tears over it, but the fir-tree did not understand them.

As Christmas drew near, quite young trees were felled, trees that were often no bigger and no older than the fir-tree of our story which knew neither peace nor quiet and was always wanting to be off. All these young trees—and they were always the most beautiful—kept their branches: they were laid on wagons, and horses dragged them away out of the forest.

'Where are they going?' asked the fir-tree. 'They're no bigger than I am—in fact, one was much smaller. Why do they keep all their branches? Where are they being taken to?'

'We know! We know!' twittered the sparrows. 'We've peeped through the windows down in the town! We know where they're taken! You can't imagine the brilliance and splendour in store for them! We've peeped in at the windows and seen them planted in the middle of warm rooms and decorated with the loveliest things—gilded apples, gingerbread, toys and hundreds of lighted candles!'

'And then?' asked the fir-tree, all its branches quivering. 'And then? What happens then?'

'Well, we haven't seen any more! But it was quite wonderful!'

'I wonder if I was born to travel such a brilliant road!' cried the fir-tree excitedly. 'It's even better than sailing over the sea! I'm quite sick with longing! If only it were Christmas! I'm tall now and well formed, with my branches stretching out like the others that were carried away last year!—Oh, if only I were on that wagon! If only I were in that warm room in all that splendour and glory! And then?—Yes, then something even better will follow, something even more beautiful—if not, why should they decorate me like that! Something even greater, even nobler, must come!—But what? Oh, how I suffer! How I long to find out! I don't know myself what's the matter with me!'

'Be happy with me!' said the air and the sunlight. 'Be happy in your fresh youth out in the open!'

But it wasn't a bit happy. It grew and grew: winter and summer it stood there, green, dark green it stood. Those that saw it said, 'That's a lovely tree!' and towards Christmas it was the first to be felled. The axe struck deep through its heart, and the tree fell with a sigh to the ground. It felt pain and a sudden weakness: it was quite unable to think of happiness, it was so overcome with sorrow at being parted from its home, the spot where it had sprung up. It knew that it would never again see its dear old companions, or the little bushes and flowers around it, or even, perhaps, the birds. Its journey was by no means pleasant.

The tree was in the courtyard, unloaded with the other trees, before it came to itself and heard a man say, 'That's a fine one! That's the one for us!'

Two men-servants in full livery came and carried the fir-tree into a fine big room. Portraits hung round the walls, and by the great tiled stove stood large Chinese vases with lions on their lids; there were rocking-chairs, silk-covered sofas, great tables full of picture-books and covered with toys worth hundreds and hundreds of pounds—at least, that's what the children said. And the fir-tree was set up in a big tub filled with sand, but no one could see it was a tub because it was draped all round with green cloth and stood on a large brightly-coloured carpet. Oh, how the tree trembled! Whatever would happen now? Men-servants and young ladies came and decorated it: they hung little baskets cut out of coloured paper on the branches, and every basket was filled with sweets; gilded apples and walnuts were hung up and looked as if they were growing there; and over a hundred little candles, red, blue and white, were fastened firmly to the branches. Dolls that looked really life-like—the tree had never seen anything like them before—swayed among the green needles, and right at the very top of the tree a big gold-tinsel star was fixed. It was magnificent, perfectly magnificent.

'This evening,' they all said, 'this evening it will be a blaze of light!'

'Oh,' thought the tree, 'if only it were evening! If only the candles were lit! And what will happen then, I wonder? I wonder if the trees will come from the forest to look at me? Will the sparrows fly up to the window? Shall I take root here and stand decorated, summer and winter?'

Yes, it could think of nothing else; it had a real bark-ache from so much longing, and a barkache is just as bad for a tree as a headache is for us.

Now the candles were lit. What radiance! What magnificence! The tree was so excited by it that all its branches quivered and one of the candles set fire to the greenery: the tree sweated with fright.

'Heaven preserve us!' screamed the young ladies as they hastily put it out.

And now the tree dared not give even the smallest quiver. What a dreadful moment it had been! It was so frightened of losing any of its finery and it was quite bewildered by all the brilliance—then the double doors opened wide and a crowd of children burst in as if they would overturn the whole tree. The grown-ups followed soberly. The little ones stood silenced—but only for a moment: then they shouted for joy till the whole room rang with their noise. They danced round the tree as one present after another was pulled off.

'What is it they're doing?' thought the tree. 'What's going to happen?' The candles burnt right down to the branches, and as they burnt down they were put out. Then the children were given leave to strip the tree. My, they rushed upon it with such violence that all its branches creaked! If it had not been firmly fastened to the ceiling by its tip and the gold star on it, it would have been pushed right over.

The children were dancing around with their lovely

toys, and no one looked at the tree except the old nurse who came peeping in among the branches, but that was only to see if a fig or an apple were still left.

'A story! A story!' shouted the children, dragging a stout little man over towards the tree. He sat down right under it. 'Now we're in the greenwood,' he said. 'And oddly enough, it may do the tree good to listen, too. But I'm going to tell only one story: do you want to hear about Ivede-Avede or about Humpty-Dumpty who fell down the stairs but for all that came to the throne and won the princess?'

'Ivede-Avede!' screamed some; 'Humpty-Dumpty!' screamed others. There was such a shouting and a screeching, and only the fir-tree remained silent. 'Aren't I going to join in?' it thought. 'Aren't I going to do anything?' But of course it had joined in: it had done all it had to do.

And the man told them about Humpty-Dumpty who fell down the stairs but for all that came to the throne and won the princess. The children clapped their hands and cried, 'Tell us another! Tell us another!' They wanted 'Ivede-Avede' as well, but they only got 'Humpty-Dumpty'. The fir-tree stood quite still and thoughtful: the birds out in the forest had never told him anything like that. 'Humpty-Dumpty fell down the stairs and for all that won the princess! Yes, yes, that's how the world goes!' thought the fir-tree, who believed it was all true because it was such a nice man who had told the story. 'Yes, who knows! Perhaps I shall fall down the stairs, too, and win a princess!' And it looked forward to being dressed up again the next day with candles and toys and gold and fruit.

'I shan't tremble tomorrow!' it thought. 'I'll enjoy myself properly in all my glory. Tomorrow I shall hear the story of Humpty-Dumpty again, and perhaps the one about Ivede-Avede as well.' And the tree stood there quiet and thoughtful the whole night through.

In the morning the men-servants and the maids came in.

'Now they'll begin to deck me out in my finery again!' thought the tree, but they dragged it out of the room, up the stairs and into the attic, and there they put it away in a dark corner where no daylight came. 'What's the meaning of this?' thought the tree. 'What am I supposed to do up here? What shall I have to listen to in this place?' And it leant up against the wall, and there it stood and thought and thought—and as the days and nights went by it had plenty of time for thinking. No one came up there, and when at last someone did come, it was only to put some big boxes away in the corner; the tree was now completely hidden and, one would imagine, quite forgotten.

'It's winter outside now!' thought the tree. 'The ground is hard and covered with snow. They can't plant me just yet, and so, no doubt, I'm to stay here under cover until the spring! That is thoughtful! Aren't people kind!—If only it weren't so dark here and so dreadfully lonely!—Not even a little hare!—Yes, it was very pleasant out there in the forest when the snow lay on the ground and the hare scampered by—even when he jumped right over me, though I didn't like it at the time. It really is dreadfully lonely up here!'

At that very moment a little mouse said, 'Squeak, squeak!' and nipped into the room. Then another little mouse followed and together they sniffed round the tree and scurried about among its branches.

'It's horribly cold!' said the little mice. 'But apart from that, it's a lovely place to be in. Isn't it, old fir-tree?'

'I'm not in the least old!' said the fir-tree. 'There are many who are much older than I am!'

'Where do you come from?' asked the mice. 'And what things do you know?' They were dreadfully inquisitive. 'Tell us about the loveliest place on earth! Have you been there? Have you been in the pantry where cheeses stand on the shelves and hams hang from the ceiling, where you can dance on tallow-candles, and go in thin and come out fat?'

'I don't know that place,' said the tree. 'But I know the forest where the sun shines and the birds sing!' And so it told them all about when it was young: the little mice had never heard anything like it before—they listened very attentively and said, 'My, what a lot you've seen! You have been lucky!'

'I?' said the fir-tree, and thought over what it had told them. 'Yes, I suppose they really were quite pleasant times!' Then it told them about Christmas Eve when it was decorated with cakes and candles.

'Oh,' said the little mice, 'how lucky you've been, old fir-tree!'

'I'm not old at all!' said the tree. 'It was only this winter I came from the forest! I'm at my very best—I'm just beginning to grow properly!'

'You do tell lovely stories!' said the little mice, and the night after they came with four other little mice to hear what the tree had to tell them, and the more it told them the more clearly it remembered it all and thought, 'Yes, they really were pleasant times! But they may come back, they may come back! Humpty-Dumpty fell down the stairs and yet won the princess: perhaps I may win a princess, too!' And as it spoke, the fir-tree thought about a pretty little birch-tree that grew out in the forest and in the eyes of the fir-tree was a really lovely princess.

'Who's Humpty-Dumpty?' asked the little mice. Then the fir-tree told them the whole story—it could remember every single word. The little mice were ready to jump to the top of the tree with pure delight. The night after that many more mice came, and on Sunday two rats as well. But they said the story wasn't amusing, and that distressed the little mice because now they thought less of it, too.

'Is that the only story you know?' asked the rats.

'The only one!' answered the tree. 'I heard it on the happiest evening of my life, though at the time I didn't know how happy I was!'

'It's an exceedingly dull story! Don't you know one about bacon and tallow-candles? No pantry-tales?'

'No!' said the tree.

'Well, thank you very much!' answered the rats, and in they went.

At last the little mice stayed away, too, and then the tree sighed, 'It was really very cosy when they sat all round me, those nimble little mice, and listened to what I told them! Now that's gone, too!—But I shall remember to enjoy myself when I'm taken out again!'

But when would that be?—It happened one morning when they came rummaging in the attic. The boxes were moved and the tree was pulled out. They threw it down on the floor—pretty hard, too—and then one of the men dragged it away towards the stairs where the daylight shone.

'Now life's going to begin again!' thought the tree. It felt the fresh air and the first rays of the sun—and then it was out in the yard. Everything happened so quickly that the tree completely forgot to look at itself, there was so much to see all round. The yard adjoined a garden where everything was in bloom: roses hung fresh and sweet-scented over the low fence, lime-trees were in flower, and swallows flew about saying, 'Tweet-tweet-tweet, my husband's come!' But it wasn't the fir-tree they meant.

'Now I'm going to live!' it cried joyfully, stretching out its branches—but alas! they were all withered and yellow, and it lay in a corner among the weeds and nettles. The gold paper star, still in place at the tip of the tree, glittered in the bright sunshine.

Two or three of the merry children who had danced round the tree at Christmas and been so delighted with it, were playing in the yard. One of the smallest of them came and tore the gold star off.

'Look what's still left on the ugly old Christmas-tree!' he said, as he trampled on the branches and snapped them under his boots.

The tree looked at the flowers, beautiful and fresh in the garden—it looked at itself, and wished it had stayed in its dark corner in the attic. It thought of its own fresh youth in the forest, of the merry Christmas Eve and of the little mice who had listened with such delight to the story of Humpty-Dumpty.

'Gone! Gone!' said the poor tree. 'If only I'd been happy when I could! Gone! Gone!'

And the man-servant came and chopped the tree into small pieces until a whole pile lay there. It blazed beautifully under the big copper; and it sighed so deeply, each sigh like a pistol-shot, that the children who were playing ran in and, sitting down in front of the fire, looked into it and cried, 'Pop! Pop!' But with each crack—really a deep sigh—the tree thought upon a summer's day in the forest or a winter's night when the stars were shining; it thought of Christmas Eve and Humpty-Dumpty, the only fairy-tale it had ever heard and knew how to tell—and then the tree was burnt up.

The boys played in the yard, and the smallest of them wore upon his chest the gold star which the tree had worn on its happiest evening. It was gone now, the tree was gone, too, and its story was over—over and done with, as all stories are, sooner or later.

The Snow Queen

Which deals with the mirror and its splinters

WELL, now, let's begin—and when we come to the end of the story we shall know more than we do now! There was once a wicked demon—one of the very worst—the Devil himself! One day he was in a really good humour because he had made a mirror which had the power of making everything good and beautiful reflected in it disappear almost to nothing, while all that was bad and ugly to look at showed up clearly and appeared far worse than it really was. In this mirror the loveliest of landscapes looked just like boiled spinach, and even the nicest people looked hideous or else they stood on their heads and had no bodies. Their faces were so changed that there was no recognizing them, and if anyone had a freckle, you could be certain it would seem to spread all over his nose and mouth. It was great fun, said the Devil. If a good and holy thought passed through a person's mind, it appeared in the mirror as a grin, and then the Devil had to laugh at his own clever invention. All those who attended the School for Demons—for he ran a School for Demons—spread the news that a miracle had happened: now for the very first time, they said, you could see what the world and mankind really looked like. They ran everywhere with the mirror, until at last there was not one land or one person that had not been distorted in it. And now they wanted to fly up to Heaven itself to make fun of Our Lord and His angels. The higher they flew with the mirror, the louder it laughed, so that they could hardly keep hold of it: higher and higher they flew, nearer to God and the angels, until at last the mirror shook so violently with laughter that it sprang out of their hands and fell down to earth, where it broke into hundreds of million, billion, and even more, pieces. For that very reason it caused much greater misfortune than before, for some of the pieces were hardly as big as grains of sand, and these flew round about the wide world, and wherever they got into people's eyes, there they stayed, and then the people saw everything distortedly, or else they had eyes only for what was bad in things, for every little splinter of glass had kept the same power that the whole mirror had. Some people even got a little bit of the mirror in their hearts, and then it was really dreadful, for their hearts became just like lumps of ice. Some pieces of the mirror were so big that they were used as window-panes, but it did not pay to look at your friends through them. Other pieces were used in spectacles, and people had a bad time of it when they put their glasses on to see properly and act justly. The Wicked One laughed until he split his sides, he was so highly tickled by it all. Small splinters of glass were still flying about in the air. So now let us hear what happened!

THE SECOND PART

A Little Boy and a Little Girl

In the big city where there are so many houses and people that there is not enough room for everyone to have a little garden, and where, therefore, most people must content themselves with flowers in pots, there were two poor children who had a garden that was a little bigger than a flower-pot. They were not brother and sister, but they were just as fond of one another as if they had been. Their parents lived right next to each other; they lived in two attics; where the roofs of the two neighbouring houses met and the gutter ran along under the eaves, two little windows faced one another, one from each house. All you need do was step over the gutter and you could get from one window to the other.

Their parents had a large wooden box outside each window, and in them grew vegetables for their use and a little rose-tree; there was one in each box, and they grew beautifully. Then their parents found that if they placed the boxes across the gutter they reached almost from one window to the other, and looked for all the world like two banks of flowers. As the boxes were very high and the children knew they must not clamber up them, they often got leave to climb out to one another and sit on their little stools under the rose-trees where they played wonderful games together.

In winter such pleasures came to an end. The windows were often completely frosted over, but then they would warm copper coins on the stove, lay hot pennies on the frozen panes and so make lovely peep-holes, perfectly round, and from behind them two sweet and gentle eyes would peep out, one from each window. It was the little boy and the little girl. He was called Kay and she was called Gerda. In summer they could be with one another in one jump; in winter they had first to climb all the way downstairs and then all the way upstairs—and outside the snow fell fast.

'That's the white bees swarming,' said the old grandmother.

'Do they have a queen-bee, too?' asked the little boy, for he knew that real bees have one.

'That they have!' said grandmother. 'There she flies, where they are swarming thickest! She is the biggest of them all, and she will never settle quietly upon the ground —up she flies again into the dark clouds. Many a winter night she flies through the streets of the town and peeps in at the windows, and then they frost over with such wonderful flower-patterns.'

'Yes, I've seen them!' said both the children, and so they knew it was true.

'Could the Snow Queen come in here?' asked the little girl.

P

'Just let her try!' said the boy. 'I should put her on the warm stove and then she would melt!'

But grandmother smoothed his hair and told them other tales.

In the evening when little Kay was home and half undressed, he climbed up onto the chairs by the window and peeped out through the little hole. A few snow-flakes were falling outside, and one of them, the biggest of them all, came to rest on the edge of one of the window-boxes. The snow-flake grew bigger and bigger, until at last it turned into a lady clothed in the finest white gauze made up of millions of star-like snow-flakes. She was very beautiful and dainty, but she was of ice, dazzling, gleaming ice, all through, and yet she was alive; her eyes shone like two clear stars, but there was no rest nor quiet in them. She nodded towards the window and beckoned with her hand. The little boy was terrified and jumped down from the chair; and then it was just as if a great bird flew past the window outside.

The next day there was a clear frost—and then the thaw set in—and then came spring: the sun shone, the green shoots peeped out, the swallows built their nests, the windows were thrown up, and the little children sat once more in their tiny garden high up in the gutter above all the floors of the house.

The roses bloomed splendidly that summer. The little girl had learnt a hymn, and in it there was a line about roses, and whenever she came to it, she thought about her own. She sang the hymn for the little boy, and he sang it with her:

'In the valley grew roses wild,
And there we spoke with the Holy Child!'

And the little ones held each other's hands, kissed the

roses, and, looking up towards God's bright sunshine, they spoke to it as though the Christ Child were there Himself. What beautiful summer days they were; how lovely it was to be outside near the fresh rose-trees that seemed as if they would never stop blooming!

Kay and Gerda sat looking at the picture-book with the animals and birds in it, and it was just at that moment —the clock was striking five in the great church tower— that Kay said, 'Oh! There's a pricking in my heart! And now I've got something in my eye!'

The little girl put her arms about his neck; he blinked his eyes: no, there was nothing to see.

'I think it's gone!' he said; but it hadn't. It was neither more nor less than one of those splinters of glass that had sprung from the mirror, the demon-mirror we remember hearing about, the evil glass which made everything great and good reflected in it grow small and ugly, and in which all that was wicked and bad stood out clearly and every blemish became immediately noticeable. Poor Kay—he had a splinter right in his heart as well— it would soon be like a lump of ice. It did not hurt any more—but it was still there.

'What are you crying for?' he asked. 'You look so ugly like that! There's nothing at all the matter with me! Pooh!' he cried in the same breath. 'That rose over there is all worm-eaten! And look, that one's quite lopsided! They really are a disgusting lot of roses—they're just like the boxes they grow in!' And then he kicked the box hard and tore off the two roses.

'Kay, what are you doing?' cried the little girl. And when he saw how frightened she was, he pulled off another rose and sprang in at his own window away from sweet-natured little Gerda.

After that, whenever she came with the picture-book, he said it was only fit for babies; and if grandmother told her tales, he was always ready to criticize—yes, and when he got the chance, he would walk behind her, put her glasses on, and talk just like her: it was a perfect imitation and it made people laugh. He could soon mimic the speech and walk of everybody in the street. Everything that was odd or unpleasant about them Kay knew how to imitate, and so people said, 'He's certainly got a remarkable head on his shoulders, that boy!' But it was the glass he had got in his eye, the glass that had pierced his heart, and that was why he teased even little Gerda who loved him with all her soul.

His games had become quite different now from what they had been before, they were so intelligent. One winter's day when the snow was falling fast, he came with a large burning-glass, held out the corner of his jacket and let the snow-flakes fall on it.

'Now look in the glass, Gerda!' he said, and every snow-flake grew much bigger and looked like a wonderful flower or a ten-pointed star—it was lovely to look at them.

'Do you see how beautifully formed they are!' said Kay. 'They're much more interesting than real flowers! And there isn't a single blemish on them: they're quite perfect —or they would be if they didn't melt!'

Soon afterwards Kay came again, with his big gloves on and his toboggan on his back: he shouted right in Gerda's ear, 'I've got leave to take my toboggan to the big square where the others are playing!' And off he went.

Over on the square the boldest of the boys would often tie their toboggans fast to the farmers' wagons and so ride behind them for quite a long way. It was great fun. When their games were in full swing, a great sledge came by: it was painted white all over, and in it sat a figure muffled in a thick white fur coat and a white fur hat. The sledge drove twice round the square, and Kay quickly managed to tie his little toboggan firmly to it. Then he rode behind it. It went faster and faster, right into the next street. The driver turned round and nodded to Kay in a very friendly fashion, just as if they knew one another. Every time Kay was about to loosen his little toboggan, the driver would nod to him again, and then Kay would remain sitting where he was. They drove right out of the city gates. Then the snow began to fall so thick and fast that the little boy could no longer see his hand in front of him as they sped along: quickly he undid the rope to free himself from the great sledge, but it was no good—his little toboggan hung on fast behind, and it went with the speed of the wind. Then he shouted as loudly as he could, but no one heard him, and the snow fell and the sledge flew on. From time to time it gave a bound as if it were flying over ditches and fences. He was completely terrified and wanted to say the Lord's Prayer, but all he could remember were his multiplication-tables.

The snow-flakes grew bigger and bigger until they looked like great white hens. All at once they swerved to one side, the great sledge pulled up, and up stood the driver with fur coat and hat made of pure snow: it was a lady, tall and proud and dazzlingly white—she was the Snow Queen.

'We've made good time,' she said. 'But are you cold? Creep under my bear-skin!' And she seated him beside her in the sledge and drew her fur coat round him—he felt as if he were sinking into a snow-drift.

'Are you still cold?' she asked him, and kissed him on the brow. Ooh! her kiss was colder than ice: it went straight to his heart, and his heart was already half-way to being a lump of ice. He felt as if he were about to die—but only for a moment, and then everything was all right again— and he no longer noticed the cold all around him.

'My toboggan! Don't forget my toboggan!' It was the first thing he thought about; it was made fast to one of the white hens, and she flew behind them with the toboggan on her back. The Snow Queen kissed Kay yet once more, and then he forgot little Gerda and grandmother and all the rest of them back home.

'And now you get no more kisses!' she said. 'Or else I shall kiss you to death!'

Kay looked at her: she was very beautiful; a wiser, lovelier face he could not imagine: now she no longer seemed made of ice as she had done when she sat outside the window and beckoned to him—in his eyes she was perfect. He felt no fear at all: he told her he could do mental arithmetic, even with fractions, and work out how many square miles there were in the country and how many people lived there. And she smiled all the time. Then he realized that he knew very little indeed. He looked up into the great vast vault of the sky, and she flew with him, high up on the dark clouds, and the stormy wind whistled and roared as though it were singing old ballads. They flew over forests and lakes, over land and sea, while below them the cold blast shrieked, the wolves howled, the snow sparkled, and over it flew the black screeching crows. But above them the moon shone large and bright, and Kay gazed upon it all through that long, long winter night. During the day he slept at the Snow Queen's feet.

THE THIRD PART

The Flower-Garden that belonged to the Old Woman who understood Magic

But what happened to little Gerda when Kay came back no more? Where could he be? No one knew, no one had any news of him. The boys could only say that they had seen him fasten his little sledge to another, a fine big one, that had driven out into the street and through the city gate. No one knew where he was: many tears flowed, and little Gerda wept long and sorely. Then they said he was dead, drowned in the river that ran close by the city. Oh, what long, dark winter days those were!

Then the spring came and the sun shone more warmly.

'Kay is dead and gone!' said little Gerda.

'I don't believe it!' said the sunshine.

'He's dead and gone!' she said to the swallows.

'I don't believe it!' they answered, and at last little Gerda did not believe it either.

'I will put my new red shoes on,' she said early one morning, 'the ones Kay has never seen, and then I'll go down and ask the river.'

It was quite early; she kissed her old grandmother who was still asleep, put on her red shoes, and went all alone out of the gate and down to the river.

'Is it true that you've taken my little playmate? I'll make you a present of my red shoes if you'll give him back to me!'

The waves, she thought, nodded very strangely. Then she took her red shoes, her most precious possession, and threw them both out into the river, but they fell close by the bank, and the small waves immediately carried them back to her. It was just as if the river, knowing it had not taken little Kay, would not take her most precious possession either. But Gerda now thought she had not thrown the shoes far enough out, and so she clambered into a boat that lay among the rushes, went right to the farther end of it, and threw the shoes again. But the boat was not made fast, and with her movements it slipped its moorings. Seeing what had happened, she hurriedly tried to

regain the bank, but before she could reach it, the boat
was a couple of feet out in the water and gliding away
ever more swiftly.

Then little Gerda was quite terrified and began to cry,
but no one heard her except the sparrows, and they could
not carry her back to land. But they flew along by the
bank and sang, as if to comfort her, 'Here we are! Here
we are!' The boat drifted downstream; little Gerda sat
quite still in her stockinged feet; her little red shoes
floated after her, but they could not reach the boat, which
was gathering speed.

It was very beautiful on both banks of the river: there
were lovely flowers and old trees and hillsides with sheep
and cattle—but not a soul to be seen anywhere.

'Perhaps the river will carry me to little Kay,' thought
Gerda. With that she felt more cheerful, and standing up,
she watched the beautiful green banks for hours on end.
At last she came to a large cherry-orchard where there
was a little cottage with odd-looking red and blue windows, a thatched roof besides, and two wooden soldiers
standing outside and shouldering arms for those that
sailed by.

Gerda shouted to them; she thought they were alive, but, of course, they did not answer. She came quite close to them; the river drove the boat right in towards the shore.

Gerda shouted louder still, and then there came out of the cottage an old, old woman leaning on a crooked stick. She had on a large sun-hat painted all over with the loveliest flowers.

'You poor little child!' said the old woman. 'How on earth did you come to be out on that great strong stream, driven far out into the wide world?' And the old woman waded right out into the water, caught hold of the boat firmly with her crooked stick, drew it to land, and lifted little Gerda out.

Gerda was glad to get back to dry land, though she was a little frightened of the strange old woman.

'Now come and tell me who you are and how you came here!' she said.

And Gerda told her everything; and the old woman shook her head and said, 'Hm! Hm!' And when Gerda had said all and asked her if she had not seen little Kay, the woman said that he had not passed that way yet, but he would come, sure enough, and she shouldn't be sad, but taste her cherries and see her flowers—they were more beautiful than any picture-book and every one of them could tell a whole story. Then she took Gerda by the hand, they entered the little cottage, and the old woman locked the door.

The windows were very high up, and the panes were red, blue, and yellow—the daylight shone strangely inside through all those colours. But on the table stood a dish of the loveliest cherries, and Gerda needed no encouragement to eat as many as she wanted. While she was eating them, the old woman combed her hair with a golden comb, and her hair curled and shone lovely and fair about her friendly little face that was so round and like a rose.

'I've been longing for a dear little girl like you!' the old woman said. 'You shall see now how well we two shall get on together!' And all the time she was combing little Gerda's hair, Gerda was forgetting her foster-brother Kay more and more—for the old woman could cast spells, though she was by no means a wicked witch and practised magic only a little for her own pleasure, and now she wanted very much indeed to keep little Gerda. And so she now went out into the garden, stretched out her crooked stick towards all the rose-trees, and, blooming beautifully though they were, they all sank down into the black earth so that you could not even see where they had been. The old woman was afraid that if Gerda saw the roses she would think of her own, and then remember little Kay and run off.

Then she took Gerda out into the flower-garden. Oh, how fragrant and lovely it was! All the flowers you could think of, flowers of every season of the year, stood there in full splendour—no picture-book could have been more gaily coloured or more beautiful. Gerda jumped for joy and played until the sun went down behind the tall cherry-trees. Then she was given a lovely bed with a red silk eiderdown stuffed with blue violets, and she slept and dreamed as sweetly as any queen upon her wedding-day.

The next day she was allowed to go out again and play among the flowers in the warm sunshine—and thus many days went by. Gerda learnt to know every flower, yet, though there were so many of them, one seemed to be missing, but which one she did not know. Then one day she sat looking at the old woman's sun-hat with its painted flowers, and the very loveliest of all was a rose. The old woman had forgotten to take it off her hat when she made the real ones disappear under the ground. But that's how it is when you're absent-minded! 'Why!' cried Gerda. 'Aren't there any roses here?' And she ran among the flower-beds, searching and searching. Her hot tears fell just where a rose-tree had sunk into the earth, and as her warm tears moistened the ground, the tree shot up at once, just as full of bloom as when it disappeared; and throwing her arms around it, Gerda kissed the roses and thought about the lovely roses at home—and with them, about little Kay.

'Oh, what a lot of time I've wasted!' said the little girl. 'I was going to find Kay!—Don't you know where he is?' she asked the roses. 'Do you think he's dead and gone?'

'No, he's not dead,' said the roses. 'We've been in the earth where all the dead are, but Kay wasn't there!'

'Oh, thank you, thank you!' said little Gerda, and she went over to the other flowers, and looking into their cups, she asked, 'Don't you know where little Kay is?'

The flowers stood in the sun, each dreaming its own tale: little Gerda heard many, many things from them, but none of them knew anything of Kay.

What was the tiger-lily saying?

'Can you hear the drum?—Boom, boom! There are only two notes—boom, boom! over and over again. Listen to the women's dirge! Listen to the cry of the priests!—In her long red robe, the Hindu woman stands on the pyre while the flames are mounting round her and her dead husband. But the Hindu woman is thinking of the living there among those that encircle her, of him whose eyes burn hotter than the flames, the fire of whose eyes penetrates her heart more deeply than the flames that will soon burn her body to ashes. Can the heart's flame die in the flames of the pyre?'

'That I don't understand at all!' said little Gerda.

'That is my story!' said the tiger-lily.

What does the convolvulus say?

'High over the narrow field-path hangs an ancient castle. Evergreen plants grow thick and close about the old red walls, leaf upon leaf, right up round the balcony where a lovely girl is standing. She leans out over the parapet and looks down to the path. No rose hanging from its stem is fresher than she, no apple-blossom borne by the wind from the tree is more graceful. How her fine silken gown rustles! "Still he does not come!"'

'Is it Kay you mean?' asked little Gerda.

'I'm speaking only of my own story, my dream,' answered the convolvulus.

What does the little snow-drop say?

'A long plank hangs by a rope between the trees—it is a swing. Two sweet little girls sit swinging—their dresses are as white as snow and long green silk ribbons stream from their hats: their brother, who is bigger than they, stands up on the swing with his arm about the rope to keep himself steady; he holds a little bowl in one hand and a clay pipe in the other, and he is blowing bubbles. The swing is in motion, and the bubbles fly away with lovely ever-changing colours, the last still clinging to the stem of the pipe and swaying in the breeze. The swing is still in motion. A little black dog, light as the bubbles, jumps up on his hind legs, wanting to join them on the swing. It flies out of his reach, the dog tumbles, barking furiously. They laugh at him, and the bubbles burst.— A swinging plank, a fleeting picture of foam—that is my song!'

'What you tell of may well be beautiful, but you speak of it so sadly and you don't mention little Kay at all. What do the hyacinths say?'

'There were three lovely sisters, delicate and dainty; the first was dressed in red, the second in blue, and the third in pure white. Hand in hand, they danced by the still lake in the clear moonlight. They were not fairy maidens, they were children of men. There was a strong sweet fragrance, and the girls vanished in the woods. The fragrance grew stronger—three coffins in which the lovely girls lay, glided from the depth of the dense woods away over the lake. Glow-worms flew shining around them like small flickering lights. Do the dancing girls sleep, or are they dead?—The perfume of the flowers tells they are corpses: the evening bell rings out for the dead!'

'You make me quite sad,' said little Gerda. 'Your scent is so strong it makes me think of those dead girls!

Ah, is little Kay really dead then? The roses have been down in the earth, and they say he's not!'

'Ding, dong!' rang the bells of the hyacinths. 'We are not ringing for little Kay—we know nothing of him! We are but singing our own song, the only one we know!'

And Gerda went over to the buttercup, gleaming from among its shiny green leaves.

'You're just like a bright little sun!' said Gerda. 'Tell me, if you can, where shall I find my play-fellow?'

The buttercup shone very prettily and looked at Gerda. What song could the buttercup sing? Not one about Kay at any rate.

'In a little courtyard God's good sun was shining warmly on the first day of spring, its rays gliding down the neighbour's white wall. Close by, the first yellow flowers were growing, gleaming gold in the warm sunbeams. Old grandmother was outside in her chair, and her pretty granddaughter, a poor servant-girl, had come home from a short visit: she kissed her grandmother. There was gold, heart's gold, in that blessed kiss. Gold on lips, and a golden flower; gold above in the morning hour! There you are, that's my story!' said the buttercup.

'My poor old granny!' sighed Gerda. 'I know she must be longing for me—she'll be just as unhappy about me as she was about little Kay. But I shall soon be home again, and then I shall bring Kay with me. It's no use asking the flowers: they know only their own songs;

they can tell me nothing!' And so she tucked up her little frock so that she could run more quickly. But as she was jumping over it, the narcissus caught her leg. She stopped short, and looking at the tall flower, she asked, 'Perhaps you know something?' She bent right down to it. And what did it say?

'I can see myself! I can see myself!' cried the narcissus. 'Oh, how beautiful my scent is!—Up in her little attic, a little ballet-dancer is standing, half-dressed, now on one leg, now on two, and kicking her leg at the whole world —but she is only an illusion. She pours water from the tea-pot on to a piece of cloth she is holding—it is her corset:—cleanliness is a good thing! Her white dress hangs on its peg—that has been washed in the tea-pot, too, and put out to dry on the roof. She puts it on, and arranges her saffron-yellow kerchief about her neck so that the white of her dress shows brighter than ever. One leg in the air: look how well she carries herself on one stalk! I can see myself! I can see myself!'

'I don't care a bit about that!' said Gerda. 'It's not at all what I want to hear!' And so she ran to the edge of the garden.

The door was shut, but she twisted the rusty fastening until it came away and the door flew open, and then little Gerda ran barefoot out into the wide world. She looked back three times, but there was no one following her. At last she could run no more, and so she sat down on a large stone, and when she looked about her, she saw that summer had gone and it was now late autumn—time had passed unnoticed in that lovely garden where there was always sunshine and flowers from every season of the year.

'Oh dear, what a time I've been!' said little Gerda. 'It's autumn already! I dare not rest any longer!' And she rose to go.

Oh, how tired and aching her little feet were! Everything round her looked cold and raw: the long willow-leaves were quite yellow, the wet mist dripped from them, one leaf fell after another. Only the sloe still bore its fruit, so sour and bitter it draws your mouth tightly together. Oh, how grey and heavy it was in the wide world!

THE FOURTH PART

Prince and Princess

Gerda had to rest once more: right in front of where she was sitting, a big crow was hopping in the snow; he had sat looking at her and wagging his head for a long time, and now he said, 'Caw! Caw!—Goo' daw! Goo' daw!' He could not say it any better, but he meant well towards the little girl and asked where she was going to, out in the wide world all alone. Gerda understood that word 'alone' only too well and felt how deep a meaning it had, and so she told the crow all the story of her life, and asked if he had seen Kay.

The crow nodded thoughtfully and said, 'It could be— it could be!'

'What?—Do you really think you have?' cried the little girl, kissing the crow so hard she very nearly squeezed him to death.

'Careful! Careful!' said the crow. 'I think it may be little Kay! But he's certainly forgotten you now for the princess!'

'Does he live with a princess?' asked Gerda.

'Yes, listen to me!' said the crow. 'But I find it very difficult to speak your language. If you understand crow-talk[1] I can tell you about it much better!'

[1] The Danish *Kragemaal*, literally 'crow-talk', means 'gibberish', like the English 'double-Dutch'. L. W. K.

'No, I'm sorry, I haven't learnt it!' said Gerda. 'But Granny used to know it, and she knew double-Dutch as well. If only I'd learnt it, too!'

'Doesn't matter!' said the crow. 'I'll tell you as well as I can, but I shall make a bad job of it all the same.' And so he told her all he knew.

'In this very kingdom where we are now sitting, there lives a princess who's terribly clever, and on top of that, she's read all the newspapers in the whole world—and forgotten them again, she's so clever. A short while ago, as she was sitting on her throne—and that's not as pleasant as you'd think, or so I'm told—she happened to be humming a song, and what should it be but, "Oh, why should I not marry?" "You know, there's something in that!" she says, and so she decided to marry, but she wanted a husband who knew how to answer when you talked to him, not one who just stood and looked distinguished, for she'd soon grow tired of that. Then she had all her ladies-in-waiting summoned by the drum, and when they heard what was in her mind, they were delighted. "Oh, what a good idea!" they said. "I was thinking the same thing, too, only the other day!"—Believe me, it's true, every word I'm telling you!' said the crow. 'I've a tame sweetheart who's free to go all over the palace, and she told me everything!'

Of course, she was a crow, too, for birds of a feather flock together, and a crow's mate is always a crow.

'The newspapers came out right away with a border of hearts and the princess's monogram. Every good-looking young man, as you could read for yourself, was free to go up to the palace and talk with the princess, and the one who talked so that you could hear he felt at home there, and spoke the best, the princess would take for her husband!—Oh, yes,' said the crow, 'believe me! As sure as I'm sitting here, people just streamed in—there was such a crush and commotion! But nothing came of it, either the first day or the second. They could all talk well enough when they were out in the street, but when they came through the palace gate and saw the guard in their silver uniforms and footmen in gold all the way up the stairs and the great halls all lit up, they were dumbstruck, and when they stood before the throne where the princess was sitting, they could find nothing to say except the last word she had spoken herself, and she wasn't really interested in hearing that again. It was just as if everybody there had got snuff on the stomach and had fallen into a stupor until they came out into the street once more— they could talk all right again then. There was a line right from the city gate to the palace. I was there myself and saw it!' said the crow. 'They grew both hungry and thirsty, but they didn't get so much as a glass of luke- warm water up at the palace. Some of the most sensible, of course, had brought sandwiches with them, but they didn't share them with their neighbours, for they thought, "If only he looks hungry enough, the princess won't have him!"'

'But Kay, little Kay!' asked Gerda. 'When did he come? Was he one of the crowd?'

'Give me time! Give me time! We're coming to him right now! It was the third day, and there came a little fellow, with neither horse nor carriage, who marched coolly up to the palace. His eyes were shining just like yours and he had lovely long hair, but his clothes were shabby!'

'That was Kay!' cried Gerda joyfully. 'Oh, so I've found him!' And she clapped her hands.

'He had a little knapsack on his back!' said the crow.

'Why, that must have been his toboggan!' said Gerda. 'He had his toboggan when he went away!'

'It might have been!' said the crow. 'I didn't look as closely as all that! But I do know from my tame sweetheart that when he came in through the palace gate and

saw the Life Guards in their silver uniforms and the footmen in gold all the way up the stairs, he wasn't in the least dismayed—he nodded and said to them, "It must be very dull standing on the stairs—I'd much rather go inside!" The halls were blazing with lights; privy councillors and excellencies were walking about barefoot, carrying golden salvers: it was enough to make anyone feel awestruck! His boots squeaked dreadfully, but he wasn't at all afraid!'

'It's certainly Kay!' said Gerda. 'I know he had new boots—I heard them squeaking in Granny's sitting-room!'

'Yes, they squeaked all right!' said the crow. 'And he went quite unconcerned straight in to the princess who was sitting on a pearl as big as a spinning-wheel; and all the ladies-in-waiting with their maids and their maids' maids, and all the gentlemen of the court with their serving-men, their serving-men's serving-men, and their serving-men's serving-men's boys were standing drawn up in order all round them—and the nearer they stood to the door, the haughtier they looked. The serving-man's serving-man's boy, who always went in slippers, looked so haughtily in the doorway, you hardly dare raise your eyes to him!'

'That must be terrifying!' said little Gerda. 'But did Kay win the princess then?'

'If I hadn't been a crow, I'd have taken her myself—in spite of being engaged. He must have talked just as well as I do when I speak crow-talk, or so my tame sweetheart tells me. He was confident and charming: he had no intention of coming to woo the princess, he had come only to listen to her wisdom, and that he found delightful—and in return, she found him delightful, too.'

'Yes, of course it was Kay!' said Gerda. 'He was so clever, he could do mental-arithmetic with fractions!—Oh, you will take me to the palace, won't you?'

'That's easily said,' replied the crow, 'but how shall we set about it? I must talk it over with my tame sweetheart —she'll no doubt be able to advise us, for I must tell you, a little girl like you would never get leave to enter in the regular way!'

'Oh, yes, I should!' said Gerda. 'When Kay knows I'm here, he'll come straight out to fetch me!'

'Wait for me by the stile there!' said the crow, wagging his head as he flew off.

The crow did not come back again until dusk had fallen. 'Caw! Caw!' he said. 'I'm to give you her greetings and best wishes! And here's a little loaf for you which she took from the kitchen—they've bread enough there, and you must be hungry!—It won't be possible for you to go into the palace, not with bare feet: the guards in silver and the footmen in gold won't allow it. But don't cry— you shall get in all the same. My sweetheart knows a little back staircase that leads to the bedchamber, and she knows where she can get the key!'

And they made their way into the garden and along the great avenue, where the leaves were falling one after another, and when the lights went out in the palace, one by one, the crow led little Gerda over to a back-door that was standing half-open.

Oh, how Gerda's heart beat with anxiety and longing! She felt just as if she were about to do something wrong, and yet she only wanted to find out if it were little Kay: yes, it must be he—she thought so vividly about his clever eyes and his long hair that she could actually see the way he used to smile when they sat together under the roses at home. He was sure to be glad to see her, to hear what a long way she had come for his sake, and to know how sad they had all been at home when he did not come back. How frightened she felt, but how glad she was, too!

They were on the stairs now; a little lamp was burning on a cupboard; in the middle of the floor stood the tame crow, turning her head this way and that, and looking intently at Gerda who curtseyed as grandmother had taught her to.

'My young man has spoken very nicely of you, young lady,' said the tame crow. 'And your biography, as they call it, is very touching!—If you will take the lamp, I'll go in front. We're going to take the shortest way, where we shan't meet anyone!'

'I think there's someone coming right behind us now!' said Gerda. Something swished past her, and there seemed to be shadows on the wall—horses with flowing manes and slender legs, huntsmen, lords and ladies on horse-back.

'They're only dreams!' said the crow. 'They come and take their lordships' thoughts out hunting—it's a good thing, too, for they can watch them better in bed. But I hope you will let me see, if you should come to honour and dignity, that you can show a grateful heart!'

'That's hardly something we should talk about!' said the crow from the woods.

They now entered the first hall, where the walls were covered in rose-red satin and beautifully worked flowers. The dreams were already rushing past them, but they swept by so quickly that Gerda failed to see the lords and ladies. Each hall was more magnificent than the last—it was not surprising it took your breath away—and then they were in the bedchamber. Here the ceiling was like a great palm-tree with leaves of glass, costly glass, and in the middle of the floor two beds hung from a thick golden stalk; each was shaped like a lily: one was white, and in it lay the princess; the other was red, and it was there that Gerda must look for little Kay. She turned one of the red petals aside, and she saw the nape of a brown neck—Oh, it was Kay!—She cried his name aloud, holding her lamp towards him—the dreams came rushing on horseback into the room again—he woke, turned his head, and—it was not little Kay.

The prince resembled him only on the back of his neck, but he was young and handsome. And the princess peeped out of the white lily bed and asked what was the matter. Then little Gerda wept and told her whole story and everything the crows had done for her.

'You poor little thing!' said the prince and princess, and they praised the crows and said they were not at all angry with them, but nevertheless they must not do it again. Meanwhile, they should have a reward.

'Would you like to fly away free?' asked the princess. 'Or would you rather have a permanent post as Court-Crows with a right to everything that falls on to the kitchen floor?'

And both the crows bowed low and asked for the permanent post, for they thought of their old age and said, 'It would be a very good thing to have something for the old man,' as they call it.

And the prince got out of his bed and let Gerda sleep in it, and more than that he could hardly do. She folded her little hands together and thought, 'Aren't people kind—and animals, too!' And then she shut her eyes and slept peacefully. The dreams all came flying in again, and this time they looked like God's angels; they pulled a little toboggan behind them, and in it sat Kay nodding to her. But it was all nothing but a dream, and so it vanished as soon as she woke.

The next day she was clothed from top to toe in silk and velvet. She was invited to stay in the palace and enjoy herself, but the only thing she asked for was a little carriage with a horse to pull it and a little pair of boots, and then she could drive out into the wide world again and find Kay.

She was given both the boots and a muff. She was dressed beautifully, and when she was ready to go, a new carriage of pure gold drove up to the door with the prince and princess's coat-of-arms gleaming on it like a star. The coachman, the footmen, and the postilions—there were postilions, too—sat there with golden crowns upon their heads. The prince and princess helped her into the carriage themselves and wished her good luck. The crow from the woods, who was now married, went with her for the first twelve or fifteen miles; he sat beside her, for he could not bear riding backwards. The other crow stood in the gateway flapping her wings; she did not go with them, for, ever since they got their permanent post and too much to eat, she suffered from headaches. The inside of the carriage was lined with sugared cakes, and on the seat were fruits and doughnuts.

'Good-bye! Good-bye!' cried prince and princess, and little Gerda wept and the crow wept.—And so the first few miles went by; then the crow said good-bye, too, and that was the heaviest leave-taking of all; he flew up into a tree and flapped his black wings as long as the carriage, shining like the sun, remained in sight.

THE FIFTH PART

The Little Robber-Girl

They drove through the dark forest, but the carriage shone like a flame, hurting the robbers' eyes until they could bear it no longer.

'It's gold! It's gold!' they shouted, and, rushing out, they seized the horses, struck the little postilions, the coachman, and the footmen all dead, and then dragged little Gerda out of the carriage.

'She's fat, she's a dainty little morsel, she's been fattened on nut-kernels!' said the old hag of a robber-woman with the long bristly beard and the eyebrows that hung down over her eyes. 'She's as good as a little fatted lamb! My, how tasty she'll be!' And she drew out her polished knife which gleamed most terrifyingly.

'Ow!' said the old hag at that very same moment: she had been bitten on the ear by her own little daughter who was hanging on her back and was so wild and out-of-hand it was a joy to see. 'You loathsome brat!' said her mother, and she had no time to kill Gerda.

'She's going to play with me!' said the little robber-girl. 'She's going to give me her muff and her beautiful dress, and sleep in my bed with me!' And then she bit her mother again, so hard that the robber-woman jumped and turned round, and all the robbers laughed and said, 'Look at her dancing with her cub!'

'I'm going to ride in the carriage!' said the little robber-girl, and she insisted upon having her own way, for she was very spoilt and very obstinate. She and Gerda sat inside, and thus they rode over stumps and thorns deeper and deeper into the forest. The little robber-girl was the same height as Gerda, but stronger, broader in the shoulders, and dark-skinned. Her eyes were quite black and had a rather sad look. She put her arm round little Gerda's waist and said, 'They shan't kill you as long as I'm not cross with you! Are you really a princess?'

'No,' said little Gerda and told her everything that had happened to her and how fond she was of little Kay.

The robber-girl gazed at her seriously, nodding her head a little, and said, 'They shan't kill you unless I get really cross with you, and then I shall do it myself!' Then she dried Gerda's eyes, and put both her hands inside the beautiful muff that was so soft and warm.

And now the carriage stopped: they were in the middle of the courtyard of a robbers' castle; the structure was split from top to bottom, ravens and crows flew out of the gaping holes, and the great bull-dogs—every one of them looked as if it could swallow a man—sprang high in the air, but they did not bark, for that was forbidden.

In the great old sooty hall a huge fire was burning in the middle of the flagged floor; the smoke drifted about under the roof and had to find its own way out; a big cauldron of soup was on the boil, and hares and rabbits were turning on the spit.

'You shall sleep here with me tonight, where all my pets are!' said the robber-girl. They got something to eat and drink, and then went over into a corner where straw and rugs lay scattered about. Above their heads, nearly a hundred doves were roosting on laths and perches; they all seemed to be asleep, but they shifted slightly when the little girls came.

'They're all mine, every one of 'em,' said the little robber-girl, promptly seizing one of the nearest, which she held up by the legs and shook so that it beat its wings frantically. 'Kiss it!' she cried, slapping Gerda in the face with it. 'There sit the scum of the forest!' she continued, pointing behind a number of slats nailed across a hole high up in the wall. 'They're forest scum, those two! They'd fly away at once if they weren't properly locked up. And here's my old sweetheart, Bae!' And she dragged a reindeer forward by the horn. It had a bright copper ring round its neck and was tied up. 'We have to keep him under lock and key as well, else he'd run away from us. Every evening of his life I tickle his neck with my sharp knife, and he's ever so frightened of it!' The little girl pulled a long knife out of a crack in the wall and let it glide over the reindeer's neck: the poor beast struck out with its legs, and the robber-girl laughed and pulled Gerda down into the bed.

'Do you want your knife with you when you're going to sleep?' asked Gerda, looking at it somewhat apprehensively.

'I always sleep with my knife!' said the little robber-

girl. 'You never know what may happen. But tell me
again what you told me before about little Kay, and why
you went out into the wide world.' And Gerda told the
story from the beginning, and the ring-doves cooed up
there in their cage, while the other doves slept. The little
robber-girl put her arm round Gerda's neck, and holding
her knife in the other hand, she fell asleep, as you could
tell by the sound of her breathing. But Gerda was quite
unable to shut her eyes; she did not know whether she
was to live or die. The robbers sat round the fire, singing
and drinking, and the old woman turned head over heels.
It was quite terrifying for the little girl to look at.

Then the ring-doves said, 'Coo, coo! We've seen little
Kay. A white hen was carrying his toboggan, and he was
sitting in the Snow Queen's sledge as it swept low over
the forest while we lay in our nest. She blew a cold blast
on us young ones, and all died except us two. Coo!
Coo!'

'What's that you're saying up there?' cried Gerda.
'Which way did the Snow Queen go? Have you any idea?'

'She was doubtless making for Lapland, for there's
always snow and ice there! But you ask the reindeer
tethered to that rope.'

'Yes, there's ice and snow, and everything is beautiful
and good!' said the reindeer. 'There you can run about
freely in the great gleaming valleys! The Snow Queen
has her summer tent there, but her stronghold lies up towards the North Pole, on the island called Spitzbergen!'

'Oh, Kay, little Kay!' sighed Gerda.

'You lie still now!' said the robber-girl. 'Or else you'll
get my knife in your belly!'

In the morning Gerda told her everything the ring-
doves had said, and the little robber-girl looked quite
serious, but nodded her head and said, 'Never mind!

Never mind!—Do you know where Lapland is?' she asked the reindeer.

'Who should know better than I?' answered the animal, his eyes shining at the thought of it. 'That's where I was born and bred and where I used to run over the snow-fields.'

'Listen!' the robber-girl said to Gerda. 'You see all our menfolk are out: the old girl's still here, and here she'll stay, but later on in the morning she'll take a drink from that big bottle and then have a little nap afterwards.—Then I'll see what I can do for you!' She now sprang out of bed and jumping round her mother's neck, she pulled her beard and said, 'Good morning, my own sweet billy-goat!' Her mother flicked her under the nose and made it red and blue—but it was all done out of pure affection.

So when her mother had had a drink from her bottle and was taking a little nap, the robber-girl went over to the reindeer and said, 'I should love to go on tickling you with my sharp knife because you look so funny when I do it, but never mind, I'm going to undo your rope and help you to get away so that you can run off to Lapland, but you must put your best foot forward and take this little girl to the Snow Queen's palace where her playmate is. I'm sure you overheard what she told me, for she talked loudly enough, and you're always eavesdropping!'

The reindeer jumped for joy. The robber-girl lifted little Gerda up and took the precaution of tying her firmly on and giving her a little cushion to sit on as well. 'Never mind,' she said, 'you can have your fur boots, for it'll be cold; but I'm going to keep the muff—it's much too nice! However, you shan't freeze: you can have mother's big mittens—they'll reach right up to your elbows. Shove your hands in!—now they look just like my ugly old mother's!'

And Gerda wept for joy.

'I can't bear to see you snivelling!' said the little robber-girl. 'You must look pleased now! You can have these two loaves and a ham, and then you won't go hungry.' They were tied on to the reindeer's back just behind her. The little robber-girl opened the door, shut all the big

dogs up, and then, as she cut through the rope with her knife, she said to the reindeer, 'Off you run now—but see you take good care of the little girl!'

And Gerda stretched out her hands with the mittens on towards the robber-girl and said good-bye, and then the reindeer sped away as fast as he could over bushes and tree-stumps, through the great forest, and over marsh and steppe-land. The wolves were howling and the ravens were screeching. 'Pop! Pop!'—there was a crackling in the sky, almost as if it were sneezing blood.

'There are my dear old Northern Lights!' said the reindeer. 'Look at the way they're shining!' and with that he ran on even more swiftly, night and day. The loaves were eaten, and so was the ham, and then they found themselves in Lapland.

The Lapp Woman and the Finmark Woman

They stopped by a little cottage: it was a wretched place with the roof reaching down to the ground and the door so low that the family had to crawl on their stomachs when they wanted to go in or out. There was no one at home but an old Lapp woman who stood grilling a fish over a whale-oil lamp. The reindeer told her the whole of Gerda's story, but he told his own first, for that seemed to be much more important, and Gerda was so overcome with cold she could not speak.

'Ah, you poor, poor things!' said the Lapp woman. 'You've still a long way to go! You'll have to go over four hundred miles into Finmark, for that's where the Snow Queen is staying in the country and burning blue lights every single evening. I'll write a few words on a dried codfish, for paper have I none, and give it to you to take to the Finnish woman up there—she can give you clearer directions than I can!'

And then when Gerda had warmed herself and had something to eat and drink, the Lapp woman wrote a couple of words on a dried codfish, and bidding Gerda take great care of it, she tied her firmly on to the reindeer's back once more, and off he ran. 'Pop! Pop!' came the crackling noise from up in the sky, and all night long the Northern Lights burned a beautiful blue. And then they came to Finmark and knocked on the Finnish woman's chimney-stack, for she had no door at all.

The heat inside was so overpowering that even the Finnish woman went about very nearly naked. She was short and grubby-looking. She at once loosened Gerda's clothing and took off her mittens and boots, otherwise she would have been much too hot. Then she laid a piece of ice on the reindeer's head and read what was written on the codfish. She read it three times, and then when she knew it off by heart, she put the fish into the saucepan, for it might just as well be eaten, and she never wasted anything.

Then the reindeer told his own story first and then little Gerda's, and the Finnish woman blinked her eyes wisely but said nothing.

'You're so clever,' said the reindeer, 'I know you can tie up all the winds of the world with a thread of cotton. When the skipper unties the first knot, he gets a good wind; when he unties the second, the wind blows sharp; and when he unties the third and fourth, a gale springs up and the woods come tumbling down. Won't you give the little girl a drink that will give her the strength of twelve men so that she can get the better of the Snow Queen?'

'The strength of twelve men!' said the Finnish woman. 'Yes, that should do the trick!' She went over to a shelf, took a large rolled-up skin from it and unrolled it. Strange letters were written on it, and the Finnish woman read until the sweat poured from her brow.

The reindeer again pleaded so strongly for little Gerda, and Gerda looked at the Finnish woman with such beseeching tearful eyes, that she once again began to blink her eyes and drew the reindeer over into a corner, where she put fresh ice on his head and whispered to him.

'Little Kay is with the Snow Queen right enough, and he finds everything to his liking there and thinks it's the best place on earth, but that's all because he's got a splinter of glass in his heart and a little grain of it in his eye. They must be got out first, otherwise he'll never be human again and the Snow Queen will keep her power over him!'

'But can't you give little Gerda something to take which will give her the power to put everything right?'

'I can't give her greater power than she has already! Can't you see how great that is? Can't you see how she makes man and beast serve her, and how well she's made her way in the world on her own bare feet? She mustn't know of her power from us—it comes from her heart, it comes of her being a sweet innocent child. If she can't find her way into the Snow Queen's palace and free little Kay of the glass splinters all by herself, then we can't help her! Eight or nine miles from here is the beginning of the Snow Queen's garden: you can carry the little girl there. Put her down by the big bush with the red berries which you'll see standing in the snow. Don't stand gossiping, and hurry back!' With that, the Finnish woman lifted little Gerda up on to the reindeer's back, and off he ran as fast as he could.

'Oh, I forgot to bring my boots! And I've left my mittens behind!' cried little Gerda. And she missed them in the stinging cold. But the reindeer dared not stop; he ran on till he came to the big bush with the red berries. There he put Gerda down, and as he kissed her on the lips, great glistening tears ran down the poor animal's cheeks. Then, as fast as he could, he ran back again. There stood poor Gerda, without shoes, without gloves, in the midst of the terrible icy cold of Finmark.

She ran on as well as she could, and then a whole regiment of snow-flakes came towards her; they had not fallen from the sky, for that was quite clear and bright with the Northern Lights; no, the snow-flakes were running along the ground, and the nearer they came, the bigger they grew. Gerda remembered, of course, how large and wonderfully made the snow-flakes had looked when she saw them once through a magnifying-glass.

R

But now they were big and frightening in quite a different way—they were alive, they were the Snow Queen's outposts. They had the strangest shapes: some looked like nasty great hedgehogs, others like masses of snakes knotted together and darting their heads out, and still others like tubby little bears with bristling hair. All were gleaming white, all were living snow-flakes.

Then little Gerda said the Lord's Prayer, and the cold was so intense she could see her own breath: it rose from her lips like a column of smoke; her breath became thicker and thicker, and formed itself into bright little angels that grew bigger and bigger as they touched the ground. They all had helmets on their heads and spears and shields in their hands. There were more and more of them, and when Gerda had finished the Lord's Prayer, there was a whole legion of them round her. They pierced the dreadful snow-flakes with their spears so that they burst into hundreds of pieces, and little Gerda went on her way safe and undismayed. The angels patted her hands and feet, and she felt the cold less keenly and went briskly forward towards the Snow Queen's palace.

But we must first see how Kay is getting on. He was certainly not thinking about little Gerda—least of all that she was standing right outside the palace.

THE SEVENTH PART

What Happened in the Snow Queen's Palace, and What Happened Afterwards

The palace walls were of driven snow, the doors and windows of cutting wind; there were over a hundred halls, all as the drifting snow had formed them, the largest stretching for many miles, and all brightly lit by the strong Northern Lights. They were vast, empty, icy-cold, and gleaming. Gaiety never came this way, no, not so much as a little dance for the bears, with the gale blowing up and the polar-bears walking on their hind legs and showing their fine manners; never a little card-party with slap-your-mouth and strike-your-paw; never a little bit of fun over coffee for the young white-fox ladies— empty, vast, and cold it was in the Snow Queen's halls. The Northern Lights flashed with such regularity that you could tell when they had reached their highest point and when they had reached the lowest. In the middle of that empty endless hall of snow there was a frozen lake; it had split into a thousand pieces, and all the pieces were so exactly alike that the whole thing looked like a trick. Whenever she was at home, the Snow Queen sat in the centre of this lake, and then she would say she was sitting in the Mirror of Intelligence, and that it was the best, the only, one in the world.

Little Kay was quite blue with cold—nearly black, in fact—but he did not notice it, for she had kissed his shivers away, and his heart was nothing but a lump of ice. He spent his time dragging sharp flat pieces of ice about, arranging them in all sorts of ways, and trying to make something out of them—it was rather like the kind of thing we sometimes do with small flat pieces of wood when we try to make patterns from them—a Chinese puzzle they call it. Kay made patterns in the same way, most elaborate ones, a sort of intellectual ice-puzzle. In his own eyes the patterns were quite remarkable and of the utmost importance—that was what the grain of glass that was stuck in his eye did for him! He would lay out his patterns to form written words, but he could never hit upon the way to lay out the one word he wanted, the word 'eternity'. The Snow Queen had said, 'If you can work out that pattern for me, you shall be your own

master, and I will present you with the whole world—
and a new pair of skates.' But he could not do it.

'Now I must fly off to the warm lands!' said the Snow
Queen. 'I must go and peep into the black cauldrons!'—
They were the fiery mountains that we call Etna and
Vesuvius.—'I must whiten them a little! It's expected of
me, and it's good for the lemons and grapes!' And so the
Snow Queen flew away, and Kay sat quite alone in the
vast empty hall of ice, many miles in length, and gazed at
the pieces of ice, thinking and thinking until his head
creaked with the effort. He sat there quite stiff and still:
you would have thought he was frozen to death.

It was then that little Gerda stepped into the palace
through the great gale of cutting wind; but she said her
evening prayers, and the cold winds dropped as if they
would fall asleep. She stepped into the vast empty cold
halls—then she saw Kay, she recognized him, she flung
herself about his neck, held him very tight, and cried,
'Kay! Dear little Kay! So I've found you after all!'

But he sat there quite still, stiff and cold. Then little
Gerda wept hot tears that fell upon his breast and pene-
trated to his heart. They thawed the lump of ice and de-
stroyed the little splinter of glass inside it. He looked at
her, and she sang the hymn,

> 'In the valley grew roses wild,
> And there we spoke with the Holy Child!'

Then Kay burst into tears; he wept so desperately that
the grain of glass was washed out of his eye; he recognized her and cried joyfully, 'Gerda! Dear little Gerda!—
Where have you been all this time? And where have I
been?' And he looked round about him. 'How cold it is
here! How empty and vast it is!' And as he clung to her
she laughed and cried for joy: it was a moment of such

bliss that even the pieces of ice danced for joy all round them, and when they grew tired and lay down again, they formed the very letters the Snow Queen had told him he must find out if he were to be his own master and she were to give him the whole world and a new pair of skates.

Gerda kissed his cheeks and the bloom came back to them; she kissed his eyes and they shone like hers; she kissed his hands and feet and he was in perfect health. The Snow Queen could come home when she liked: his reprieve lay written there in gleaming pieces of ice.

They took one another by the hand, and, as they made their way out of that vast palace, they talked about grandmother and the roses on the roof; and as they walked along, the winds lay still and the sun broke through. When they reached the bush with the red berries, the reindeer was standing there and waiting for them. He had another reindeer with him, a young doe whose udders were full, and she gave the children her warm milk and kissed them on the lips. Then the reindeer carried Kay and Gerda to the Finnish woman's, where they warmed themselves in the heat of the room and were given directions for their journey home, and then to the Lapp woman who had made them new clothes and got her sledge ready.

The reindeer and the young doe ran along by their side and kept them company until they came to the boundary of that land: there the first green shoots peeped forth, and there they took their leave of the reindeer and the Lapp woman. 'Good-bye!' they all said. The first little birds began to twitter, there were green buds in the forest, and out of it came riding on a splendid horse—which Gerda recognized, for it had been harnessed to her golden coach—a young girl with a bright red cap on her head and pistols before her. It was the little robber-girl who had grown tired of being at home and had made up her mind to travel northwards first and then, if she did not like it there, in some other direction afterwards. She recognized Gerda at once, and Gerda recognized her: they were very glad to see one another.

'You're a fine sort to go wandering off like that!' she said to little Kay. 'I'd like to know whether you deserve to have someone running to the ends of the world for your sake!'

But Gerda stroked her cheek and asked after the prince and princess.

'They've gone travelling to foreign parts!' said the robber-girl.

'And the crow?' asked little Gerda.

'Oh, the crow's dead!' she answered. 'His tame sweetheart's a widow now and goes about with a bit of wool round her leg; she's always moaning and complaining, but it's all put on!—But tell me how you got on, and how you came across him!'

And Gerda and Kay both told her their stories.

'And fiddle-di-fiddle-di-dee!' said the robber-girl. She took them both by the hand, and promised that if she ever passed through their town, she would come up and visit them. Then she rode away out into the wide world, but Kay and Gerda walked on hand in hand, and as they went along, the spring was beautiful with flowers and fresh green leaves. The church bells were ringing, and they recognized the high towers and the great city: it was there that they lived, and on they went till they came to grandmother's door. They went up the stairs and into the living-room, where everything stood in the same place as before, and the clock said 'Tick! Tock!' and the hands turned round. But as they entered the door, they realized that they had grown up. The roses in the gutter were thrusting their flowers in at the open window, and their little stools were still standing there. Kay and Gerda sat down in their own seats and held each other's hands. They had forgotten like a heavy dream the cold empty splendour of the Snow Queen's palace. Grandmother was sitting there in God's bright sunshine and reading aloud from the Bible, 'Except ye become as little children, ye shall not enter into the kingdom of heaven!'

And Kay and Gerda looked into each other's eyes, and all at once they understood the old hymn:

> 'In the valley grew roses wild,
> And there we spoke with the Holy Child!'

There they sat together, grown up, yet children still, children at heart—and it was summer, warm and beautiful summer.

Eldermother

THERE was once a little boy who had a cold: he had gone and got wet feet, but no one could imagine where he had got them from, for it was perfectly dry weather. His mother undressed him and put him to bed. Then she had the tea-kettle brought in to make him a good cup of elder-tea—that would be sure to warm him! At that very moment the old man who lived right at the top of the house came in at the door. He lived all alone, for he had neither wife nor child, but he was very fond of children, and they thought him great fun and were always delighted to see him because he could tell so many fairy-tales and stories.

'Now drink your tea!' said mother. 'Then perhaps you'll hear a fairy-tale!'

'Yes, if only I knew something fresh!' said the old

man, nodding gently. 'But where did the little fellow get wet feet?' he asked.

'Yes, where did he!' said mother. 'That's what no one can make out!'

'Am I going to get a story?' asked the boy.

'Yes, but there's something I must know first: can you tell me, more or less, how deep the gutter is in the little street where you go to school?'

'Exactly half-way up my legs,' said the boy, 'but only when I step in the deep hole!'

'Well, that's where we got our wet feet!' said the old man. 'And now I really ought to tell you a story, but I don't know any more!'

'You can make one up as you go along,' said the little boy. 'Mother says you can turn everything you look at into a fairy-tale and make a story out of everything you touch!'

'Yes, but those fairy-tales and stories aren't any good. No, the right sort—they come by themselves: they tap me on the forehead and say, "Here I am!"'

'Will one tap soon?' asked the little boy, and his mother laughed as she put the elder-tea into the pot and poured boiling water over it. 'Go on, tell me one!'

'I would if a fairy-tale would come, but that sort are stand-offish and come only when they think they will!— Stop!' he cried all of a sudden. 'There's one now! Look out, now it's in the tea-pot!'

And the little boy looked over at the tea-pot. The lid was lifting higher and higher, and elder-flowers were coming out fresh and white; great long branches were shooting forth, even from the spout, spreading out on all sides and growing bigger and bigger until there was a lovely elder-bush, a whole tree that pushed into the bed and thrust the curtains aside. Oh, how it blossomed and

what a perfume it had! In the middle of the tree sat a
kindly old woman in a strange dress, perfectly green like
the leaves of the elder-tree and covered with large white
elder-flowers—you couldn't tell at first glance whether it
were made of cloth or of real live leaves and flowers.

'What's the lady called?' asked the little boy.

'Well,' said the old man, 'the old Greeks and Romans
used to call her a dryad, but that's a name that doesn't
mean very much to us. Over in Nyboder they have a
better one for her: there she's called Eldermother, and
she's the one you must now pay attention to: just listen
and look at the beautiful elder-tree!

'There's a big flowering tree, just like this one, over in
Nyboder; it grows in the corner of a poor little courtyard.
One afternoon two old people were sitting under this
tree in beautiful sunshine—an old, old sailor and his old,
old wife. They were great-grandparents and they would
soon be celebrating their golden-wedding, but they
couldn't quite remember the date. Eldermother was
sitting in the tree looking happy and contented, just as
she's doing now. "I know when your golden-wedding
is!" she said, but they did not hear her for they were
talking of old times.

'"Yes, can you remember," the old sailor was saying,
"the time when we were quite small children, running
about and playing? It was in this very same courtyard
where we're sitting now, and we put slips into the ground
and made a garden."

'"Yes," said the old woman, "I remember it well! And
we watered the slips, and one of them was a slip of elder-
berry which took root and sent out green shoots—and it
grew into the big tree we old folk are sitting under now."

'"Yes, that's right!" he said. "And over there in the
corner was a water-butt where my ship used to lie. I

carved her myself and a trim craft she was, too! But I soon took to sailing after a very different fashion!"

'"Yes, but we went to school first and learnt our lessons!" she said. "And then we were confirmed: it made us both cry, but in the afternoon we walked hand in hand to the top of the Round Tower and looked all round over Copenhagen and the sea; then we walked to Frederiksberg where the King and Queen were sailing up and down the canals in their fine boat."

'"But I took to sailing after a very different fashion, and for many a year I was far away on long voyages!"

'"Yes, and I often wept for you!" she said. "Many a time I thought you were dead and gone, lying at the bottom of the deep sea! Many a night I got up to see if the weather-cock had turned round: it turned right enough, but you didn't come! Then one day—I remember it all so clearly!—it was pouring with rain; the dustman was outside the house where I was in service and I came down with the dust and stood waiting by the door. What dreadful weather it was!—And as I was standing there, the postman came up to me and gave me a letter. It was from you: what a way it had come! I tore it open and read it: I laughed and cried, I was so happy! You'd written to say you were in warm parts where coffee-beans grow! A beautiful land that must be! You wrote of so much and I could see it all as the rain was pouring down and I was standing there with the dust—and just then someone put an arm round my waist—"

'"Yes, and you gave him a good box on the ear and made it ring!"

'"But I didn't know it was you! You'd arrived at the same time as your letter, and you were so handsome—you still are—and had a big yellow silk handkerchief in your pocket and a hard shiny hat on: you did look smart! But oh, what weather it was and what a state the street was in!"

'"Then we got married!" he said. "Do you remember? And then we had our first little boy, and after that Marie and Niels and Peter and Hans Christian!"

'"Yes, and now they're all grown up, all good-hearted honest folk that everybody likes!"

'"And their children, too, they've got their own little ones now!" the old sailor said. "There's good stuff in those great-grandchildren of ours!—It must have been about this time of year, I think, that we had our wedding!"

'"Yes, this very day is your golden-wedding day!" said Eldermother as she thrust her head right in between the two old people who thought it was the woman from next door nodding to them. They looked at each other and held each other by the hand. Shortly after came their children and grandchildren: they knew it was their golden-wedding day and had already been to congratulate them that morning. But the old folk had forgotten, though they remembered so clearly all that had happened many years before. The elder-flowers smelled so strong and sweet, and the sun, which was on the point of setting, shone right into the old people's faces, giving a ruddy glow to their cheeks. The youngest of their grandchildren danced round them, shouting gleefully that there was going to be a real feast that evening with hot potatoes for everybody. Eldermother nodded from the tree and cried, "Hurrah!" with the rest.'

'But that wasn't a fairy-tale!' said the little boy who had been listening to the story.

'It is when you understand it!' said the old man who had been telling it. 'Let's ask Eldermother what she thinks!'

'No, that wasn't a fairy-tale!' said Eldermother. 'But

there's one coming now! It's just out of ordinary every-day things that the most wonderful fairy-tales grow—otherwise my lovely elder-bush could never have sprung out of the tea-pot!' Then she took the little boy out of bed, his head resting upon her breast, and the elder-branches, full of flower, closed round them.· There they sat in a closely-woven arbour that flew away with them through the air—it was inexpressibly lovely. Eldermother had suddenly become a pretty little girl, but her dress was still of the same green cloth covered in white flowers that Eldermother had worn; on her breast she had a real elder-flower and about her fair curly hair a whole wreath of them; her eyes were big and blue—oh, she was so lovely to look at! She and the boy kissed, and there they were, both of the same age and sharing the same pleasures.

They walked hand in hand out of the arbour, and now they were standing in the beautiful flower-garden at home. There by the fresh green lawn was father's walking-stick tethered to a stake; for the children there was life in that stick—as soon as they sat astride it, the shiny knob turned into a splendid whinnying head, its long black mane streaming in the wind and four strong slender legs shooting out. The steed was strong and fiery: off they went round the lawn at a gallop—hurrah! 'Now we'll ride miles and miles away!' said the boy. 'We'll ride to the manor-house where we were last year!' They rode round and round the lawn, and as they did so the little girl, who, as we know, was none other than Eldermother, cried out, 'Now we're in the country! Can you see the farmhouse with its big baking-oven—it looks just like a great big egg sticking out of the wall towards the roadway! The elder-berry branches are leaning over it, and the cock's walking about scraping for the hens—look at the way he's strutting! Now we're by the church! It stands high on the hill among the great oak-trees, one of them half-dead! Now we're by the smithy with its fire burning and men, stripped to the waist, swinging their hammers and making the sparks fly all round them! Away, away to the fine manor!' And as the little girl who sat behind him on the stick talked, everything she spoke of flew past, and the boy saw it all, though they were only riding round the lawn. Then they played on the path and scratched a little garden in the soil; she took an elder-flower from her hair and planted it, and it grew—exactly like the one that had grown for the old people in Nyboder when they were young and that we heard about before. They walked hand in hand just as the old people had done when they were children, but not up the Round Tower, not to Frederiksberg gardens—no, the little girl took the boy round the waist and they flew all over Denmark. It was spring, and spring turned to summer; then it was autumn, and autumn changed into winter. A thousand pictures were reflected in the boy's eyes and heart, and all the time the little girl sang to him, 'That's something you will never forget!' And all through their flight the elder-tree smelled sweet and lovely. The boy noticed the roses and fresh beeches, of course, but the elder-tree smelled even more wonderfully than they did because its flowers hung against the little girl's heart, and there, as they flew, he would often lay his head.

'It's lovely here in the spring-time!' said the little girl as they stood in the beech-wood where the trees had burst into new leaf, the green woodruff smelling sweetly under their feet and the pale pink anemones looking lovely among the green. 'Oh, if only it were always spring-time in the sweet-scented Danish beech-woods!'

'It's lovely here in the summer!' she said as they passed by old manor-houses from the days when knights were bold, their red walls and stepped gables reflected in moats where swans were swimming and peering up cool old avenues. In the fields corn billowed like the sea, the ditches were covered in red and yellow flowers and the hedgerows with wild hops and flowering bindweed. In the evening, as the moon rose big and round, the haystacks in the meadows smelled sweetly. 'No one could forget that!'

'It's lovely here in the autumn!' said the little girl. The sky seemed twice as high and blue; the woods took on the loveliest tints of red and yellow and green; the hounds were in full cry; whole flocks of wild fowl flew screeching over the barrow where brambles clung about the ancient stones; the sea was dark blue with white sails upon it; and in the barn sat old women, girls and children picking hops into a vat—the youngsters were singing ballads and the old folk were telling fairy-tales of goblins and trolls. 'What could be better!'

'It's lovely here in the winter!' said the little girl. All the trees stood covered in frost and looking like white coral, the snow crackled underfoot as if you had new boots on all the time, and shooting-stars fell from the sky one after another. In the living-room the Christmas-tree was lit, and there were presents and good humour everywhere. Out in the country the sound of the violin came from the farmhouse where doughnuts were thrown for all to scramble for—even the poorest child could say, 'It's really lovely in winter!'

Yes, it was lovely, and the little girl showed the boy everything, and all the time the elder-tree smelled sweetly and the red flag with the white cross, the flag the old seaman in Nyboder had sailed under, fluttered in the breeze. The boy grew into a lad, and the time came for him to go out into the wide world, far away to the warm lands where coffee grows. And as they parted, the little girl took an elder-flower from her breast and gave it to him to keep. He put it in his hymn-book, and whenever he opened the book while he was in foreign lands, it was always at the place where the keepsake lay, and the more he looked at it, the fresher it grew—he would seem to smell the perfume of the Danish woods, and he would see, quite clearly, the little girl peeping from among the petals with her bright blue eyes, and then she would whisper, 'It's lovely here in spring-time, in summer, in harvest-time and winter!' and hundreds of pictures would flit through his thoughts.

And so many years passed by, and he was now an old man sitting with his old wife under a flowering tree: they were holding one another by the hand, just as great-grandfather and great-grandmother had done over in Nyboder, and they were talking just like them of the old days and their golden-wedding. The little girl with the blue eyes and the elder-flower in her hair was sitting up in the tree: she nodded to them both and said, 'Today's your golden-wedding day!' Then she took two of the flowers from her wreath and kissed them: they shone first like silver, then like gold, and as she placed them on the old people's heads, each flower became a golden crown. There they both sat like a king and queen under that sweet-scented tree that looked every bit like an elder, and he told his old wife the story of Eldermother just as he had been told it when he was a little boy, and they both thought there was a great deal in it that was like their own story, and those were the parts they liked best.

'Yes, that's how it is!' said the little girl in the tree. 'Some call me Eldermother, others call me a dryad, but my real name is Memory. Here I am sitting in the tree as it grows and grows: I can remember everything, I can tell you everything! Let me see if you still have your flower!'

The old man opened his hymn-book: there lay the elder-flower as fresh as if it had only just been put there. Memory nodded, and the two old people with their golden crowns on sat there in the red evening sun: they shut their eyes, and—and then—yes, that was the end of the story!

The little boy lay in his bed, not knowing whether he had dreamed it or heard the story told. The tea-pot was standing on the table, but there was no elder-tree growing out of it and the old man who had been telling the story was just about to go out of the door—and out he went.

'That was lovely!' said the little boy. 'Mother, I've been in hot countries!'

'I'm not at all surprised!' said his mother. 'When you've got two great cups of elder-tea inside you, you must expect to find yourself in hot countries!'—And she covered him up well so that he should not catch a chill. 'You were asleep while I sat arguing with him whether it were a true story or a fairy-tale!'

'Where's Eldermother?' asked the boy.

'She's in the tea-pot!' said his mother. 'And there she can stay!'

The Darning-Needle

THERE was once a darning-needle who put on such airs that she imagined herself a sewing-needle.

'Now just you mind what you're holding!' said the darning-needle to the fingers as they picked her up. 'Don't drop me! If I should fall on to the floor, I'm quite likely never to be found again, I'm so fine!'

'Well, I wouldn't go as far as that!' said the fingers, as they held her tightly round the waist.

'Look, I'm coming with my train!' said the darning-needle, pulling a long thread after her—but it had no knot in it.

The fingers guided the needle straight towards the kitchen-maid's slipper, which had a tear in the uppers that now had to be sewn up.

'What common work!' said the darning-needle. 'I shall never go through that! I shall snap! I shall snap!'—And snap she did. 'Didn't I tell you so!' said the darning-needle. 'I'm much too fine!'

'She's no good for anything now!' thought the fingers, but they had to keep hold of her while the kitchen-maid dropped a spot of sealing-wax on her and stuck her in the front of her scarf.

'Look, I'm a brooch now!' said the darning-needle. 'I always knew I should rise to a high position! When you are something, you always will be something!' Then she laughed inwardly—you will never see a darning-needle laugh outwardly. There she sat, as proud as if she were riding in her own carriage, and looked all round her.

'May I have the honour of asking if you're made of gold?' she inquired of the pin who was her neighbour. 'You've a handsome appearance, and your own head, too, though it's a small one! You must see to it that it grows, for we can't all be topped with sealing-wax!' And with that, the darning-needle drew herself up so proudly that she came right out of the scarf and fell into the sink just as the kitchen-maid was rinsing it out.

'Now we're going on our travels!' said the darning-needle. 'If only I don't get lost!' But she did.

'I'm too fine for this world!' she said, as she lay in the gutter. 'But I'm very conscious of what I am, and there's always some pleasure in that!' And as she spoke, the darning-needle held herself upright and refused to lose her good humour.

All kinds of things went sailing by overhead, sticks and straws and bits of newspaper. 'Look at them sailing along!' said the darning-needle. 'They little know what's hidden underneath them! I am, and here I lie! Look, there goes a stick thinking of nothing in the world but "stick", and that's himself. There's a straw floating along—look at it swaying and turning! Don't think so much of yourself—you might run into the kerb!—And here comes a newspaper drifting past!—Everything in it's forgotten, but it spreads itself out and shows off all the same!—And here am I lying here quietly and patiently! I know what I am, and nothing can change that!'

One day there was something shining very prettily near

by, and the darning-needle thought it must be a diamond. But it was a bit of broken glass, and as it glittered, the darning-needle spoke to it, introducing herself as a brooch. 'You must be a diamond?'—'Yes, something of the sort!' So each believed the other to be very valuable, and they talked of how much pride there was in the world.

'Yes, I've been living in a casket at a young lady's house,' said the darning-needle, 'and the young lady was a kitchen-maid. She had five fingers on each hand, but I've never known anything quite so conceited as those five fingers—and yet they were only there to hold me and take me out of my casket and put me back again.'

'Were they at all brilliant?' asked the bit of broken glass.

'Brilliant!' said the darning-needle. 'Oh, no, but they were proud enough! They were five brothers, all born "Fingers", and they stuck very close together, though they differed in height. The first, Tom Thumb, was short and stout and something of an outsider. He had only one joint in his back and so he could bow only in one place, but he used to say if a man had him chopped off he was quite unfit for military service. Lickpot dipped into bitter and sweet and pointed at sun and moon, and it was he who held the pen tight whenever they were writing. Longman looked over the others' heads, Goldbrand wore a gold ring round his stomach, and little Peter Playboy did nothing at all and was proud of it. But it was all boasting, nothing but boasting, and so I fell into the sink!'

'And now here we sit and glitter!' said the bit of glass, but at that moment a rush of water overflowed the gutter and washed it away.

'Well, it's been moved higher up now,' said the darning-needle, 'and I'm left behind! I'm too fine—but I'm proud of it, and a proper pride it is!' And there she lay, stiff and upright, thinking many thoughts.

'I could almost believe I was born of a sunbeam, I'm so fine; and doesn't the sun always seem to be looking for me under the water? Ah, I'm so fine my mother can't find me—if I had my old eye that snapped off, I think I could cry—except that I wouldn't do it: crying's not refined.'

One day some street-urchins lay poking about in the gutter where they found old nails, pennies and such things. They made themselves filthy, but they enjoyed it.

'Aw!' said one as he pricked himself on the darning-needle. 'There's a fine fellow for you!'

'I'm not a fellow; I'm a young lady!' said the darning-needle, but no one was listening. The sealing-wax had worn off and she had turned black, but black is slimming and so she thought she was finer than ever.

'Here comes an egg-shell sailing along!' said the boys, and so they stuck the darning-needle firmly into the shell.

'White walls and myself in black!' said the darning-needle. 'That's very smart! Everyone will see me now! —If only I'm not sea-sick: I shall snap if I am!'—But she wasn't sea-sick, and she didn't snap.

'A steel stomach's good for sea-sickness, and then one must always remember one is a little above the common run of people! The sickness has quite gone now—the finer one is, the more one can stand!'

'Crack!' said the egg-shell as a loaded wagon went over it. 'Ooh, how it squeezes!' said the darning-needle. Now I shall be sea-sick! I'm snapping! I'm snapping!' But she didn't snap although a loaded wagon had gone over her: she was lying full length on the ground—and there she can stay!

The Red Shoes

THERE was once a little girl who was very pretty and dainty, but in the summer-time she always had to go barefoot because she was poor, and in the winter she wore big wooden clogs that made her little ankles quite red—and that looked dreadful.

In the middle of the village lived old Mother Cobbler; she sat and sewed a pair of little shoes as well as she could out of old strips of red cloth—they were very clumsy, but they were well meant and the little girl was to have them. The little girl was called Karen.

She got the red shoes and had them on for the first time the very day her mother was buried. They were hardly the right thing for mourning, but then she had no others, and so with them on her bare feet she walked behind the poor coffin.

Then at that moment a large old carriage came by, and in it there sat a large old lady: she looked at the little girl

and felt sorry for her, and so she said to the parson,
'Listen, give that little girl to me and I'll be good to her!'

And Karen thought it was all on account of her red
shoes, but the old lady said they were dreadful and so
they were burnt. Karen was dressed in neat clean clothes
and she had to learn to read and sew: people said she was
pretty, but the mirror said, 'You're much more than
pretty—you're beautiful!'

Then one day the queen was travelling through the
land, and with her she had her little daughter who was a
princess. Streams of people came and stood outside the
palace, and Karen was there, too. The little princess,
dressed in white, stood at a window to let herself be
seen: she had neither train nor golden crown, but she did
have lovely red morocco-leather shoes—they were quite
different from the ones Mother Cobbler had made for
little Karen. There was nothing in the world like red
shoes!

Karen was now old enough to be confirmed. She was
given new clothes, and she was to have new shoes as well.
The wealthy shoemaker in the town took the measure-
ments of her little foot: he did it at home in his own
sitting-room where large glass-fronted cupboards stood
full of beautiful shoes and shining boots. They looked
lovely, but the old lady could not see very well and so
she found little pleasure in them. Right in the middle of
the shoes stood a pair of red ones, just like those the
princess had worn—how beautiful they were! And the
shoemaker said they had been made for the daughter of a
count but had not fitted.

'They must be made of very highly polished leather!'
said the old lady. 'Look at the way they shine!'

'Yes, they shine beautifully!' said Karen. They fitted
her and they were bought—but the old lady did not know

they were red, for she would never have allowed Karen to be confirmed in red shoes. But that is just what happened.

Everybody looked at her feet, and, as she walked up the aisle towards the choir, even the old pictures on the tombs, portraits of parsons and their wives in starched ruffs and long black gowns, seemed to her to fix their eyes upon her red shoes. They were all she thought about. The parson laid his hand upon her head and spoke to her of holy baptism and her covenant with God; he told her that she must now be a good Christian; the organ played solemnly and the sweet voices of the children were raised in song and the old choir-master sang with them—but the red shoes were all that Karen thought about.

During the afternoon everybody told the old lady that Karen had had red shoes on, and she said it was very naughty and most improper and in future when Karen went to church, she must always go in black shoes, even if they were old ones.

The next Sunday there was communion. Karen looked at the black shoes and she looked at the red ones—and then she looked at the red ones again and put them on. It was lovely bright sunny weather and Karen and the old lady walked along the path through the corn-fields which were rather dusty.

By the church door stood an old soldier with a crutch and a strange long beard: it was more red than white—in fact, it was quite red. He bowed right down to the ground and asked the old lady whether he might dust her shoes. And Karen stretched out her little foot, too. 'What pretty dancing-shoes!' said the soldier. 'Stay fast when you dance!' And as he spoke, he patted the soles of her shoes.

The old lady gave the soldier a small coin and went into the church with Karen.

Everybody present looked at Karen's red shoes, and all the pictures looked at them, and as Karen knelt before the altar and put the golden chalice to her mouth, the red shoes were all she was thinking of and they seemed to be swimming round the chalice in front of her—she forgot to sing the hymn: she forgot to say the Lord's Prayer.

Now they all came out of church, and the old lady stepped into her carriage. As Karen raised her foot to step in after her, the old soldier who was standing close by said, 'What pretty dancing-shoes!' Then Karen could not help dancing a few steps, and once she had begun, her legs went on dancing as if the shoes had some power over them. She danced round the corner of the church and she could not stop. The coachman had to run after her and take hold of her: he lifted her into the carriage, but her feet went on dancing and she kicked the good old lady dreadfully. At last they got her shoes off and her legs lay quiet.

When they got home, the shoes were put away in a cupboard, but Karen could not help going to look at them.

The old lady now lay ill and they said she would not live. She had to be nursed and looked after, and if it was anybody's duty to do this, it was Karen's. But there was a great ball in the town, and Karen was invited. She looked at the old lady, who would not live long anyway; she looked at the red shoes, and thought there could be no harm—she put the red shoes on: she could surely do that. —But then she went to the ball and began to dance.

But when she wanted to turn to the right, the shoes danced to the left; and when she wanted to go up the room, the shoes danced down the room, down the stairs, through the street and out of the town gate. Dance she did and dance she had to, right out into the dark woods.

Then she saw something shining among the trees, and she thought it was the moon for she could see a face, but it was the old soldier with the red beard. He was sitting and nodding his head, and he said, 'Look at those pretty dancing-shoes!'

Then she was frightened and wanted to pull the red

shoes off but they were stuck fast; she tore her stockings off, but the shoes had grown to her feet: and dance she did and dance she had to over field and meadow, in rain and sunshine, by night and by day—but it was most terrifying at night.

She danced into the open churchyard, but the dead there were not dancing—they had something much better to do than dance. She wanted to sit down on the pauper's grave where the bitter tansy grew, but there was neither rest nor peace for her, and, as she danced towards the open church door, she saw an angel there in long white robes and with wings that reached from his shoulders down to the ground. His face was stern and serious and in his hand he held a sword, broad and shining.

'Dance you shall!' he said. 'You shall dance in your red shoes till you grow pale and cold, till your skin shrinks and your body is like a skeleton! You shall dance from door to door and wherever vain, conceited children live, you shall knock that they may hear you and be afraid! Dance you shall, dance—'

'Mercy!' cried Karen. But she did not hear what the angel answered for the shoes carried her through the gate, out into the fields, along highways and byways, and still she had to go on dancing.

Early one morning she danced by a door she knew well: from within came the sound of hymn-singing, and a coffin, decorated with flowers, was carried out. Then she knew the old lady was dead, and she felt herself forsaken by all and cursed by the angel of God.

Dance she did and dance she had to, dance through the dark night. The shoes carried her away through thorn and stubble where she tore herself till the blood ran. Away she danced over the heath to a little lonely house. Here she knew the executioner lived, and she tapped on the window with her fingers and said, 'Come out! Come out!—I can't come in because I'm dancing!'

And the executioner said, 'You surely don't know who I am? I cut off the heads of wicked men, and I can feel my axe quivering!'

'Don't cut my head off!' said Karen. 'For then I can't repent of my sin! But cut off my feet and the red shoes with them!'

And then she confessed all her sins, and the executioner cut off her feet and her red shoes with them; but the shoes, with her little feet inside them, danced away over the fields into the deep forest.

He carved wooden feet for her and made her a pair of crutches; he taught her a hymn that sinners always sing, and she kissed the hand that had wielded the axe and went away over the heath.

'I've suffered enough now for the red shoes!' she said. 'I'll go to church now so that they can see me!' And she walked as fast as she could towards the church door, but as she came near, the red shoes danced in front of her and she was frightened and turned away.

The whole week through she was sad and shed many heavy tears, but when Sunday came she said, 'There now! Now I've suffered and striven enough! I expect I'm just as good as many of those that sit and hold their heads high in church!' And so she plucked up courage and went, but she got no farther than the gate when she saw the red shoes dancing in front of her: she turned back in terror, repenting her sin deep in her heart.

She went over to the vicarage and asked if she could go into service there. She would work hard and do all she could; she did not mind about wages as long as she had a roof over her head and could live with good people. The parson's wife took pity on her and took her into service, and she was hard-working and grateful. In the evening she would sit quietly and listen to the parson reading aloud from the Bible. The children were all fond of her, but when they talked of fine clothes and dressing up and looking as lovely as a queen, she would shake her head.

The next Sunday, when they were all going to church, they asked her if she would like to go with them, but with tears in her eyes she looked sadly at her crutches, and so the others went to hear God's word while she went alone to her own little room. It was just big enough to hold a bed and a chair, and there she sat down with her hymn-book, and as she was reading in it with a devout heart, the wind carried the sound of the organ over to her from the church. She raised her tear-stained face and said, 'Oh God, help me!'

The sun shone brightly and right in front of her stood the angel of God in his white robes, the one she had seen that night in the church door. But he was no longer holding his sharp sword: instead he carried a lovely green bough full of roses. With it he touched the ceiling and it rose to a great height, and where he had touched it there shone a golden star: he touched the walls and they opened out, and she saw the organ playing, she saw the old pictures of parsons and their wives. The congregation were sitting in their carved and painted pews, singing from their hymn-books.—For the church itself had come home to the poor girl in her narrow little room—or else she had gone to the church. She was sitting in the pew with the rest of the parson's family, and when the hymn came to an end and they looked up, they nodded and said, 'You did right to come, Karen!'

'It was through the grace of God!' she said.

The organ played and the voices of the children in the

choir sounded soft and sweet. Bright sunshine streamed warm through the window into the pew where Karen was sitting: her heart was so full of sunshine, of peace and joy, that it broke. Her soul flew on the sunshine up to God, and there there was no one who questioned her about her red shoes.

The Shepherdess and the Chimney-Sweep

HAVE you ever seen a really old cabinet, black with age and carved into scroll-work and foliage? One just like that used to stand in the living-room, handed down from great-grandmother and carved from top to bottom with roses and tulips: it had the oddest scrolls, and in between them small harts with spreading antlers poked their heads out. But in the middle of the cabinet the figure of a man was carved full length: he was really funny to look at—he was grinning himself: you could hardly call it laughing—for he had billy-goat's legs, small horns on his forehead and a long beard. The children of the house always used to call him 'Field-marshal-major-general-commander-sergeant Billy-Goat's Legs' because it was a difficult name to say and there are not many who are given that title—but then it was something of an honour to have him carved there like that. Anyway, there he was, and he was always looking over at the table under the mirror where there stood a beautiful little shepherdess made of porcelain: her shoes were gilt, her dress prettily looped up with a rose, and besides that she had a golden hat and a shepherd's crook—she

was lovely! Close by her stood a little chimney-sweep as
black as coal but nevertheless made of porcelain, too;
he was just as neat and clean as anyone else, and as for his
being a chimney-sweep, that was only something he was
supposed to be—the potter could just as well have made
a prince of him, for it was all the same to him.

He stood there very charmingly with his ladder, his
face pink and white like a girl's—and that was a proper
mistake for he could very well have been a little black.
He stood quite close to the shepherdess: they had both
been put where they stood, and as they were now
permanently placed there, they had become engaged.
They were well suited to each other—they were
both young, made of the same china clay and equally
fragile.

Close by them stood yet another figure, three times as
big: it was an old Chinaman who could nod his head.
He was made of porcelain, too, and said he was the little
shepherdess's grandfather, but this he could not prove.
He insisted, however, that he was responsible for her,
and so he had nodded his consent to Field-marshal-major-
general-commander-sergeant Billy-Goat's Legs who had
proposed to her.

'There you'll have a husband,' said the old Chinaman,
'a husband who, I'm almost certain, is made of mahogany.
He can make you Lady-field-marshal-major-general-com-
mander-sergeant Billy-Goat's Legs, and he's a whole
cupboard full of silver, besides what he has tucked away
in secret drawers.'

'I'm not going into that dark cupboard!' said the little
shepherdess. 'I've heard tell that he's eleven porcelain
wives in there already!'

'Then you can be the twelfth!' said the Chinaman.
'Tonight as soon as the old cupboard creaks you shall be

married, as sure as I'm a Chinaman!' And with that he nodded his head and fell asleep.

But the little shepherdess wept and looked at her beloved, the porcelain chimney-sweep.

'I think I'll ask you,' she said, 'to go out into the wide world with me, for we can't stay here!'

'I'll do everything you wish,' said the little chimney-sweep. 'Let's go straight away—I'm sure I can earn you a living by my trade!'

'If only we were safely down from the table!' she said. 'I shan't be happy until we're out in the wide world!'

And he comforted her and showed her where to put her little foot on the carved edges and the gilt foliage round the table leg. He made use of his ladder to help, too, and so at last they were down on the floor, but as they looked over at the old cabinet there was such a commotion—the carved harts were all poking their heads farther out, raising their antlers and turning their necks round as Field-marshal-major-general-commander-sergeant Billy-Goat's Legs sprang high in the air and shouted over to the old Chinaman, 'They're running away! They're running away!'

Then they were a little frightened and quickly jumped into the drawer under the window-seat.

Here lay three or four incomplete packs of cards and a little toy theatre which had been set up as well as possible. A play was going on, and all the queens—diamonds and hearts, clubs and spades—were sitting in the front row fanning themselves with their tulips. The knaves were standing behind them, each with two heads, one at the top and one at the bottom—playing-cards are like that. The play was about two people in love who were prevented from being together, and the shepherdess wept over it because it was just like her own story.

'I can't bear any more of it!' she said. 'I must get out

T

of the drawer!' But when they reached the floor and looked up at the table, the old Chinaman had woken up and was rocking his whole body—the lower part of him was all in one piece.

'The old Chinaman's coming!' screamed the little shepherdess, and she was so distressed she fell right down on her porcelain knees.

'I've an idea!' said the chimney-sweep. 'Let's creep inside that big pot-pourri jar that stands in the corner: we can lie down among the roses and the lavender and throw salt in his eyes if he comes!'

'That won't be any good!' she said. 'Besides, I happen to know the old Chinaman and the pot-pourri jar were once engaged, and when two people have been as close as that there's always some sympathy left between them. No, there's nothing else for it but to go out into the wide world!'

'Have you really enough courage to go out into the wide world with me?' asked the chimney-sweep. 'Have you thought how big it is and that we could never come back here again?'

'Yes, I have!' she said.

The chimney-sweep looked hard at her and then he said, 'The way I'm going is up the chimney! Have you really enough courage to crawl through the stove with me—through the body of the stove and the flue? Then we shall come out into the chimney, and once there I know what I'm about! We shall climb so high they won't be able to reach us, and right at the top there's a hole that leads out into the wide world!'

And he led her across to the stove door.

'It looks very black!' she said, but she went with him, through the body of the stove and the flue, where the darkness was like a pitch-black night.

'Now we're in the chimney!' he said. 'Look! Look! There's the loveliest star shining right over our heads!'

And there really was a star in the sky shining right down on them as if to show them the way. They crawled and they crept—a dreadful journey it was, up and up, higher and higher. But he lifted her and helped her up, he held her and showed her the best places to put her little porcelain feet, and so at last they got right up to the top of the chimney, and there they sat down, for they were very tired, as well they might be.

The sky with all its stars was over their heads and below them all the roofs of the town; they could see far and wide all round them, right out into the wide world; the poor shepherdess had never imagined it was anything like that—she laid her little head on her chimney-sweep's shoulder and wept so bitterly that the gilt came off her sash.

'It's too much!' she said. 'I can't bear it! The world is much too big! If only I were back again on the little table under the mirror! I shall never be happy until I'm there again! I've followed you out into the wide world, and now, if you really love me, please follow me home again!'

The chimney-sweep spoke to her sensibly, reminding her of the old Chinaman and Field-marshal-major-general-commander-sergeant Billy-Goat's Legs, but she sobbed so pitifully and kissed her little chimney-sweep so that he could do nothing but give in to her, foolish though it was.

So they crawled back again with great difficulty down the chimney and they crept through the flue, which wasn't at all pleasant, and at last they found themselves standing in the dark stove. There they hid behind the door to find out how things stood in the living-room. It was quite still: they peeped out—oh dear, there in the middle of the floor lay the old Chinaman! He had fallen down off the table as he attempted to go after them, and now he lay broken into three pieces: the whole of his back had come off in one piece and his head lay where it had rolled into a corner. Field-marshal-major-general-commander-sergeant Billy-Goat's Legs was standing where he had always stood, and was deep in thought.

'It's dreadful!' said the little shepherdess. 'Old grandfather's broken to bits and it's our fault! I shall never get over it!' And she wrung her tiny little hands.

'He can be riveted, though!' said the chimney-sweep. 'He can be riveted perfectly well!—Now don't get so excited about it! When they've glued his back together and put a good rivet in his neck, he'll be as good as new again and quite able to say all sorts of disagreeable things to us!'

'Do you think so?' she said. And then they climbed up on to the table again where they had stood before.

'Well, we've been a long way!' said the chimney-sweep. 'And we might have spared ourselves the trouble!'

'If only old grandfather were riveted!' said the shepherdess. 'Will it be very expensive?'

But he was riveted. The family had his back glued on, a good rivet was put in his neck, and he was as good as new, but he could no longer nod his head.

'You've grown pretty proud since you were broken to bits!' said Field-marshal-major-general-commander-sergeant Billy-Goat's Legs. 'But it doesn't strike me you've got so much to be proud of! Well, am I going to have her, or aren't I?'

The chimney-sweep and the little shepherdess looked very anxiously at the old Chinaman. They were very much afraid he would nod, but he couldn't, and he found it very disagreeable to tell a stranger that he had a permanent rivet in his neck. And so the porcelain pair were left together, and they blessed grandfather's rivet and loved each other until they broke to pieces.

The Little Match-Girl

IT was so dreadfully cold! It was snowing, and the evening was beginning to darken. It was the last evening of the year, too—New Year's Eve. Through the cold and the dark, a poor little girl with bare head and naked feet was wandering along the road. She had, indeed, had a pair of slippers on when she left home: but what was the good of that? They were very big slippers—her mother had worn them last, they were so big—and the little child had lost them hurrying across the road as two carts rattled dangerously past. One slipper could not be found, and a boy ran off with the other—he said he could use it as a cradle when he had children of his own.

So the little girl wandered along with her naked little feet red and blue with cold. She was carrying a great pile of matches in an old apron and she held one bundle in her hand as she walked. No one had bought a thing from her the whole day; no one had given her a halfpenny; hungry and frozen, she went her way, looking so woe-begone, poor little thing! The snow-flakes fell upon her long fair hair that curled so prettily about the nape of her neck, but she certainly wasn't thinking of how nice she looked. Lights were shining from all the windows, and there was a lovely smell of roast goose all down the street, for it was indeed New Year's Eve—yes, and that's what she was thinking about.

Over in a corner between two houses, where one jutted a little farther out into the street than the other, she sat down and huddled together; she had drawn her little legs up under her, but she felt more frozen than ever, and she dared not go home, for she had sold no matches and hadn't got a single penny, and her father would beat her. Besides, it was cold at home, too: there was only the roof over them, and the wind whistled in, although the biggest cracks had been stopped up with straw and rags. Her little hands were almost dead with cold. Ah, a little match might do some good! If she only dared pull one out of the bundle, strike it on the wall, and warm her fingers! She drew one out— Whoosh!—How it spluttered! How it burnt! It gave a warm bright flame, just

like a little candle, when she held her hand round it. It was a wonderful light: the little girl thought she was sitting in front of a great iron stove with polished brass knobs and fittings; the fire was burning so cheerfully and its warmth was so comforting—oh, what was that! The little girl had just stretched her feet out to warm them, too, when—the fire went out! The stove disappeared—and she was sitting there with the little stump of a burnt-out match in her hand. Another match was struck; it burnt and flared, and where the light fell upon it, the wall became transparent like gauze; she could see right into the room where the table stood covered with a shining white cloth and set with fine china, and there was a roast goose, stuffed with prunes and apples, steaming deliciously—but what was more gorgeous still, the goose jumped off the dish, waddled across the floor with knife and fork in its back, and went straight over to the poor girl. Then the match went out, and there was nothing to see but the thick cold wall.

She struck yet another. And then she was sitting beneath the loveliest Christmas-tree; it was even bigger and more beautifully decorated than the one she had seen this last Christmas through the glass doors of the wealthy grocer's shop. Thousands of candles were burning on its green branches, and gaily coloured pictures, like those that had decorated the shop-windows, were looking down at her. The little girl stretched out both her hands—and then the match went out; the multitude of Christmas-candles rose higher and higher, and now she saw they were the bright stars—one of them fell and made a long streak of fire across the sky.

'Someone's now dying!' said the little girl, for her old granny, who was the only one that had been kind to her, but who was now dead, had said that when a star falls a soul goes up to God.

Once more she struck a match on the wall. It lit up the darkness round about her, and in its radiance stood old granny, so bright and shining, so wonderfully kind.

'Granny!' cried the little girl. 'Oh, take me with you! I know you'll go away when the match goes out—you'll go away just like the warm stove and the lovely roast goose and the wonderful big Christmas-tree!'—And she hastily struck all the rest of the matches in the bundle, for she wanted to keep her granny there, and the matches shone with such brilliance that it was brighter than daylight. Granny had never before been so tall and beautiful; she lifted the little girl up on her arm, and they flew away in splendour and joy, high, high up towards heaven.

And there was no more cold and no more hunger and no more fear—they were with God.

But in the corner by the house, in the cold of the early morning, the little girl sat, with red cheeks and a smile upon her lips—dead, frozen to death on the last evening of the old year. The morning of the New Year rose over the little dead body sitting there with her matches, one bundle nearly all burnt out. She wanted to keep herself warm, they said; but no one knew what beautiful things she had seen, nor in what radiance she had gone with her old granny into the joy of the New Year.

The Old Street Lamp

HAVE you ever heard the story of the old street lamp? It really isn't so extraordinarily amusing, but it will always bear listening to once. There was an honest old street lamp which for many, many years had given good service but now had to retire. It was the last evening it would sit on its post and shine there in the street, and it felt like an old ballet-dancer giving her last performance and knowing that tomorrow she would be on the shelf. The lamp felt just that kind of dread at the thought of the next day, because then, it knew, it would have to appear for the first time in its life at the Town Hall, and the Town Council would have to consider whether it were still serviceable or not. It would then be decided whether it should be sent out to one of the suburbs to give light there or to a factory in the country—perhaps it would go straight to an iron-foundry to be melted down, and then, of course, it might be turned into anything; and it was worried because it did not know whether it would still remember that it had once been a street lamp. But whatever happened, it would be parted from the watchman and his wife whom it quite looked upon as its family. It had been made a lamp when he was made watchman. At that time his wife had thought rather a lot of herself: only during the evening did she look at the lamp as she walked past—never in the day-time. During those last years, however, when they had all three grown old, the watchman, his wife and the lamp, she had looked after it, too—she had polished the lamp and filled it with oil. Honest folk they were, the man and his wife: they had never cheated the lamp of a single drop. It was its last evening in the street, and the next day it would have to go to the Town Hall: those were the two dark thoughts in the lamp's mind, and so you can imagine how it burnt. But other thoughts passed through its mind, too: there was so much it had seen, so much that had given it pleasure—perhaps just as much as the Mayor and Corporation had experienced, but it did not say so, for it was an honest old lamp and would not offend anyone, least of all the powers that be. It remembered so much, and now and then the flame would flare up inside it as if it felt that it would be remembered, too. 'There was that handsome young man, many years ago now, who

came by with a letter—a letter on the finest rose-pink paper with gilt edges and beautifully written in a lady's hand. He read it through twice and kissed it, and then he looked up at me with eyes that said, "I'm the happiest man in the world!"—Only he and I knew what was written in that first letter from his beloved.—I remember, too, another pair of eyes—it's odd how one's thoughts jump from one thing to another! There was a magnificent funeral here in the street—a beautiful young lady lay in her coffin in a hearse draped with velvet; there were so many flowers and wreaths and so many flaring torches that I was quite overcome by it; the whole pavement was crowded with people all walking in the funeral procession. But when the torches were out of sight and I looked round me, one of the mourners still stood leaning against my post and weeping—I shall never forget those two eyes full of sorrow as they looked up at me!'—Many thoughts like these passed through the mind of the old street lamp as it shone that evening for the last time. The sentry, when he is relieved, at least knows the man who is taking over from him and can pass a few words with him, but the lamp did not know what would take its place, and that was a pity, for it could have given it a tip or two about rain and rough weather and told it how far across the pavement the moonlight would reach and from what corner the wind would blow.

On the kerb stood three who had presented themselves before the lamp in the belief that it had the choosing of its own successor. One of these three was a herring's head: it shone in the dark and it considered it would be a real saving of oil if it were appointed to the lamp-post. The second was a bit of rotten wood: it shone, too, and, as it said itself, better at least than a dried codfish. Moreover, it was the last bit of a tree that had once been the pride of the forest. The third was a glow-worm. Where it had come from the lamp had no idea, but there it was, and giving light, too, though the bit of rotten wood and the herring's head took their oath upon it that it shone only at certain times and could not therefore be considered.

The old lamp said that none of them shone brightly enough to be a street lamp, but this they refused to believe, and when they heard that the lamp did not make the appointment, they said it was just as well since it was obviously much too doddery to make a proper choice.

At that moment, the wind came whistling from the corner of the street through the old lamp's cowl and said,

'What on earth is this I hear? Are you really leaving us tomorrow? Is this the last evening I shall meet you here? Well then, you must have a present! I'll air your brains and then you'll be so clear-headed you will not only remember clearly everything you've seen and heard, but you'll be able to see, as if it were actually happening, whatever's spoken or read about in your presence!'

'Well, that's wonderful!' said the old street lamp. 'Thank you very much! If only I'm not melted down!'

'That won't happen yet,' said the wind. 'And now I'll blow into you and refresh your memory—if you can get more gifts like this, you'll be able to enjoy a very pleasant old age!'

'If only I'm not melted down!' said the lamp. 'Or can you preserve my memory even if I am?'

'Now be reasonable, old lamp!' said the wind as it blew. At that moment the moon came out. 'What are you going to give the lamp?' asked the wind.

'I shan't give it anything!' it said. 'I'm on the wane, as you can see. The lamps have never shone for me, but I've shone for them!' And with that the moon went behind the clouds again for it did not want to be bothered. Then a drop of water fell right on the cowl: it looked as if it had dripped off the roof, but it said it came from the grey clouds and was a gift, too—perhaps the best of all. 'I shall penetrate into you and then you'll have the power, whenever you wish, to rust through in one night. Then you'll disintegrate and be nothing but dust.' But the lamp thought that was a poor gift and the wind thought so, too. 'Is there nothing better, nothing better than that?' it cried, blowing as hard as it could. Then a bright shooting-star fell, leaving a long trail of light behind it.

'What was that?' cried the herring's head. 'Wasn't that a star falling down? I think it went into the lamp!—Ah, well, if we're up against that sort of competition for the job, we may as well clear off and go to bed!' And that's what it did—and the others with it. But the old lamp at once shone with a wonderful brightness: 'That was a lovely gift!' it said. 'The bright stars that have always given me so much pleasure and shine so much more beautifully than I've ever really been able to—even though I've put all my effort into it—have taken notice of me, poor old lamp that I am, and one of them has been sent down with a gift for me, the power to make those I love see everything that I myself remember and see so clearly! And that's the only true happiness there is, for a joy's only half a joy if you can't share it with others!'

'The thought does you credit!' said the wind. 'But perhaps you don't know that you need a wax candle. Unless a wax candle is lighted inside you, you won't be able to make the others see what you can. The stars didn't think of that—they think everything that shines has at least one wax candle in it. But I'm tired now,' said the wind. 'I want to lie down!' And lie down it did.

The next day—well, we can pass over the next day: the next evening then, the lamp was lying in an armchair, and where do you think it was?—In the old watchman's room. He had asked the Mayor and Corporation if he might, in view of his long and faithful service, keep the old lamp. They laughed when he made this request and gave it to him, and now the lamp lay in an armchair close by the warm stove—it really seemed to have grown bigger as a result, for it all but filled the chair. The old couple sat at supper and glanced kindly at the lamp as if they would willingly have made room for it at the table. It was a basement they lived in, four feet below the surface of the ground; you had to go through a paved entrance to get into the room, but it was cosy inside for there were strips of cloth fastened round the door. Everything was neat and clean; there were curtains round the bed and in front of the little windows, and on the window-sills stood two strange flower-pots. Christian the sailor had brought them home from the East or West Indies: they were two china elephants and where their backs should have been they were filled with earth; fine chives grew in one of them—that was the old couple's kitchen-garden—and a large flowering geranium in the other—and that was their flower-garden. On the wall hung a large coloured picture of the Congress of Vienna where they had all the kings and emperors gathered together. A Bornholm clock with heavy lead weights went 'Tick-tock! Tick-tock!' It always went fast, but that was better, the old couple would say, than going slow. They ate their supper, and the old street lamp lay, as we said, in the armchair close by the warm stove. The lamp felt as if the whole world had been turned upside down. But when the old watchman looked at it and spoke of what they two had been through together, in rain and rough weather, in the bright brief summer nights, and when the snow drifted down so that it was good to get back to the shelter of the basement, then the old lamp felt that everything was in place again—it saw it all as if it were still taking place: yes, the wind had indeed made its memory burn bright.

They were so careful and hard-working, that old couple,

that not an hour was entirely wasted. On Sunday after-
noons a book would be brought out, preferably a book
of travels, and the old man would read aloud about
Africa with its great forests and its elephants that roamed

about wild, and the old woman would listen to him and
steal a glance at the china elephants that served as flower-
pots. 'I can almost see it!' she would say. And the lamp
would wish so deeply that a wax candle were lit and
placed inside it so that she could see everything exactly
as the lamp saw it—the tall trees, the close interwoven
branches, the naked black men on horseback, and whole
herds of elephants crushing reeds and bushes under their
broad feet.

'What's the use of all my gifts when there are no wax

candles!' sighed the lamp. 'They've only oil and tallow candles, and they're not good enough!'

One day a whole bundle of wax candle stumps appeared in the basement: the biggest bits were burnt and the old woman used the smallest to wax her thread when she was sewing. There were wax candles now, but it did not occur to them to put a little bit in the lamp.

'Here I stand with all my rare gifts!' said the lamp. 'I've everything within me, but I can't share it with them! You don't know that I can change these white walls into the loveliest tapestries, into rich forests, into anything you wish!—You don't know that!'

Meanwhile, the lamp stood neatly polished in a corner where it always caught the eye. People said, naturally enough, that it was a cumbersome old thing, but the old couple took no notice—they were fond of the lamp.

One day—it was the old watchman's birthday—the old woman went over to the lamp, smiled a little and said, 'I'll light up for him!' The lamp's tin hat cracked with excitement, for it thought, 'Now they'll really see!' But oil was put in it, not a wax candle: it burnt right through the evening, but it now knew that the gift the stars had given it—the best gift of all—was a hidden treasure as far as this life goes. Then it fell into a dream—and when you have gifts like that you can certainly dream: it dreamed the old couple were dead and that it was itself sent to an iron-foundry to be melted down. It felt just as nervous as when it had to appear at the Town Hall to be considered by the Council, but although it possessed the power to disintegrate into rust and dust whenever it wished, yet it made no use of it, and so it found itself in the smelting-oven and was made into the loveliest candlestick anyone could wish to put a wax candle in. It was shaped like an angel carrying a bouquet. The wax candle

U

was put in the middle of the bouquet, and the candle-stick was placed on a green writing-table. The room was very comfortable; there were many books and there were lovely pictures on the walls: it was a poet's room and everything that he thought and wrote seemed to un-fold itself there—the room changed into a deep dark forest, a sunlit meadow where the stork strutted, the deck of a ship high above the swell of the sea.

'What rare gifts I have!' said the old lamp as it woke up. 'I could almost long to be melted down!—But no, that mustn't happen as long as the old couple are alive! They're fond of me for my own sake! I'm really like a child to them: they've scoured me and given me oil, and I live as comfortably as the Congress in the picture there —and they're dignified enough!'

From that time the honest old street lamp had more peace within itself, and it thoroughly deserved it.

The Old House

ACROSS the road there was an old, old house: it was nearly three hundred years old, as you could read for yourself on the beam where the date was carved along with tulips and hop-vines. Whole verses stood there in old-fashioned spelling, and in the beam over each window was carved a wry, mocking face. The upper storey projected a long way over the lower, and just under the roof was a lead gutter with a dragon's head on it: the rainwater was supposed to run out of its jaws, but actually it ran out of its belly, for there was a hole in the guttering.

All the other houses in the street were so new and so neat with their large window-panes and smooth walls, that it was easy to see they did not want to have anything to do with that old house. No doubt they thought, 'How long is that monstrosity going to cumber up the street! That top-front bay sticks out so far that no one can see from our windows what's happening on the other side of it! The steps are wide enough for a palace and high enough for a church tower. The iron railing certainly looks like the gateway to an old tomb, and it has brass knobs, too! It does look silly!'

The houses straight across the road were new and neat as well, and they thought like the others, but a little boy with fresh red cheeks and bright shining eyes was sitting at the window, and he definitely liked the old house best, both in sunshine and moonlight. And if he looked across at the wall where the plaster had peeled off, he could discover the most wonderful pictures from where he sat: he could see exactly how the street had looked long ago, with its steps and bay-windows and steep gables; he could see soldiers with their halberds, and gutterings that ran along under the roofs like dragons and serpents.—It really was a house worth looking at! An old man lived over there: he went about in knee-breeches, had a coat with big brass buttons, and wore a wig which you could see was a real one. Every morning an old fellow arrived to tidy up for him and run errands; otherwise, the old man in the knee-breeches was quite alone in the old house. From time to time he would cross over to the window and look out, and the little boy would nod to him, and the old man would nod back again. And so they made each other's acquaintance and became friends, although they had never spoken to one another, not, of course, that that mattered.

One day the little boy heard his parents say, 'The old man over there is very comfortably off, but he's so dreadfully lonely!'

The next Sunday the little boy took something and wrapped it in a piece of paper, went down to the gateway, and as the old chap who ran errands came by, he said to him, 'Listen, will you take this from me to the old man across the road? I've two tin-soldiers—that's one of them: he can have it, for I know he's so dreadfully lonely.'

And the old fellow looked quite pleased, nodded, and took the tin-soldier over to the old house. Afterwards there came a message asking whether the little boy wouldn't like to come over himself and pay a visit: he got leave to go from his parents, and so he went over to the old house.

The brass knobs on the railings shone much more brightly than usual—you might have thought they had been polished in honour of his visit—and the carved trumpeters—for there were trumpeters standing in the tulips carved on the door—seemed to be blowing with all their might, their cheeks puffed out rounder than ever. Yes, they were blowing, 'Tatterata! The little boy's coming! Tatterata!' And then the door was opened. The hall was hung all over with old portraits, knights in armour and ladies in silken gowns—and the armour rattled and the silk gowns rustled. And so they came to a staircase that went a long way up and a little way down, and then led them on to a balcony which was obviously very frail with great holes and long cracks in it. But through the holes and cracks grass and green leaves grew, for the whole of the balcony outside the walls of the house was so overgrown with greenery that it looked like a garden, though it was only a balcony. Old flower-pots with faces and asses' ears stood there; and the flowers grew in wild disorder. One pot was overflowing with pinks, or rather with green shoots, one tumbling upon another and saying quite clearly, 'The air has caressed me, the sun has kissed me and promised me a little flower on Sunday, a little flower on Sunday!'

And then they entered a room with its walls covered in pigskin tooled with gilt flowers.

> 'Though gilding fade fast,
> Yet pigskin will last!'

said the walls.

And there were armchairs with great high backs and carving all over them. 'Sit down! Sit down!' they said. 'Ooh, how I creak! Now I shall have rheumatism like that old cupboard! Rheumatism in the back—ooh!'

And then the little boy entered the sitting-room where the bay-window was and where the old man was sitting.

'Thank you for the tin-soldier, my little friend!' said the old man. 'And thank you for coming over to see me!'

'Thanks! Thanks!' or 'Creak! Creak!' said all the furniture; there was so much of it that the pieces very nearly got in each other's way in their efforts to see the little boy.

And in the middle of the wall hung a picture of a lovely lady, young and happy, but dressed in the fashion of days gone by, with powdered hair and stiff clothes; she said neither 'Thanks' nor 'Creak', but looked at the little boy with her gentle eyes; and he at once asked the old man, 'Where did you get her?'

'Over at the second-hand shop!' said the old man. 'There are a great many pictures hanging up over there; no one knows them or cares about them, for the people are all dead. But in the old days I knew her, and now she has been dead and gone for half a century.'

Under the picture a bouquet of withered flowers hung behind glass; they must have been half a century old, too, so old did they look. And the pendulum of the great clock went to and fro, and the hand turned, and everything in the room was even older than before, though none of them noticed it.

'They say at home,' said the little boy, 'that you're dreadfully lonely!'

'Oh,' he said, 'old thoughts, and what they bring with them, come and visit me, and now you've come, too!—I've nothing to complain of!'

And then he took a picture-book down from the shelf; there were great long processions, the strangest-looking coaches such as you never see nowadays, soldiers looking like the Jack of clubs and citizens with waving banners; the tailors had on theirs a pair of scissors borne by two lions, and the shoemakers carried not a boot, but an eagle with two heads, for shoemakers have to have everything like that so that they can say, 'It's a pair!'—What a fine picture-book it was!

And the old man went into the other room to fetch sweets and apples and nuts—it was all very pleasant over in the old house.

'I can't stand it!' said the tin-soldier who was standing on the bureau. 'It's so lonely and sad! No, when you've been used to family-life, you can't accustom yourself to this sort of thing! I can't stand it! The days are so long, and the evenings longer still! It isn't a bit like it is over at your house, with your father and mother talking so pleasantly and you and all the other sweet children making such a lovely row. My, what a lonely life the old man leads! Do you suppose anyone kisses him? Do you suppose anyone looks at him kindly or gives him a Christmas-tree? There's nothing for him but the grave!—I can't stand it!'

'You mustn't take it so badly!' said the little boy. 'I

think it's lovely here, and all the old thoughts, and what they bring with them, do come visiting!'

'Well, I don't see them, and I don't know them!' said the tin-soldier. 'I can't stand it!'

'But you must!' said the little boy.

And the old man came back with the happiest face and the loveliest sweets and apples and nuts, and so the little boy thought no more about the tin-soldier.

Happy and pleased, the little boy returned home, and the days went by and the weeks went by, and nods were exchanged with the old house, and then the little boy went over there again.

And the carved trumpeters blew, 'Tatterata! It's the little boy! Tatterata!' and in the pictures of the knights sword and armour rattled and the silken dresses rustled, the pigskin spoke and the old chairs had rheumatism in the back—'Aw!'—it was exactly like the first time, for over there one day or one hour was just like another.

'I can't stand it!' said the tin-soldier. 'I've wept tears of tin! It's much too sad here! Let me go to war and lose arms and legs—I'd much rather—and it would be a change! I can't stand it! I know what it is now to be visited by old thoughts and what they bring with them! I've been visited by mine, and, believe me, there's no pleasure in it in the long run—in the end I came near jumping off the bureau. I saw all of you over there in the house as plainly as if you'd really been here. It was that Sunday morning again—you know the one I mean! All you children were standing in front of the table and singing your hymn, just as you do every morning; you were standing with your hands folded devoutly, and your father and mother were just as solemn, and then the door opened and your little sister Maria, who isn't two yet and who always dances whenever she hears music or singing, no matter what kind it is, stepped in—which she shouldn't have done, of course—and then she began to dance, but she couldn't pick up the time, for the notes were so long, and so she stood first on one foot and leant her head right over, and then on the other foot and leant her head right over, but still she couldn't manage it. You stood there looking very serious, all of you, though it must have been a difficult job, but I laughed to myself and so I came to fall off the table and get a dent which I still have, for it wasn't right of me to laugh. But it all goes through my mind again, together with everything else I met with: and that must be old thoughts and what they bring with them.—Tell me, do you still sing on Sundays? Tell me something about little Maria! And how's my comrade getting on—the other tin-soldier? Yes, he's a lucky fellow, and no mistake!—I can't stand it!'

'But you've been given away as a present!' said the little boy. 'You'll have to stay—don't you realize that?'

And the old man came back with a drawer full of many things to look at—powder-boxes, scent-sprays, and old playing-cards, much larger and more lavishly gilded than you will ever see them now. And large drawers were opened, and the spinet was opened—it had a landscape painted on the inside of the lid, and it sounded so hoarse when the old man played on it; and then he hummed a song.

'Yes, she used to sing that!' he said, as he nodded towards the portrait he had bought from the second-hand shop, and the old man's eyes were shining very bright.

'I want to go to war! I want to go to war!' shouted the tin-soldier at the top of his voice, as he tumbled down on to the floor.

Where had he got to? The old man searched, the little boy searched: he was lost, and lost he remained. 'I shall find him no doubt!' the old man said, but he never did: there were far too many gaps and holes in the floor. The tin-soldier had fallen through a crack, and there he lay in an open grave.

And that day came to an end, and the little boy went home, and the week passed by, and several more weeks, too. The windows were quite frozen over: the little boy had to sit and breathe on them to make a peep-hole for him to see over to the old house, and snow had drifted into all the carved decorations and inscriptions. It lay right up over the steps just as if there were no one at home, and there wasn't either, for the old man was dead.

In the evening a carriage stopped outside, and he was carried down to it in his coffin; he was to be taken out into the country to lie in his grave. And so he was driven away, but no one followed, for all his friends were dead. And the little boy blew a kiss after the coffin as it drove off.

Some days later there was a sale at the old house, and from his window the little boy watched the things being taken away—the knights and the ladies of days gone by, the flower-pots with the long ears, the old chairs and the old cupboards—some went this way and some that. Her portrait, which had been found in the second-hand shop, went back to the second-hand shop, and there it remained, for no one knew her any more, and no one cared for the old picture.

In the spring the house itself was pulled down, for it was an unsightly old place, they said. From the street you could see right into the sitting-room, right to the pigskin covering of the walls, now gashed and torn. And the green plants on the balcony hung in wild disorder about the falling beams.—And so it was cleared away.

'That's better!' said the houses round about.

And a handsome house was built there with large windows and smooth white walls, and in front, where the old house had actually stood, a little garden was planted, and up against the neighbours' walls wild vines grew. In front of the garden were tall iron railings with an iron gate; it looked very fine, and people would stand still and peep inside. And the sparrows hung by the score in the vines, all chattering as hard as they could at the same time, but it was not about the old house, for that they could not remember—that had been gone for so many years that the little boy had grown up to manhood. Yes, he was a fine man who gave his parents real cause for pleasure. He had just been married, and had moved with his little wife into the house where the garden was. He stood by her side as she planted a wild flower which she found very beautiful. She planted it with her own little hand and patted the earth about it with her fingers.—Oh! What was that? She pricked herself. Something sharp and pointed was sticking right up out of the soft earth.

It was—just think!—it was the tin-soldier, the one who had been lost up in the old man's room, and had rumbled and tumbled among timbers and rubble, and finally had lain for many years in the earth.

And the young wife dried the soldier, first with a green leaf and then with her own fine handkerchief that had such a lovely perfume! And the tin-soldier felt just as if he had wakened up from a trance.

'Let me see him!' said the young man, laughing and shaking his head. 'No, he can't possibly be the same one after all this time, but he reminds me of a story about a tin-soldier I had when I was a little boy!' And so he told his wife about the old house and the old man and the tin-soldier he had sent him because he was so dreadfully lonely, and he told it in such detail, just as it had really happened, that the young wife felt tears come into her eyes over that old house and the old man who had lived there.

'But it could be the same tin-soldier!' she said. 'I shall keep it and remember all that you've told me. But you must show me the old man's grave!'

'I don't know where it is,' he said, 'and no one knows where to find it. All his friends were dead, there was no one to look after his grave, and I was only a little boy!'

'How dreadfully lonely he must have been!' she said.

'Dreadfully lonely!' said the tin-soldier. 'But it's nice not to be forgotten!'

'Nice!' cried something close by; but the tin-soldier was the only one who saw that it was a scrap of pigskin covering; it had lost all its gilding and looked like damp mould, but it still had something to say, and it said it,

'Though gilding fade fast,
Yet pigskin will last!'

But the tin-soldier refused to believe it.

The Shirt Collar

THERE was once a fine gentleman whose only household equipment was a boot-jack and a comb, but he had the smartest shirt collar in the world, and it is about this collar that we are going to hear a story.—The collar was now old enough to think of marriage, and it so happened that he found himself in the wash-tub with a lady's garter.

"'Pon my word,' said the collar, 'never have I seen any-one so slim and delicate, so soft and charming! May I ask your name?'

'I'm not going to tell you!' said the lady's garter.

'Where do you live?' asked the collar.

But the garter was very bashful and felt too shy to answer.

'You must be a girdle!' said the collar. 'The sort of girdle ladies wear underneath! I can see you are both use-ful and decorative, little lady!'

'You mustn't speak to me!' said the garter. 'I'm sure I've given you no encouragement!'

'But you have!' said the collar. 'When anyone's as pretty as you are, that's encouragement enough!'

'Stop coming so near me!' said the lady's garter. 'You look much too like a man!'

'Yes, indeed, I'm a fine gentleman!' said the collar. 'I have a boot-jack and a comb!' Now that wasn't true: it was his master that had those, and he was just boasting.

'Don't come near me!' said the garter. 'I'm not used to that sort of thing!'

'Prude!' said the collar, and at that point they were taken out of the wash. He was starched, hung over a chair in the sunshine and afterwards laid on the ironing-board. Then came the hot iron.

'Madam!' said the collar. 'Little widow! I'm getting quite hot! I'm beginning to feel a different person—I'm losing all my wrinkles! You're burning a hole in me! Oh!—Will you marry me?'

'Old rag!' said the iron, passing haughtily over the collar. She fancied she was a steam-engine and ought to be out on the railway-lines pulling a train.

'Old rag!' she said.

The collar was a little frayed at the edges, and so along came a pair of scissors to snip off the loose threads.

'Oh!' said the collar. 'You must be a prima ballerina! How you can stretch your legs! That's the most charming thing I've seen yet! I'm sure no human being can do that as well as you can!'

'I know that!' said the scissors.

'You ought to be a countess!' said the collar. 'All I have is a fine gentleman, a boot-jack and a comb—if only I had an earldom!'

'Is he proposing?' said the scissors. She was cross now and gave him a real snick, and so he was sent about his business.

'Well, I shall have to propose to the comb!' said the

collar. 'It's remarkable how you keep all your teeth, little lady! Have you ever thought of becoming engaged?'

'Why, yes, of course I have!' said the comb, 'I'm engaged to the boot-jack!'

'Engaged!' said the collar. And now there was no one left to propose to, and so he began to look upon the whole idea with contempt.

A long time passed, and then one day the collar found himself in a box at the paper mill. There was a great gathering of rags there, the fine ones separated from the coarse, as is only right and proper. They all had a great deal to say, but the collar said the most for he was a regular braggart.

'I've had a frightful lot of girls in love with me!' said the collar. 'They gave me no peace at all! Of course, I was a fine gentleman, you know, always well starched! And I had both boot-jack and comb, though I never used them!—You should have seen me in those days, especially when I lay at ease on my side! Never shall I forget my first sweetheart—she was a lady's girdle, very delicate, very soft, very charming: she threw herself into a wash-tub, and all on account of me!—There was a widow, too: she was red-hot, but I left her to cool off and she turned quite black! Then there was the prima ballerina: she gave me this little scratch I still bear, fury that she was! My own comb was in love with me, too: she lost all her teeth through being crossed in love. Oh, yes, I've had many experiences of that kind! But I chiefly regret the garter—I mean the lady's girdle—who went into the wash-tub. I've a great deal on my conscience: I really do need to be made into white paper—a clean sheet, you know!'

And he was—all the rags were made into white paper, but the collar was made into this very piece of white paper we are looking at now, the one this story is printed on, and that was because he boasted so frightfully of things that had never happened. And we must take good care that we don't behave like that, for we can't really be sure that we shan't one day end up in the rag-box, too, and be made into white paper with the whole of our story, even our closest secrets, printed on it, and have to run round telling it to everybody, just like the collar.

The Goblin at the Provision-Dealer's

THERE was a student—an unmistakable student —who lived in the attic and owned nothing; there was a provision-dealer—equally unmistakable—who lived on the ground-floor and owned the whole house, and he was the one the goblin attached himself to, for every Christmas Eve he gave him a dish of porridge with a great lump of butter in it. The provision-dealer could easily spare it, and so the goblin stayed in the shop—and there was much to be learnt from it.

One evening the student came in by the back door to buy himself some candles and cheese—he had no one to send and so he came himself. He got what he wanted and paid for it, and the provision-dealer and his wife nodded 'good evening'—the wife was a woman who could do more than nod, for she had the gift of the gab!—and the student nodded back and then stood reading the bit of paper the cheese was wrapped in. It was a page torn out of an old book which should never have been torn up at all, an old book full of poetry.

'There's more of that lying about!' said the provision-dealer. 'I gave an old woman some coffee-beans for it. If you'd like to give me sixpence, you can have the rest.'

'Thank you,' said the student. 'You can let me have it instead of the cheese! I can make do with bread and butter. It would be sinful to tear the whole book to pieces. You're a fine man, a practical man, but you understand no more about poetry than this cask here!'

Now that was a rude thing to say, especially as far as the cask was concerned, but the provision-dealer laughed and the student laughed, for of course it was said as a kind

x

of joke. But the goblin was annoyed that anyone dared speak like that to a provision-dealer who was the landlord of the house and sold the best butter.

That night, when the shop was shut and everyone but the student was in bed, the goblin went in and took the wife's gift of the gab—she had no use for it while she was asleep —and whatever object in the room he put it on received the power of speech and could express its thoughts and feelings just as well as she could. But only one at a time could have it, and that was a blessing, for otherwise they would all have talked at once.

And the goblin placed the gift of the gab on the cask where the old newspapers were kept. 'Is it really true,' he asked, 'that you don't know what poetry is?'

'Yes, of course I do,' said the cask. 'It's something you find at the bottom of the page in the newspaper and cut out. I should think I've more of it inside me than the student has, and I'm only a poor cask compared with the provision-dealer.'

And the goblin placed the gift of the gab on the coffee-mill—my, how it went! And he put it on the butter-tub and the till—they were all of the same opinion as the cask, and what most people are agreed upon you have to respect.

'Now I'll try it on the student!' And so the little goblin

went quite quietly up the back stairs to the attic where the student lived. There was a light inside his room, and the goblin peeped through the key-hole and saw the student reading the tattered book from downstairs. But how bright it was in the room! A bright beam of light rose out of the book and grew into a trunk, a mighty tree that rose up high and spread out its broad branches over the student. Every leaf looked so fresh, and every flower was the head of a lovely girl, some with eyes so dark and shining, others with eyes so blue and strangely bright. Every fruit was a shining star, and there was a sound of wonderfully beautiful singing.

The little goblin had never even imagined anything so glorious, let alone seen and experienced it. And so he stayed there, standing tip-toe and peeping and peeping, until the light in the room went out: the student must have blown out his lamp and gone to bed, but the little goblin stayed where he was, for the song still sounded soft and lovely in his ears, a beautiful lullaby for the student who had lain down to rest.

'It's wonderful here!' said the little goblin. 'I hadn't expected anything like this!—I think I'll stay with the student—' And he thought about it—and thought about it very sensibly, and then he sighed and said, 'The student hasn't any porridge!'—and so off he went—yes, he went down again to the provision-dealer. And it was a good thing he did, for the cask had very nearly used up the good lady's gift of the gab telling everybody all that was inside it. It had already done this once from one angle, and now it was just about to turn over so that it could repeat it from the other angle, when the goblin came and took the gift of the gab back to the good lady. But from that time the whole shop, from the till to the firewood, based its views on what the cask said, and they held it in such high esteem and had such confidence in it that ever after when the provision-dealer was reading the art criticisms and theatre notices from the evening paper, they thought he had it all from the cask.

But the little goblin no longer sat quietly listening to all the wisdom and good sense down below: no, as soon as the light shone from the room in the attic, its beams were just like strong anchor-chains dragging him upstairs, and off he had to go and peep through the key-hole, and there he was overpowered by a sense of greatness, such as we feel when we stand by the rolling sea and God passes over it in the stormy blast; and he would burst into tears—he did not know himself why he was crying— but there was something very blessed in those tears.—How wonderfully delightful it would be to sit under that tree with the student!—But that could never be: and he was glad he had the keyhole. He would still stand there in the cold passage when the winds of autumn were blowing down from the skylight and it was so very, very cold, but the little fellow would not feel it until the light went out in the attic and the sound of music died away in the wind. Ooh! Then he would freeze and creep downstairs again into his warm corner—how cosy and comfortable it was!—And then his Christmas porridge came with its great lump of butter.—Yes, the provision-dealer was the master for him.

But in the middle of the night the goblin was awakened by a frightful banging on the window-shutters: people outside were thumping on them; the watchman was blowing his whistle; a great fire had broken out and the whole street was lit up by the flames. Was it in this house or next door? Where was it? What a panic there was! The provision-dealer's wife was so flurried that she took her gold ear-rings out of her ears and put them into her pocket so that she might at least save something; the provision-dealer ran for his bonds, and the maid for her silk mantilla—for she was well enough off to have one: everyone wanted to save what he prized most, and so, too, did the little goblin. In a couple of bounds he was up the stairs and in the attic with the student who was standing quite calmly by the open window and looking out at the fire which was in the house across the road. The little goblin seized the wonderful book from the table, put it into his red hood, and held it tight in both hands: the most precious treasure in the house had been rescued. Then off he went, right out on to the roof, right up the chimney-stack, and there he sat lit up by the flames of the burning house opposite and holding closely in both hands his red hood and the treasure that lay inside it. Then he knew where his heart lay, whom he really belonged to. But when the fire had been put out and he had become more level-headed, well—'I'll divide my time between them!' he said. 'I can't give up the provision-dealer entirely, on account of the porridge!'

And that was really quite human!—We, too, go to the provision-dealer's—for porridge.

What the Old Man Does is Always Right

I'M now going to tell you a story that I heard when I was small, and every time I've thought about it since, it's seemed to me much better than before; for it's true of stories, as it is of many people, that they grow nicer and nicer with age—and that's very pleasant!

You've been out in the country, of course, and no doubt you've seen a really old country cottage with a thatched roof overgrown with moss and weeds. There's a stork's nest on the roof-ridge—we can't do without the stork; the walls are uneven and the windows low, and only one of them will open; the baking-oven bulges out like a tubby little tummy, and the elder-bush hangs over the fence where there's a little pond with duck and ducklings right under the gnarled willow-tree. And then, of course, there's the watchdog barking at all and sundry.

There was a cottage just like this out in the country, and two people lived in it, a countryman and his wife. However little they had, they nevertheless had one thing they could do without, and that was a horse that used to go and graze in the ditch alongside the road. Father used to ride to town on it, the neighbours would borrow it and he would get other services in return, but it would still pay them better to sell the horse or exchange it for something or other that would be of more use to them. But what?

'You know best, old man!' said his wife. 'It's market-day in town; ride over and get money for the horse or make a good bargain with it! Whatever you do always turns out right. Now ride off to market!'

And with that she tied his neckerchief, for that at least she could do better than he could; she tied it with a double bow that looked very smart, and then she brushed his hat with the flat of her hand and kissed his warm lips. Then off he rode on the horse that he was going to sell or exchange. Oh, yes, the old man would do that all right!

The sun was burning hot and there wasn't a cloud in the sky. The road was dusty—there were so many people going to market, in carts, on horseback, and on their own feet. It was very hot and there was no shade at all on the road.

A man came along driving a cow, as pretty a cow as you could wish to see. 'She'd give lovely milk for certain sure!' thought the countryman. 'It'd be a real good bargain to get her!—I say! You with the cow!' he said. 'Shall we have a little chat together? Look, I know a horse costs more than a cow, but I don't mind about that! I could make more use of a cow. Shall we swop?'

'Right you are!' said the man with the cow, and so they swopped.

It was done now, and the countryman could have turned back again, for he had done what he set out to do, but as he had made his mind up to go to market, to market he would go, if only to have a look at it. So on he went with his cow. He walked along briskly, and the cow walked along briskly, and they soon found themselves walking beside a man leading a sheep. It was a good sheep in good condition with a good fleece.

'I'd like to have that!' thought the countryman. 'It'd not want for grazing along the side of our ditch, and in winter we could take it indoors with us. When all's said and done, it'd be more proper for us to keep a sheep than a cow. Shall we swop?'

Yes, the man who had the sheep was only too willing, so the bargain was made, and off went the countryman with his sheep along the high road. There by the stile he saw a man with a big goose under his arm.

'That's a fine big 'un you've got there!' said the countryman. 'He's well covered with feathers, and fat, too! He'd look well, tethered by our pond! It'd be something for mother to save her scraps for! She's often said, "If only we had a goose!"—And now she can have one— and she shall and all! Will you swop? I'll give you the sheep for the goose, and a "Thank you" into the bargain!'

The other man was quite willing, and so they swopped and the countryman got his goose. He was near the town now and the road was growing more and more crowded with throngs of men and beasts: they were trudging along the road and overflowing into the ditch right up to the turnpike-keeper's potato-patch where he had tethered his hen so that she shouldn't run away with fright and get lost. She was a short-tailed hen who blinked one eye and looked in good fettle. 'Cluck, cluck!' she said: what she was thinking about, I can't say, but when the countryman saw her, he thought, 'She's the prettiest hen I've ever set eyes on—she's prettier than the parson's brood-hen. I'd like to have her! A hen'll always find a bit of corn: she could almost fend for herself! I think I'd make a good deal of it if I got her for the goose. Shall we swop?' he asked. 'Swop?' said the other. 'Yes, that wouldn't be at all a bad idea!' And so they swopped. The turnpike-keeper got the goose and the countryman got the hen.

He had got through a lot of business on his way to town, it was hot and he was tired. He was in need of a drink and a bite of bread, and there, close at hand, was an inn, but as he was going in, the barman was coming out and ran smack into him in the doorway with a sack crammed full.

'What have you got there?' asked the countryman.

'Rotten apples!' answered the barman. 'A whole sack-ful of 'em for the pigs!'

'That's a terrible lot! I wish mother could have a sight of that! Last year we'd naught but a single apple on that old tree by the peat-shed. We were going to keep that apple and it stood on the chest of drawers till it burst. "At least it's a crop!" says our mother, but she could see a proper crop here! Ah, I wish she might have it!'

'Well, what will you give for it?' asked the barman.

'Give? I'll give you my hen!' And so he gave him the hen in exchange, took the apples and went into the tap-room and over to the bar. He leaned his sack of apples up against the stove: the fire was lit, but that hadn't occurred to him. There were many strangers in the room—horse-dealers, cattle-dealers, and two Englishmen who were so rich their pockets were bursting with gold: they were fond of a wager, too, as you shall now hear!

'Hiss-s-s! Hiss-s-s-s!' What was that noise over by the stove? The apples were beginning to roast!

'What's that?' They weren't long finding out: they heard the whole story of the horse that was swopped for the cow, right down to the rotten apples.

'My word, the old woman'll give you a hiding when you get home!' said the Englishmen. 'There'll be the devil to pay!'

'She'll give me no hiding!' said the countryman. 'Our mother'll give me a kiss and say, "What the old man does is right!"'

'Shall we bet on it?' they said. 'Gold coins by the barrel, a hundred pounds to the ton!'

'A bushel will do!' said the countryman. 'I can only lay a bushel of apples, with me and the old woman thrown in—and that's more than flat-measure, that's top-measure!'

'Done!' they said, and the bet was made.

The landlord's cart was brought out: in went the Englishmen, in went the countryman, in went the rotten apples, and off they went to the countryman's cottage.

'Good evening, mother!'

'Thank you, father!'

'Well, I've done a deal!'

'Ah, you're a right good 'un for that!' said his wife, giving him a hug and ignoring the sack and the strangers.

'I swopped the horse for a cow!'

'Thank God for the milk!' said his wife. 'Now we shall have milk to cook with and butter and cheese on the table. That was a real good bargain!'

'Yes, but I swopped the cow for a sheep!'

'But that's even better!' said his wife. 'You're always so thoughtful! We've got just the right grazing for a sheep. Now we can have sheep's milk and sheep's milk cheese and woollen stockings—and woollen nightgowns,

too! A cow wouldn't give them: a cow loses her hair!
You're a wonderful deep-thinking man!'
'But I swopped the sheep for a goose!'
'What, my old dear, shall we really have a goose for

Martinmas this year! You're always thinking up something to please me! That was a lovely thought! We'll
tether the goose and it'll be fatter still by Martinmas!'
'But I swopped the goose for a hen!' said her husband.
'A hen! That was a good bargain!' said his wife. 'The
hen'll lay eggs and hatch 'em, and then we shall have
chickens and a proper poultry-yard! That's just what
I've been longing for!'
'Yes, but I swopped the hen for a sack of rotten apples!'
'Oh, now I really shall have to give you a kiss!' said his
wife. 'Oh, thank you, thank you, my own dear husband!
Now I must tell you something. After you'd gone, I

thought I'd make a real nice supper for you, an omelette with chives in it. I had the eggs, but I'd got no chives. So I went over to the schoolmaster's: I know they've got chives there, but the wife's an old skinflint and so I asked her just to lend me some. "Lend you some?" she said. "Nothing grows in our garden, not even a rotten apple!" There I was and I couldn't lend her one in return! But now I can lend her ten—a whole sackful, if need be! That's real funny, that is, father!' And with that she kissed him right on the mouth.

'That's what I like to see!' said the Englishmen. 'Going downhill all the time and just as pleased as ever! It's worth the money!' And so they paid a ton of gold coins to the countryman who had got a kiss instead of a hiding.

Yes, it always pays when the wife realizes and makes it clear to others that the old man is the wise one and what he does is right.

Well, there's the story! I heard it when I was small, and now you've heard it, too, and you know that what the old man does is always right.

The Tea-Pot

ONCE there was a proud tea-pot—it was proud of its fine porcelain, proud of its long spout, proud of its broad handle: it had something in front of it and something behind it—its spout at the front and its handle behind—and it talked about it. But it didn't talk about its lid—it was cracked, it was broken, it had a bit missing—and you don't willingly talk about your shortcomings: others are only too ready to do it for you. Cups, milk-jug, sugar-basin, the whole tea-set, were much more inclined to remember the frailty of the lid and talk about it than they were the good handle and the excellent spout: and the tea-pot knew it.

'I know them!' it said to itself. 'And I know my short-comings, too, and I admit them, and there lies my humility, my modesty. We all have our faults, but we have our gifts as well. The cups were given handles, the sugar-basin a lid: I was given both, and a thing in front, too, which they will never have—I was given a spout, and that makes me Queen of the Tea-Table. It is granted to the sugar-basin and the milk-jug to be the handmaids of good taste, but I am the Giver, the Mistress: I pour out my blessings for thirsting humanity; in my inward parts, the leaves from China are prepared in boiling tasteless water.'

All this the tea-pot spoke in the confidence of youth. It was standing on the table which had been laid for tea, it was lifted by the daintiest of hands, but the daintiest of hands was clumsy—the tea-pot fell, the spout was broken off, the handle was broken off, and the lid wasn't worth talking about—it's been talked about enough already. The tea-pot lay swooning on the floor, the boiling water running out of it. It was a hard blow it received, and the hardest part of it was that they laughed—and it was the tea-pot they were laughing at, not the clumsy hand.

'I shall never get that memory out of my head now!' said the tea-pot when it was later telling the history of its life. 'I was called a casualty and put away in a corner, and the next day I was given away as a present to a woman who came to beg some dripping. I came right down in the world; there I stood, destitute and aimless, both within and without; but even as I stood there, my better life began: you are one thing, and then you become something quite different. Earth was put inside me—and for a tea-pot that's as much as being buried—but in the earth a bulb was planted—who put it there, who gave it to me, I do not know, but given it was, a compensation for the China leaves and the boiling water, a compensation for the handle and spout that had been broken off. And the bulb lay in the earth, the bulb lay inside me—it became my heart, my living heart, and such a thing I had never had before. There was life in me, there was strength and force; my pulse beat, shoots sprang from the bulb as if it were unable to contain its thoughts and feelings, and they burst into flower. I saw it, I bore it; I forgot myself in its loveliness. A blessed thing it is to forget oneself in others! It did not thank me, it did not think about me— it was admired and praised. I found such joy in it in any case. One day I heard someone say it deserved a better pot. I was broken in two; it hurt dreadfully, but the flower was put in a better pot—and I was thrown out into the yard, and there I lie like an old crock—but I have my memories, and they're something I shall never lose!'